HEARTWARMING

The Police Chief's Pitch

—

Janice Sims

HARLEQUIN
HEARTWARMING

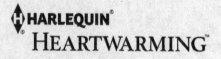

HARLEQUIN®
HEARTWARMING™

ISBN-13: 978-1-335-47568-8

The Police Chief's Pitch

Copyright © 2024 by Janice Sims

Recycling programs for this product may not exist in your area.

For questions and comments about the quality of this book, please contact us at CustomerService@Harlequin.com.

Harlequin Enterprises ULC
22 Adelaide St. West, 41st Floor
Toronto, Ontario M5H 4E3, Canada
www.Harlequin.com

Printed in U.S.A.

"How is signing my son up for Little League good for you?"

"I'm the coach," Dave said. "If you bring him to the games, at least you and I will be around one another. You'll see I'm a not-too-weird guy and maybe after a while decide to go out with me. Sound reasonable?"

"Sounds like a long shot..." Darla said, with a humorous glint in her eye. "But I'll ask Bastian if he wants to participate and see what I can do. That's all I'm promising."

"You're a fair woman," he said, rising. He took his wallet out of his back pocket and handed her a business card. "I know it's old-fashioned, but I think it's much more personal than exchanging cell phone numbers."

When she took it, their fingers touched. Her eyes met his at that moment, and once again, his heart skipped a beat...

Dear Reader,

The people we love shape us in ways we may not even be aware of. While I was writing *The Police Chief's Pitch*, my mother passed away. I was understandably bereft. It was only until I read the final draft that I realized my grief had been translated to this story of forgiveness and redemption. I cried several times while writing it. Therefore, I'm formally apologizing to you for making you sad, should you suddenly burst into tears while reading. But there are also warm, funny moments, too. Those laugh-out-loud moments reminded me that life is like that: sad one moment and hilarious the next.

Continued blessings,

Janice

Janice Sims is the author of over forty titles ranging from romance to romantic suspense to speculative fiction. She won two Romance in Color awards: an Award of Excellence for her novel *For Keeps* and the Novella of the Year Award for her short story "The Keys to My Heart." She won an Emma Award for Favorite Heroine for her novel *Desert Heat*. She has been nominated for a Career Achievement Award twice by *RT Book Reviews*. Her novel *Temptation's Song* was nominated for Best Kimani Romance Series in 2010. Her novel *Safe in My Arms*, the second novel in the Gaines Sisters series, won the 2014 RT Reviewers' Choice Award for Kimani Romance. She was the 2016 recipient of the Francis Ray Lifetime Literary Award from BRAB, Building Relationships Around Books. She lives in Central Florida with her family.

Visit the Author Profile page
at Harlequin.com for more titles.

This book is dedicated to two wonderful women who passed away in recent months: my mother, Lillie Jean, who not only gave me life, but informed my life with love, a sense of adventure and generosity.

Also, to Gwendolyn Osborne, who, when my first book was published, contacted me and told me she liked my style of writing. She subsequently went on to become a dear friend.

CHAPTER ONE

CHIEF OF POLICE David Harrison strode purposefully along the sparsely crowded sidewalk in downtown Port Domingo on Saturday morning, heading to the new supermarket. It was his day off; however, one of his officers had a crisis at home, so until another officer could come relieve him, he was filling in for her as security at the store. In the past few months, lots of positive changes had been made in the town that had started out as a small fishing village on Florida's Emerald Coast. First, the supermarket had opened, taking pride of place in the downtown area. Then Mason's Bed and Breakfast, due to a partnership with the Nishimura Group, had gone through a transformation, adding more accommodations for the influx of visitors. The inn even boasted a peaceful Japanese tea garden on the grounds that had lately become the "in" spot for weddings. Dave was glad of the changes but worried that with more visitors and new residents spilling into Port Domingo, the crime rate would increase.

"Mornin', Chief! Don't you look dapper. What's with the new hat?" Wanda Garrett, owner of the bakery he was passing, stepped outside, halting him in his tracks. He should have known he wasn't going to get past her. Wanda always found a way to flirt with him whenever she glimpsed him. It was all harmless, though. She was a happily married woman.

A tall, buxom redhead in her forties, Wanda gave him a warm smile. She was wearing a long-sleeved blouse over blue jeans and her customary white athletic shoes. Her green eyes sparkled in her attractive face as she waited expectantly for his response.

"Good morning, Mrs. Garrett," Dave said, smiling back and touching the brim of his tan cowboy hat with its dark brown band in a gentlemanly gesture. "This is, indeed, a new hat. It's my mother's opinion that the chief should not be wearing a Braves baseball cap while carrying out his duties, but something with a little more dignity."

Wanda regarded him with a critical eye.

He felt kind of naked for a moment, and in spite of the pleasant, mild temperatures this March morning, he suddenly wished he was wearing more than his long-sleeved blue-and-white-checked shirt, open at the collar, with a pair of jeans, his favorite brown cowboy boots and his new hat. He wasn't in uniform because he was supposed to be able to pass for a shopper today instead of a law enforcement officer.

After much consideration, Wanda said, "I'm a Braves fan, therefore I have to disagree with Miss Margaret. But don't tell her I said so because I don't want to be told to mind my own business in Italian. I wouldn't know what she was saying, but I'm sure it would be delivered with gusto."

They laughed.

It was true, his mother, Anna Margherita Caruso-Harrison, an Italian immigrant who'd married a Southern Irish-American and become known as Margaret due to the fact that the people in this part of the country found Margherita hard to pronounce, was known for lapsing into fiery Italian when she got excited.

"Yeah, it's best not to go there."

Wanda nodded in the direction of the new supermarket. "They're going to put me out of business before long."

Dave gave her a sympathetic smile. "I know they have a bakery in there, but it doesn't compare to yours. You have lots of loyal customers."

"Loyal customers who might want to save money on their treats. I can't compete with a chain."

"The quality of your baked goods is way above theirs," Dave stated with conviction, hoping to allay her worries.

Wanda laughed softly. "This coming from a policeman who doesn't even eat donuts," she playfully scoffed.

"I've got to watch my waistline," Dave said. They'd had this conversation before and it had always ended on a light note. Her comment did make him wonder how the new supermarket was going to affect the small shop owners, though. He'd hate to see any of them go out of business due to the competition.

"My department will always patronize your bakery," he promised her. He might not eat pastries but plenty of others on his staff did.

That put a bigger smile on Wanda's face. "And you all have been good customers over the years. I'm sorry for being so glum. It's one of those days."

"Well, cheer up," Dave said with a quick nod at the tall gentleman walking across the street and making his way toward the bakery. Mayor Tom Steadman stopped in front of Dave and Wanda. His brown eyes focused on Wanda.

"Good morning, pretty lady."

"Good morning, Mayor," Wanda said cheerfully.

"Two dozen of your finest, please. I can't start my day without one of your delicious confections."

Wanda beamed. "Right away." And she hurried back inside of the bakery to fill his order.

"Good morning, Tom," Dave said to the mayor in her absence.

Tom, a tall, muscular African American in his late forties, attired in his usual suit and tie with highly polished leather dress shoes, had strands of gray in his close-cropped Afro, a pleasant face given to smiling and brown eyes that reflected his emotions. So

Dave knew that something was bothering the mayor when he turned his gaze on him.

"Dave," Tom said, raking his big palm across his moist forehead as he spoke. "The supermarket has been open only a few months and I've been told they've already got a shoplifting problem over there. Kids, probably. But we've got to nip that in the bud. If the kids are doing it as a prank, we've got to set them straight. And if they're doing it because they're hungry, why, we've got programs in this town to address that problem."

Dave nodded in agreement. His officers were on the case. In fact, one of his people was always in the supermarket in plain clothes, keeping an eye on everything. Two teen boys had been caught stealing minor things and sternly spoken to and released into their parents' care. In both instances it had been a first-time offense. They'd been given a warning of what would happen if they committed another violation. Both had promised to never do it again.

"We're aware, and we're on it," Dave assured the mayor. "I'm heading there now to fill in for one of my officers."

Tom laughed shortly. "I'm sure your presence will make any shoplifter think twice, but as for blending in? I don't think so. Everyone knows you, Dave."

Dave smiled. "Oh, believe me, I don't expect to see any action this morning."

Then he touched the brim of his hat in farewell to Tom. "Have a nice day, Mayor."

"You, too, Chief," Tom said, his eyes still lit by laughter.

DARLA CRAMER WAS in the produce section of the supermarket, choosing a cantaloupe, when she heard someone say her name. At first she thought someone was calling to her. But then she glanced to her left and saw two women she didn't recognize with their heads together, one of them with a hand cupped at the side of her mouth as though it would muffle her words.

No such luck. Darla heard the woman whisper, "She should be ashamed to show her face, the way she treated Sebastian." The acoustics in this new supermarket were excellent.

It wasn't the first time Darla had encountered people gossiping about her since moving back to her hometown around six months ago to get to know her son, Bastian. Bastian's father, Sebastian, had been decent toward her. He had been kind enough to let her back into Bastian's life. However, some people couldn't resist expressing their disappointment in her behavior.

Maybe if they knew how disappointed she was in herself, they'd be willing to give her a break. Because no one was harder on her than she was when it came to heaping recriminations on her head.

The mere fact that she'd missed the first five years of Bastian's life was enough to keep her up nights, calling herself all kinds of a fool for running away instead of toughing it out when she found herself in a panic after giving birth to Bastian.

What's more, she had known nothing about postpartum depression back then and believed her pessimism and lack of joy at being a new mother made her an aberration. Wasn't becoming a mother a time for celebrating, not panicking and thinking that your life, as you knew it, was over?

She knew now how off her reasoning had

been. Because when you become a mother, your life as you know it is indeed over.

But in a good way. You change, you grow. That new life enhances yours and you learn so much from one another. Today, she wouldn't trade Bastian for anything in the world. Every day she found a new reason to love him more. And the love he gave her in return gave her life.

If only she had confided in someone back then, instead of internalizing everything and letting the emotions build until she wound up doing something desperate. That desperate thing turned out to be running away with a rock guitarist whose career was waning and who needed an ego boost in the form of a starry-eyed groupie whose only goal was to escape her life. When she came to her senses, she left him. But she was too ashamed to go back home.

It took her almost five years to get up the courage to go back to Port Domingo. She worked on herself while she was away. She trained as a nurse so that she would have marketable skills and be able to support herself and Bastian. She worked at fast-food restaurants to fund her education. Finally, when she felt she had something to offer Bastian, she came home and asked Sebastian to let her back into Bastian's life. Oh, it hadn't been that easy. She'd bungled her initial meeting with Sebastian because she'd been nervous and they'd wound up in a shouting match. But soon, they'd understood each other and Sebastian was willing to share Bastian with her.

Today, they worked well together. They had agreed that Bastian would live with Sebastian and his wife, Marley, on weekdays during the school year, coming to her on weekends, then would spend the summer months with her. They all lived in Port Domingo, so arrangements were a breeze to manage. She was happy now. She was still living with her mother, though, and was saving to get her own place. However, she had a well-paying job as a private nurse for a gentleman of means in town who had an advanced case of Parkinson's but wanted to remain in his own home instead of going to an assisted-care facility. Her existence was quiet and ordered. Just like she liked it.

The women continued to whisper to each other, casting furtive glances in her direction. She moved away from the cantaloupes and pushed her cart out of the produce section, thinking if she ignored them, they'd be happy with a few chosen words of contempt and things wouldn't escalate.

ABOUT TWO HOURS after he'd gone undercover at the supermarket, Dave was more than ready to be relieved by Officer Plummer. He'd never spent this much time in a supermarket before. Usually he dashed in and picked up a few items and was out of here. He didn't know how shoppers with carts filled to the brim could stand the Muzak in the background or the constant hum of human voices and babies crying. Josh had texted that he was on the way, so Dave figured he'd be out of here in about five minutes.

He strolled into the produce section, and that was when he spotted her: Darla Crammer, looking beautiful in just jeans, a T-shirt and tennis shoes. He hadn't seen her since he and his deputies had assisted in finding her son, Bastian, the day he decided to go on an adventure by climbing his grandmother's backyard fence and following a puppy home almost six months ago.

His heartbeat sped up. Then it slowed down as he got ahold of himself. He sighed softly. No use entertaining romantic thoughts about Darla Cramer. It was a hard habit to break, though, because he'd had a crush on her since they were in high school.

He surreptitiously studied her face. She looked sad but somehow resigned. He followed her gaze. Two women were engaged in conversation. One of them was Joyce Hines, whom he'd also known since high school. Joyce had been a bully back then. Mean-spirited, selfish and always making trouble for someone else. He'd been able to avoid her in recent years.

That evil expression in Joyce's eyes told him she was up to no good right now. He saw Darla push her cart out of the produce section and breathed a sigh of relief. Maybe the situation had all been in his imagination. But then Joyce and the other unidentified woman followed Darla. He followed them.

By the time he rounded a corner, the two women had Darla's cart trapped between their shopping carts.

"Well, if it isn't Beyoncé," he heard Joyce say to Darla, her tone dripping with acid. She addressed the woman who was with her. "When we were in high school, Miss Darla here and two of her friends sang together and Darla was the one in the middle. The glamorous one."

Then back to Darla. "I heard J. J. Starr kicked you out years ago. What took you so long to come crawling back home?"

To her credit, Darla didn't even wince at Joyce's nasty words. Dave watched as Darla drew herself up to her full height. Which was about five-five. Still, he was impressed with the steely expression in her lovely brown eyes.

Darla smiled at Joyce. "You know, I didn't recognize you a moment ago. But now I do. Joyce Hines." From his vantage point, he saw the smile on her face be replaced by a more serious countenance. "You remember when Marley, Kaye and I used to sing together, huh? Well, I was a naive kid in high school. I was so convinced that I was going to be a star. But, you know, I've grown up since then. That moment of madness I experienced when I took off with J. J. Starr taught me a few things about life. One thing it taught me was that your problems can't be solved by running away from them. You have to stick around and face them. What about you, Joyce? How is life treating you these days?"

Her smile returned, brighter than ever, as she awaited Joyce's reply. But Joyce looked stunned. Dave supposed it was because Joyce had expected Darla to spout vitriol right back at her. She had no comeback for Darla's calm, measured response to her hatred. Joyce just stood there with an "Ah…" coming out of her mouth, and nothing else.

Since apparently Joyce wasn't capable of communicating at the moment, Darla said to the anonymous friend, "Tell Joyce it was a pleasure seeing her again."

Then she turned her back on the two women and pushed her cart down another aisle. Of course, that was when she looked up and locked eyes with him. He was grinning so wide, he was sure he looked like a fool, but he couldn't help it. He was proud of her. He hadn't figured out how he was going to de-fuse the situation should it turn into an altercation. Now he saw that Darla hadn't needed his help at all.

Darla shocked him by laughing out loud and saying "Chief! I'm so happy I ran into you. Are you busy right now? If not, would you like to have a cup of coffee with me? I've been meaning to properly thank you for helping to bring Bastian home safely when he decided to break out of prison."

Dave was thunderstruck again by her invitation, but tried to play it off by chuckling himself and saying, "Is that what you call it, a prison break? And, yes, I'm totally free. I'd love to have a cup of coffee with you." He glanced down at her shopping cart. "But aren't you shopping?"

Darla shrugged. "I haven't put anything in there that won't keep for a few minutes. I'll come back later and finish shopping." She parked the cart out of the way of other shoppers.

Dave was suddenly distracted by Officer Josh Plummer walking toward them, looking like he was getting ready to say something to him once he got closer. Dave threw Josh a thumbs-up sign. Josh acknowledged with a thumbs-up of his own.

"That sounds great," he said, meeting Darla's eyes.

"I like your hat," she said brightly as they began walking toward the supermarket's exit. He was beginning to think of it as his lucky hat.

CHAPTER TWO

DARLA'S HEART WAS thumping so hard as she and the chief walked across the street to Wide Awake, Port Domingo's only coffeehouse, that she was sure he could hear it. Her exchange with Joyce had left her a ball of nerves. In spite of the cool facade she'd been able to pull off, her flight-or-fight response was still pretty much on flight.

Gazing up at the chief helped a little. He reminded her of Jason Momoa before he grew the long hair and beard. The chief had curly dark brown hair, gorgeous brown eyes, full lips and deeply tanned skin. He was tall, too, and whereas he had been kind of lanky in high school, he'd bulked up over the years. More importantly, he had a reputation of being a good, loyal friend. He and her ex, Sebastian, had been friends in school and, as far as she knew, were still friends to this day.

"Mean ole Joyce strikes again," he commented offhandedly as they stepped onto the sidewalk in front of Wide Awake. The tables out front were round and topped with forest green umbrellas.

"How much did you hear?" she asked, pausing beside one of the empty tables to take a deep breath.

"Pretty much everything after they caught you between their shopping carts."

Darla's face grew hot with embarrassment. She looked him in the eyes. "So, you were getting ready to step in if things got heated."

"I think you could have taken her, but it was two against one," he said lightly.

Darla chuckled and turned toward the coffeehouse's entrance. "I promised you coffee."

They walked inside and got in line behind several other customers, two of whom called out greetings to the chief. He returned their hellos but immediately gave her his undivided attention again.

"You weren't chief when I left town," Darla said. "How did that happen?"

The chief's thick brows rose in a questioning expression, and she hastily added, "Not that I don't think you make a fine leader. It was just a surprise the day that Bastian disappeared and you showed up and introduced yourself as the chief of police. Chief Donaldson was an institution in this town."

The chief smiled. "Matt wanted to retire and I happened to be the most qualified officer to succeed him. Admittedly, I was young at thirty, but I'd joined the marines right out of high school. Was military police for a number of years, got my bachelor's degree in criminal justice. I was his second in command for three years before he decided he wanted to spend his golden years fishing instead of chasing bad guys. So, with the support of the mayor and the city commissioners, I was in. It's a five-year term, which is renewable if I keep my nose clean."

Darla stared up at him in amazement. "I'm always astounded by people who know what they want out of life, go after it and actually achieve it. I'm still figuring it out."

This got a laugh out of the chief. "Believe me, I'm still figuring it out, too."

Finally, it was their turn to order and after their orders had been taken, they found a table toward the back of the coffeehouse.

Their coffees would be brought to them by a server.

The chief helped Darla with her chair, then after hooking his hat on a nearby coatrack, sat down himself. They sat across from one another for a few moments, just smiling.

The chief broke the silence with "Would you please call me Dave? So many people call me chief, it would be nice to hear my name every now and then."

Darla felt as if she was seeing David Harrison for the first time; although, to be honest, she'd known him since they were in elementary school, at least by sight. She hadn't associated with him. He was the guy she saw in the hallways at school. Or, during their high school years, watched on the football field along with the rest of the players on the team. Her ex, Sebastian, had been quarterback his senior year. She didn't remember which position Dave played.

Now she wished she'd paid more attention to him back then.

"Dave it is," she promised. "Although I'll save it for when it's just the two of us. If anyone else is around, it's back to chief."

Dave chuckled. "Deal."

"Now that that's settled," Darla continued, "I wanted to thank you for being such a calming force when Bastian ran away. I, on the other hand, was a basket case. I had him in my care for one day, and I let him disappear."

"Children are like cat burglars," Dave said. "They're incredibly quick and slippery. I have a nephew who has been escaping from his crib and going to sleep with the dog in the living room since he was a year and a half. His parents finally just let the dog sleep in his room at night to keep him in bed."

Darla couldn't help laughing as the image of a toddler climbing out of his crib in the middle of the night appeared in her mind's eye. "I'm learning," she said after she'd gotten control of her laughter. "And have you noticed how they have the ability to change the laws of physics? Sometimes when you pick them up and they don't want to be picked up they can miraculously change their body density by relaxing every muscle in their bodies and appearing to weigh twice as much."

Dave was nodding and laughing along.

"Yes, I've noticed that. I don't have any of my own, but I'm the uncle of two who've been known to pull that trick on me."

"Yeah," Darla said. "Kids are a handful. A wonderful handful, but a handful nonetheless. I know now that I can't let my guard down until Bastian goes away to college."

"The way I hear it, not even then," Dave said.

The server, a petite young woman with pink streaks in her short brown hair, glided up to their table. "Chief, your coffee and the young lady's," she said smartly, placing their coffees in front of them. "Enjoy!"

"Thanks, Gemma," Dave said with a smile.

Darla saw the girl blush before she quickly said "My pleasure" and walked away as fast as her tiny feet could carry her.

Meanwhile, the chief—no, Dave—was looking her directly in the eyes and smiling like he could think of no place else he would rather be. Which, frankly, scared her. What had she gotten herself into by suggesting they have coffee together? She sincerely hoped he was not reading more into her invitation than she had meant. And how was she going to extricate herself from the situation should her instincts be right?

She took a sip of her coffee and silently prayed it wouldn't come to that.

"YOU DON'T OWE me any thanks for Bastian's safe return," Dave said after placing his mug back on the table and regarding her again. "It was Sebastian and Marley who followed his trail back to Claude Benson's farm."

Was that a wince he'd seen on her face? What had he said? It couldn't have been the mention of Claude Benson's name. Perhaps she and Sebastian and Marley weren't on the best of terms?

"Is something wrong?" he asked. "You seemed to be in pain."

"Oh, no," Darla denied. "I'm fine. I was just remembering how scared I was that Sebastian was going to tear into me that day after I'd lost Bastian. But you know what? He was so understanding. He said it was just the beginning of my adventure as a parent and to get used to it. And Marley! She was just the best. I don't deserve how nice they were to me that day."

This statement caused him to wince this

time, but with sympathy. Why did she think so little of herself? Yes, he'd heard the gossip. Who hadn't? It had been the juiciest to hit Port Domingo in years. The wife of the most successful guy in town running off with a rock star she'd just met at the town's yearly seafood/music festival. When he'd heard it, he hadn't wanted to believe it was true because he really liked Sebastian and thought highly of Darla. Like a lot of people, he thought they made a lovely couple and everyone had wished them well on the birth of their perfect baby boy.

"You know," he said slowly, choosing his words carefully, "when I was serving in Afghanistan, I never knew what the day would bring. All I could do was hope I'd be able to cope with whatever happened. I'm lucky that my actions always ended in a positive way. I might save a life one day. I might come close to death the next but walk away, which is the desired outcome when you're in that kind of situation. But even though I fooled myself into thinking I was in control? I never actually was. I was just winging it and hoping for the best.

"I say all of this to say, I don't know where

your head was at the time you made the decision to leave with J. J. Starr. But I'd be willing to bet it wasn't as clear as it is today. We all make mistakes. And when we attempt to correct them, we deserve the chance to try. The people who really love you will support you in that."

Tears sat in her eyes, and he knew he'd said something that had gotten through to her. He just didn't know what it had been.

Darla took a deep breath and wiped the tears that had fallen onto her cheeks with a napkin. She met his eyes. "I had postpartum depression and didn't recognize it. I only found out later when I was in Portland, Oregon, and in nursing school. One of my instructors and I were talking one day and I described my symptoms and she told me that's what I probably had. I just thought I was unfit to be a good mother. And then, to add credence to my delusion, I met J.J., who told me I was beautiful and that I had a good voice. I didn't know until later on that he told all the girls that. Also, at that time, Sebastian was working ten-hour days. But even through those long hours he always found time to bond with Bastian. Bastian responded positively to him, whereas with me, he cried all the time. I felt like a third wheel. I didn't know what I was doing wrong."

"You didn't think to talk to someone about it?" Dave asked softly.

"And admit I was a freak of nature who couldn't even stop her own child from crying? No, I just panicked more until one day my mother came over and told me to get out of the house, she would take care of Bastian. She must have noticed I was going crazy, but she isn't the type to offer advice if it isn't asked for. She thinks she's meddling. And I was too afraid to ask."

"You were overwhelmed," Dave offered. "Lots of new parents feel incapable of coping those first few months."

She offered him a wan smile. Dimples appeared in her reddish-brown face and she self-consciously brushed a wayward lock of long, curly black hair behind her ear.

"Don't be kind, Dave. Yeah, okay, I might not have known I was suffering from postpartum depression but even a fool knows that you don't flirt with another man when you're married. And I'm guilty of that."

She stopped suddenly and regarded him

with a frown. "What do you remember about me from our high school days?"

Dave smiled, but he was worried that he would say the wrong thing. So he kept it general and complimentary. "You loved to sing. You were popular. One of the girls the other girls wanted to be like, and guys wanted to date."

"In other words, I was a selfish, materialistic person who cared more about my outfits than about other people."

"I didn't say that," he began.

"You didn't have to," Darla said. "I was an insecure pretty girl who craved attention. Now, why I craved the spotlight, I never figured out. It wasn't that my mom didn't give me enough attention. She did the best she could after our dad died. I don't know, maybe it was seeing her struggle that lit a fire under me to become rich and famous, no matter what it took." She paused again. "What am I doing, telling you all of this? You didn't come here to hear my sad story."

"I really don't mind," Dave assured her, and meant it. She was talking to him and that was enough for him. "And I promise you, nothing you say will be repeated by me."

She seemed to relax after that statement, breathing a sigh of relief and taking another sip of her coffee before continuing. "Thanks. I haven't been able to talk to anyone who is totally uninvolved in this situation and can be absolutely unbiased about it."

Dave wasn't sure how unbiased he could be since he was very attracted to her. But he was willing to try.

A song by Adele drifted through the air. It was quiet otherwise because the other customers were either lost in their laptops and cell phones or had earphones on while they enjoyed their drinks.

"I know people are wondering if I knew all along that Marley was in love with Sebastian years ago. But I had no idea. I like to think that, deep down, I would have stepped aside if I'd known. We used to be good friends. Marley, Kaye and I not only sang together, we dreamed together. Marley was the most talented. She was playing gigs around the area when she was a teen. She was a great guitarist, too. Kaye had the soulful Mahalia Jackson gospel voice. She could really move you. And I could carry a tune, but I admit that I depended on my looks more and didn't develop my singing talent as much as they did. I really miss them." She ended with a longing-filled sigh.

"You're not friends anymore?" he asked, his tone soft.

"Kaye has reached out, but I'm too ashamed to go talk to her," she stated sadly. "And trying to rekindle my friendship with Marley is complicated. She's really pleasant when we see each other, but I'm afraid to go any further because even if she wants to be my friend, I'm not sure how comfortable Sebastian would be if his present wife and his ex-wife started hanging out together."

Dave nodded slowly. "I can see your point. But look, Darla, you know who you are as a person. Don't let what someone else might think of you color your own opinion of yourself. Know who you are and stand by that. Be proud."

"I can see where you're going with this. I guess I should stop second-guessing what others think of me. What's important is what I think of myself. It's just hard to do, Dave," Darla said. She finished off her coffee and set the cup down. "Well, I've bent your ear enough for one day. I'd better get back to my shopping and let you get on with your day."

She sat for a moment, just smiling at him. "Thank you for listening to my woes, Dave."

He watched as she picked up her shoulder bag and prepared to rise, possibly to walk out of his life forever. "Let me be your friend," he said, the words coming out in a heated rush.

And when he looked up and saw she was still there, he added, "In fact, I've admired you for a long time and I was wondering if you'd like to have dinner with me sometime."

Darla, who had half risen out of her chair, sat back down and rehung her shoulder bag onto the back of her chair by its strap.

Afterward, she looked him straight in the eyes and said, "Dave, haven't you been listening to me? I'm the bad girl of Port Domingo. I'm sure Miss Margherita has warned you about women like me. If not, then I will—stay far, far away from me. Besides, I don't date. I've been honest with you in hopes that, in case you were thinking of asking me out, you would think twice. I haven't been out with anyone since J.J. And that's been nearly five years. Frankly, with trying to be a good mother to Bastian, my job and making sure I don't do something else that will embarrass my dear, sweet mother, I'm pretty much booked until the next millennium."

Dave laughed softly at her "next millennium" comment. Then he recalled she had referred to his mother as Miss Margherita instead of Miss Margaret. He took that as a good sign. She paid attention and out of respect for his mother, used her birth name, not her Americanized name. "So, it's because you're busy that you won't go out with me. It's not because you don't like me."

She laughed, too. "Did you see how that cute server looked at you? Dave, you're adorable. I'm sure plenty of women around here would give their eye teeth to go out with you. I'm just not one of them. Sorry."

"It's not because my grandfather, a former chief of police of this town, was a known racist and made the lives of Black and brown citizens a living hell?"

This, he saw, drained the laughter right out of her. She sat up straighter in her chair and met his eyes. "So what if your grandfather was a legendary racist around these parts? You can't choose your relatives. You come from good parents. The racist attitude obviously skipped your dad. I like your mother. I know your father only by sight, but your mother and my mother belong to the same charitable organization in town. They help the elderly by making sure they get hot meals and do repairs on their houses when they need it. I've participated in the past and gotten to know Miss Margherita a little. I know you're nothing like your grandfather, Dave."

"So, you're okay with the interracial thing," he said, wanting to be clear on the subject.

She smiled. "Yes, but that's neither here nor there. I'm not ready to date anyone, Black, white, or in your case half Italian and half Irish."

Dave sat smiling at her, with her smiling right back at him. Her dark brown, almond-shaped eyes sparkled. It told him that although she definitely wasn't ready to start dating again, she found his company entertaining. He was banking on that.

He cleared his throat. "Okay, so, you won't go out with me. How about signing Bastian up for Little League? It would be a good way for you to bond with him and get to know some other parents with kids his age. Sign-up starts soon. He's about six, right? The kids in his age group are in the Tee Ball Division, and the teams are coed—girls and boys play together. It's a lot of fun for the kids." He laughed shortly. "And it teaches the parents how to play well with others, too."

Still smiling at him, she astutely asked, "And how does my signing Bastian up for Little League benefit you?"

"I'm the coach," he told her. "If you bring him to the games, at least you and I will be around one another. You'll see I'm a not-too-weird guy and maybe after a while you'll take pity on me and decide to go out with me. Sound reasonable?"

"Sounds like a long shot," she said, but with that humorous glint in her eye. "But I'll ask Bastian if he wants to participate and if he does and it's all right with his father, I'll see what I can do. That's all I'm promising."

"You're a fair woman," he said, rising. He took his wallet out of his back pocket and retrieved one of his business cards from it and handed it to her. "I know it's old-fashioned, but I think it's much more personal than exchanging cell phone numbers. Besides, this gives you the option of contacting me and you won't have to worry about my stalking you since I won't have your number. Safety first."

When she took it, their fingers touched. Her eyes met his at that moment and, once again, his heart skipped a beat.

"You're such a chief," she murmured and slipped the card into her shoulder bag. She gave him a beautiful smile before turning and walking away, leaving him standing at their table. He sat back down and sighed. He was rusty when it came to matters of the heart. Rusty, and wholly lacking in that mythological charm men from the South were supposed to possess. As was his nature, though, he immediately perked up. Maybe his being without guile and an ulterior motive would work in his favor. Darla had apparently had enough of charm and manipulation from her experience with J. J. Starr. After all, Mr. Starr had put her off men for almost five years.

CHAPTER THREE

"KAYE, I CAN'T believe I let you talk me into this," Darla hissed at her old friend as they got out of Kaye's car in the Saint Domingo Catholic church parking lot on a Tuesday night. There were several other vehicles of various makes and models in the well-lit parking lot. Darla assumed they belonged to Kaye's fellow choir members.

The weather tonight was cool and breezy. Darla was glad she'd worn a long-sleeved shirt with her jeans.

Kaye Johnson, five-three and full-figured, tossed her natural, abundant black braids with golden highlights over her shoulder and laughed. "Now, don't start getting cold feet. You're just auditioning for soprano in a choir, not for *America's Got Talent*." She pressed the locking function on her key fob.

"But what if they hate me? People haven't been real friendly since I came back home."

Kaye gave her a fierce look. "And you're going to take that lying down? No, no, my friend. No one in this town is gonna make you afraid to live your life. Who do they think they are? Matthew, chapter seven, verse one says anyone who condemns others will be condemned themselves!"

"Oh, here we go, she's already quoting the Bible," said a feminine voice to Darla's left. Darla was startled by the sound of the voice: Marley.

"Where have you two been? I've been waiting out here for at least ten minutes," Marley complained lightly. She went and hugged Kaye and before Darla could protest, hugged her, too.

Marley stood with her hands on her hips, practically defying Darla to protest her sudden appearance. Darla noticed all three of them were dressed in jeans, casual blouses and athletic shoes, similar to what they wore daily back in high school. It made her feel nostalgic.

Darla stared at Marley, whose natural, curly black hair had grown even longer in the few months she'd been home. "Is this a setup?" she asked.

"Yes," Marley said, not trying to deny it. "Kaye and I got together recently and we decided that you've been a chicken long enough."

"How would you know I've been chickening out?" Darla asked, knowing the answer before the words were completely out of her mouth. "Momma's been talking to your grandmother."

"You've got it," said Marley. "Miss Evie told Eula Mae that if you're not working or running errands, you just stay home redecorating her house. Not that she's not appreciative of your efforts but, frankly, she thinks you're wasting your life with all the self-flagellation going on. Those were her words. You know how ex-schoolteachers like your mom and my grandmother like using SAT words every now and then to prove they know more than us common folk."

The three of them laughed.

"Yeah, she couldn't just say that I'm super critical of myself?" Darla said.

Kaye leaned her butt against the door of her late-model Toyota Camry. This told Darla to get comfortable. Their conversation was going to last awhile.

"I see you two intend to get to the bottom of what my problem is and solve it in one night," Darla said, a bit defensively. She was fighting against the urge to just spill her guts to them, she was so happy they still considered her worthy of their friendship. But she had her pride.

Marley hopped onto the hood of Kaye's Toyota and crossed her legs. "Uh-huh, that's about the size of it. You're not some fading wallflower, Darla Mae Cramer. Why is it that people in the South love to name their females Mae? Anyway, Kaye and I've known you since you were a toddler. You're a fighter."

Darla was the only one still standing all stiff as if she had to be on guard against another assault to her spirit. But with Marley's assertion that she was a fighter deep down, she felt the tension leave her body and she went and planted her butt against Kaye's Toyota, too, and got ready to have a talk fest with her longest-lasting friends.

"It's like this," she told them. "I know you and Sebastian have been polite and everything, but I can't help feeling that because of what I did, we're never going to really feel comfortable around one another again. By the way, does he know where you are?"

Marley smiled at her. "Of course he does. We don't have any secrets between us."

"And he's okay with it?" A spark of hope fired in Darla's chest.

"After I told him I was going to come anyway, he got okay with it," Marley bluntly told her. "Look, he's been hurt by you in the past and it's going to take him a while to be convinced he can trust you again. All of that's going to take time. But when I told him we all need to get along for Bastian's sake, he agreed with me. For Bastian's sake, the adults have to behave like civilized human beings. Plus, for the sake of our future children. Mine and Sebastian's and yours and whomever you wind up with in the future. They will all be Bastian's brothers and sisters."

"Oh, I'm not having any more children," Darla stated emphatically.

"You'll change your mind when you meet someone, fall in love and want to reproduce with him," Kaye joked.

"Nope," Darla insisted.

Marley sighed. "Let's leave that discussion for another time, ladies."

Darla and Kaye harrumphed and silently agreed to table the discussion. So Marley continued, "Darla, I want to know exactly why you believe that our relationship might be strained forever."

Darla turned to face her so that she would be looking Marley in the eyes. She wanted to see her reactions close-up when she confessed what had been on her mind.

"First of all, I want you to know how grateful I am that you were there for Sebastian and Bastian when I took off. Momma told me she offered to step in and help with Bastian, but Sebastian told her that you had already volunteered. You became a surrogate mother to him."

She spoke swiftly, afraid to let Marley get a word in, because if she were interrupted, she might lose her nerve and clam up. "I have wracked my brain trying to recall any time in the past when I noticed that you were attracted to Sebastian and I can't remember an instance. If I'd known you were in love with him, I'd like to think I would have stepped aside and let you have him. I loved you that much. I know I did. Why didn't you ever tell us you loved him? Kaye and I told you about our crushes when we were in high school."

Marley suddenly climbed off the hood of Kaye's car and went and hugged Darla. "Are you tormenting yourself over that?"

When she held Darla away from her, Darla saw that tears rolled down her cheeks. "I didn't tell anyone," Marley said. "Not even Father Rodriguez!

"Besides," Marley continued, "Life isn't a fairy tale. Sebastian was in love with you. He didn't love me then. He saw me as a little sister. It took him a while to fall in love with me."

Kaye went and made it a group hug. "Y'all need to stop this crying. I'm not looking forward to having to reapply my eye liner."

After some sniffing, they got their crying under control and Marley looked Darla in the eyes. "Is that it? You wanted to make sure I don't hate you for taking my man?"

Darla nodded. "It sounds silly now, but yeah, that was it."

"Then we're good?" Marley pressed.

"Yes, we're good," Darla answered sheepishly.

"Excellent," said Kaye. "There's still time for you to audition."

Darla froze. She'd forgotten all about the audition to join the choir. In fact, after being ambushed by Marley, she'd assumed the audition had been a ruse to get her here.

"What do you mean? The audition is real?" Her voice rose in panic.

"Of course it's real," said Kaye smiling. "Singing has always been your happy place. Our happy place. So, come on, let's go. I told you to choose a song and practice it, remember?"

"Oh, good, which song did you choose?" Marley asked excitedly.

Darla's palms were sweating by now. "'His Eye Is on the Sparrow,'" she said. "But I'm in no shape emotionally to sing now. You two have drained me with this stunt."

"Oh, diva, please," said Marley. "You know you want to get up there and sing."

Darla calmed down because Marley was right, as usual. She loved to sing. So what if she wasn't Whitney Houston? The joy she felt when performing made up for the lack of technical expertise.

She brightened. "Okay, but only if you two will sing with me."

"No problem," Marley immediately agreed.

"That song's in my repertoire," Kaye said. "Which version did you settle on?"

"The version in *Sister Act 2*," Darla said, excited by the prospect now. "Would you listen to me before we go in and give me your honest opinions?"

"We'll do better than that," Kaye said. "We'll be your backup."

"Yeah," Marley agreed. "We'll blend together on the chorus."

They each stood up straight and gave each other space, assuming the correct posture, chests held high but not strained, shoulders back, abdomen firm and ready to expand when they sang from their diaphragms. All things they had been practicing for years, because the voice was an instrument and a singer learned how to play it as such.

Darla began singing, "'Why should I feel discouraged…'"

On the night air, her voice sounded clear and true. She loved the words of the gospel song, which, according to her google search, was written in 1905. She liked knowing the origins of songs she sang. It made her feel more connected to them. It was also a song she was very familiar with because it was her go-to one to sing when she needed a boost of encouragement.

Her emotions were high due to her reunion with Kaye and Marley, so she sang from her heart. And when she came to the chorus, Kaye and Marley joined her: "'I sing because I'm happy…'"

Hearing all three of their voices raised in song again was almost her undoing. It was like coming home after a long, arduous journey completely devoid of rest or a friendly gesture from another human being.

They sang on, reaching new heights. This felt like a celebration to her. She hadn't been this happy in a long time, her joy punctuated by melodious notes she belted out. Kaye and Marley were supporting her, lifting her up, buoying her spirit.

When they finished singing, from behind them they heard applause, shouts of praise and good-natured ribbing from one choir member Darla heard say, "Don't they know we have a perfectly good rehearsal hall inside?"

Thirty or so choir members from inside the sanctuary had heard them singing and decided to come investigate.

The choir director, a dreadlocked Black man in his late twenties of average height and stocky build, wearing jeans and a T-shirt with *I Sing for the Lord* written across his chest, came forward. "Kaye," he said, "when I agreed to listen to your friend sing, I thought you were going to bring her inside. But this will do. You're in, Darla."

To which the choir members applauded again. Then Kaye started introducing Darla to everyone, after which they began making their way back inside the church to resume choir rehearsal.

Darla couldn't have imagined a more perfect night, despite the biting mosquitoes.

"WHEN DID YOU notice some of your display jewelry was missing?" Dave asked Joy Henderson, owner of Joy's Crystals and Healing Emporium.

Joy, in her sixties, was tall and thin with short, spiky white hair. Dave noticed she was usually attired in flowy dresses and sandals and accessorized with her own hand-made jewelry. Her shop had been downtown for about ten years and, unlike many jewelry stores, she didn't use locked display cases. Her entire stock was on shelves for easy browsing by her customers. Which, in his opinion, made her an extremely trusting person.

Admittedly, her jewelry was not made of precious stones like diamonds or rubies or emeralds. She used crystals and other natural gemstones like the moonstone, amethyst, tourmaline and turquoise. He doubted anything in the shop sold for over fifty dollars. She must do well for herself, though, because she had customers coming from all over the county and a fair number of tourists who frequented her store.

Dave knew all of this because his mother worked part-time at Joy's shop. And she was always complaining about the lack of security. Joy was just too trusting. She had not even had cameras installed. According to his mother, she believed that if anyone stole from her they must have a good reason to do it. Perhaps they needed it more than she did. She called it giving back to the universe that had so generously blessed her.

In fact, it had been his mother who had reported the crime and insisted he come investigate.

He had agreed but told her to make herself scarce. He didn't want her putting her two cents worth in. He only wanted to speak with the owner.

Joy cleared her throat and looked up at him. "To tell the truth, I wasn't the one who noticed. Margherita told me about it and I double-checked. She was right. A pair of sterling silver turquoise dangle earrings and a matching necklace are missing. Together they're worth about sixty dollars."

"That was the sale price on them?"

"No, that's what they cost me to make," Joy said.

"Then how much were you selling them for?"

"Seventy," Joy said.

Now, Dave knew the woman was a saint. He would wager that most jewelry stores' markups were way more than that. No wonder his mother was worried about her boss and friend.

"You know, Miss Henderson," Dave said, putting his notepad and pen that he'd been taking notes with back in his uniform's shirt pocket. "These days, technology being less expensive, cameras might be a good idea for you. I'm sure your insurance company would appreciate your having a bit more security in your place of business. They might even lower your rates if you did that."

Joy smiled, and for a moment he thought he saw interest in her brown eyes. But it didn't last long. Joy shook her head no. "I don't want my customers thinking I don't trust them."

"It's routine for businesses to have cameras on the premises," Dave offered. "No one would think you're accusing them of being untrustworthy."

"Yeah, but that's not how I've run my business all these years and I'm doing fine."

Dave smiled. He was obviously not getting anywhere. Who was he to argue the point? It was her business, and she made the rules.

"Okay, then, I'll be going," he told her, heading for the exit.

She walked him to the door. "Thank you for coming, Chief. But it isn't as if this was a big-city jewelry heist. Some kid probably took it to give to his mother or his girlfriend. I hope whoever winds up wearing it enjoys it."

Dave sighed. Yes, she was one of the nicest people he'd ever met. "You enjoy the rest of your day, Miss Henderson."

"You, too, Chief," she said gaily.

Dave began his walk back to the police station. He loved that Port Domingo was so conducive to bipedal mobilization, as his dad called walking.

And he was appreciative of the fact that crime was not running rampant in their beautiful town. Sometimes he thought of his job as the most boring on earth, with five minutes of heart-pounding drama every once in a while. He tried his best to cope with the interminable hours spent day after day, and he prayed he'd be ready when the inevitable emergencies and life-threatening scenarios presented themselves. In life, he told his staff, a police officer had to be prepared for anything.

So when a teenage boy sprinting out of the supermarket nearly knocked him down, he quickly assessed the situation and took off after the kid. One of his newer officers came barreling out right behind the kid and yelled, "Chief, it's the Spivey kid again. This time he snatched a woman's purse out of her shopping cart."

Dave's first thought, after hearing the officer's report, while he was pounding the sidewalk, was that the store had signs posted warning customers not to leave their purses unattended in shopping carts. His next thought was that he was glad he ran every morning before work because this kid was fast. "Damien," Dave yelled at the boy, "don't make this harder than it has to be. I know where you live."

A few minutes later, he and Damien Spivey were in a residential neighborhood, having run clear through the downtown area. The boy wasn't even looking back. He had his head down as though he was running a marathon.

Suddenly, a car backing out of a yard blocked the youth's path. He tried to maneuver around it and tripped over his own feet. He landed face-down on someone's lawn.

Dave grabbed him by the arm and pulled him to his feet.

The boy was so winded, he didn't put up a fight. Dave, who was grateful the pursuit was over with, handcuffed him. By that time, his backup had caught up with them. He turned the boy over to the officer. "Read him his rights and hold on to him. I'm calling for a cruiser to pick him up."

"Chief, you were really moving," the young officer, also breathing hard, complimented him with a grin.

Dave laughed. "I'm getting too old for this."

When Dave got back to the police station, the officer manning the front desk, Laraine Winslow, stopped him before he could head back to his office. "Chief," she said brightly, "you have a message."

She handed him a slip of paper. He thanked her and continued on to his office. A glance at what was written on the paper made him pause in his steps.

"Yes," the message read, "Bastian wants to join your Little League team. You can call me with the details."

He smiled. She'd left her number. It had been two weeks since his encounter with Darla and he'd just about given up hope that she would actually respond to his offer. He felt like dancing, but there were too many staff around who would never let him live it down. So he calmly walked into his office, closed the door and then in the privacy of his inner sanctum, he cried, "Yes, that's what I'm talking about!" But not too loudly because Laraine's desk was only a few feet away.

CHAPTER FOUR

DAVE'S HEART SWELLED with pride as he glanced around him while he flipped burgers. It was a beautiful late March day on a Saturday, and he and nearly all thirty of his officers were enjoying their annual Family Day Picnic surrounded by their loved ones. Of course, some of the officers had to work today, but even they would be relieved of duty at intervals so that they could come join the fun.

The noise level was high as kids ran wild, chasing one another, and competing in sack and three-leg races with their parents. Later, there would be a softball game pitting adults against the kids. The menu consisted of burgers and hotdogs with various side dishes. Garret's bakery provided the desserts.

Dave's parents were holding court beneath one of the three huge tents where picnic tables were set up. His dad, David Jr., (he was number three), was playing cards with a few other seniors, and from the way his dad was slapping those cards down onto the tabletop, he was enjoying himself.

"Medium rare, please," his sister, Maria, jokingly said as she sidled up to him. She'd just gotten there with her husband, Grant, and their two children: Sadie, four, and Ben, six.

Maria was almost the spitting image of their mother, Margherita. She was tall at around five-ten, dark-haired and dusky-skinned, like him. Both of them tanned easily. Looked like she'd been spending a lot of time outdoors.

"Sis, Grant, kids, I'm glad you could make it," Dave greeted them while simultaneously moving some burgers from the grill into the huge aluminum pan keeping the others warm. "And it's self-serve. All the fixings are on that table, so eat up. Someone else is going to take over for me in a few minutes because we're getting ready to start the softball game soon."

Grant grinned. He was around the same height as Maria with curly light brown hair and hazel eyes. Both their kids had inherited their mother's coloring and dark brown hair, although they favored their dad more, both having his almond-shaped eyes and dimples in their chins.

"I don't have to be told twice," Grant said and grabbed a paper plate and began building a humongous burger. Ben followed his dad, while Sadie shyly clung to one of her mom's legs, peeking around at the other children ripping and running everywhere.

Dave finished transferring the cooked burgers, then put other patties onto the grill. This done, he wiped his hands on a dish towel and went and picked Sadie up and kissed her loudly on her cheek. She giggled. He adored his niece and nephew and wished he had more time to spend with them.

"How's my sweet Sadie?" he said as she wrapped her arms around his neck and returned his kiss.

"Good," she said.

"She's hooked on books. She wants me to read to her all the time," Maria proudly told her brother. "I can't keep up with her."

"Is that so?" Dave said, looking his niece in the eyes. "What's the title of your favorite book?"

"My Grandma Lives in Florida," Sadie answered, smiling.

"I can guess who gave you that one," Dave said.

"Grandma Margie," Sadie said. Margie was what she called her grandmother Margherita.

As if thinking about her had conjured her, his mother strode up to them and commandeered her granddaughter. She grabbed Sadie out of his arms and began raining kisses on Sadie's plump cheeks. "Sadie, Sadie, you're just in time to be my partner in the three-legged sack race."

"Hi, Mom," Maria said. Dave noted her tone and figured she was feeling a little neglected. When her grandkids were around, his mother ignored everyone else.

"Oh, hi, Maria, Grant," his mother said. However, her eyes were on Ben, who was trying his best to bite into his hamburger, but his little mouth didn't open wide enough, so he wound up nibbling on the edges instead.

"Are you having trouble with that big burger?" Margherita asked. She set Sadie down and went to cut the sandwich Grant had made for Ben into manageable pieces. Ben gazed up at his grandmother in wonder. "Thanks, Grandma," he said, and dived in.

This done, Margherita got down on one knee to regard Sadie on her level. "Are you hungry, too, baby? Or will you go with grandma and have some fun?"

Sadie went into her arms and Margherita walked off with her, looking back at the others with a triumphant expression on her face. "That woman would steal my children if I let her," Maria grumbled with a laugh.

"Sometimes," Grant said, "that's a good thing." Then he turned his attention to his burger like his son, who was happily devouring his sandwich.

Dave went over to the grill to turn the fresh burgers. Maria stuck close by. Dave, who knew his sister's facial expressions, guessed that she had something she wanted to talk to him about.

"Go on," he told her as he flipped the burgers. "What's on your mind?"

"Darla Cramer." She said Darla's name in her annoying singsong fashion that took him right back to their childhood.

"What about Darla?" He kept his tone light and airy.

"Mom told me about you and her."

"How did Mom find out? I haven't spoken with her about Darla. Actually, there is no me and her. She hasn't even gone out with me yet."

"Who knows where Mom gets her information. I don't even want to know. But you do want to go out with her?"

"Indeed, I do."

"I'm happy for you."

Dave glanced up. "Why?"

"Because you haven't shown any interest in anyone since Macy, and I'm glad you're finally trying to get back into dating."

"I'm over Macy."

"She broke your heart."

"It mended."

Maria sniffed derisively. "I guess I'm not over it. I wanted to dropkick her into next week. Saying you weren't enough of a bad boy for her? You're chief of police. What was she wanting? For you to rob a bank, commit a murder, scam a bunch of old folks out of their retirement? Talk about a ditz!"

Dave cleared his throat. "Listen, sis, Macy

wants what Macy wants and I didn't fit the bill. Let's move on. I'm just glad she let me know how she felt before it went further. Divorces can get messy." He was glad Macy Patterson had moved to Atlanta, where, in a city that size, she probably had her choice of bad boys. There were slim pickings in Port Domingo.

Maria took a cleansing breath and smiled at him. "You're right. I know you're right. Just, truth be told, I wanted to tear her hair out for dissing my brother."

"You are your mother's daughter," Dave teased her.

She punched him in the arm, hard. "Take that back!"

"Ouch!" Dave rubbed his arm with a mock scowl on his face. "Don't injure the best player before the game starts."

Maria laughed at his claim that he was the best player.

She took a step back and pointed at her glaringly white athletic shoes. "I didn't wear these babies just to look good. I'm going to be the best player on that field today."

Laraine Winslow, who was the police department's front desk officer and sometime dispatcher, and the employee who had the most seniority at the Port Domingo Police Department, cleared her throat behind them. Dave turned and smiled at Laraine. She was a petite African American woman in her fifties with beautiful, flawless dark brown skin and black eyes. She wore her natural black hair in a short Afro and today she was dressed in all white. A sleeveless white blouse and white jeans. Her athletic shoes were as spotless as Maria's.

"Hey, Laraine," Maria said, smiling. "You look fabulous!"

Laraine flashed a white-toothed smile. "So do you. I see your boys, but where is that cutie Sadie?"

"With her grandmother," Maria answered, pulling a face.

Laraine laughed at her expression. "There's no one better to teach her the ways of the world."

Dave was touched. His mother was loved by a lot of people in Port Domingo. Even when her brutal honesty put her on someone's bad side. But she was also generous and kind, so they tended to quickly forgive.

And she was the first person to lend a hand when someone was in need.

"I couldn't agree more," Maria said. "If only she wouldn't gloat about it so much."

"But then she wouldn't be Margherita," Laraine said with a smile. "The world needs diversity in human beings. Otherwise things would get boring. Say what you will about your mother, but she's never boring."

Then Laraine turned her attention to Dave, her expression serious. "I came to make sure you weren't cooking these burgers to death. Remember last year?"

"That was a fluke, and you know it," Dave said. Last year he'd burned a few burgers when he'd gotten distracted. He guessed that was why Laraine was commandeering the grill. He dutifully handed her the long-handled spatula.

Taking it, Laraine said, "Now, go start the ball game. I'm looking forward to seeing my grandkids embarrass you old folks."

Dave remembered Laraine had five grandkids: three boys and two girls and every last one of them were great athletes. Just like their grandmother.

"BATTER UP!" shouted Dave from behind home plate, where he'd taken up position as umpire.

The adults were in the field. The kids had won the coin toss and after their parents made sure their safety helmets were on, the game was about to begin. He was excited because this was the first time this baseball diamond would be used. This park, located about a three-minute drive from downtown Port Domingo, had been inaugurated just last month. There was a playground with swings, a slide and a sandbox, as well as a basketball court, a tennis court and the baseball field they were presently getting ready to play ball on. And, of course, there were public toilets at both entrances.

Dave tugged his cap's bill down farther to protect his eyes from the bright sun and got ready for the first pitch. Rob Conrad's son, Mark, stepped up to home plate. Seven years old, with a determined grimace on his brown face, he got into batter stance, wiggled his slim hips a bit, as though he were a seasoned pro loosening up his muscles. He raised the bat and waited for the pitch.

Pitching was Josh Plummer, a tall, muscular police officer who knew what he was doing, but somehow failed to get the ball over the plate with his initial pitch.

"Outside ball," Dave called.

"That was good," Josh protested.

"It was way outside," Kayla Conrad, Mark's mother, called from the sidelines, her hand resting on her baby bump.

Dave got into position again. "Right here, Josh," he said, holding his glove up.

Josh threw another pitch and this time it was right over the plate. Mark swung and hit a line drive that flew past Josh's head and straight to the outfield, where several adult players scrambled to retrieve it. Meanwhile, Mark gleefully ran to first base, and seeing that no one had the ball yet, kept running until he landed on second base.

The onlookers cheered. A group of moms started chanting and clapping, "Way to go, Mark. Show them what you've got."

Next up to bat was one of Laraine's grandsons, Dwayne. Dave thought he appeared to be around twelve, despite his height, and he was in great shape.

The kid approached home plate slowly, as if he were weighing his options. He glanced at Dave and nodded at him. Dave nodded back. He scrutinized the sky for a moment and squinted in the sun's bright light. Then he boldly pointed in the direction of the fence that surrounded the park. That fence was fifty yards away. Dave didn't think the kid could hit a ball that far.

Josh wiped the sweat off his brow and wound up to pitch. He threw the ball. Dwayne stepped forward and just tapped the ball with the bat. He'd faked them out. He was bunting, not swinging for the fence. Josh leaped for the ball and missed it.

"Do you have a hole in your glove?" shouted Margherita and everyone laughed.

Dwayne easily made it to first base before the ball was recovered and was once again safely in Josh's hand.

Dave smiled to himself. He loved it when the kids used their brains as well as their prowess to outsmart the adults.

Now there was one kid on first base, and one kid on third because Mark had safely made it to third after Dwayne's bunt.

The next batter up was Brandi McCammon, a lovely blond girl of ten. Her mom was Misty McCammon, one of two women on the police force. She was so delicate looking that Dave worried she wouldn't be able to hit the ball. However, her mother was one of his toughest officers, so he wouldn't be surprised if she landed a home run.

Brandi quietly adjusted her helmet, straightened her hitting gloves and assumed the batter's stance. Josh threw a high ball. She let it go. Dave caught it and returned the ball to Josh. Josh then threw a solid pitch.

Brandi hit the ball with all her strength behind her swing. The ball soared through the air. Everyone out there followed its trajectory straight over the fence.

"That's my girl!" yelled Misty, jumping up and down. Her husband, Jim, was jumping right alongside her. Brandi ran at breakneck speed around the bases, smiling all the way. Now the kids had three points.

Dave was cheering along with everyone else. This was what he loved about baseball. Practically anyone could play the game and fall in love with it.

After Mark, Dwayne and Brandi cleared home plate, the three of them gave each other high fives.

From the sidelines, Dave heard Laraine say, "If the first five minutes of this game is any indication, you adults are going to get your butts beat today!"

Thirty minutes later, Dave had to admit that Laraine was onto something. The kids were leading 7–0.

And they held on to the lead, wrapping up the game with a final score of 13–3. The kids were over the moon, and the adults were just glad they could sit down and have a cool glass of lemonade. Everyone had had a blast. He couldn't wait until Little League practice started, when Bastian and Darla could join in the fun.

LATER, DAVE'S MOTHER insisted he come home with her and his father. She'd baked his favorite lasagna, and since Maria, Grant and the kids weren't able to join them for dinner, she was hoping he'd come share a meal with his elderly parents. When she referred to herself and his father as elderly, he knew she was milking it for all she could. She'd wasted the effort, though. He loved his parents and enjoyed spending time with them. Also, he couldn't resist her lasagna. It had been her mother Lucia's recipe and it was worth the mile he'd have to run in the morning to burn the extra calories. Besides, he wanted to grill her on Maria's claim that she was already gossiping about him and Darla.

He stayed after to help clean up, and made it to his parents' southern-style bungalow at around 6:00 p.m.

His dad met him at the door, moving slowly and yawning every few seconds. "What's up, Dad?" he said cheerfully. "Mom put you through your paces today."

His dad closed the door and gestured toward the kitchen of the open floor plan. His mother was retrieving something from the oven. There were wonderful aromas emanating from the kitchen. "I thought we were retired," his dad said. "Some days, though, she has me up at dawn and out and about. That part-time job of hers isn't enough. She needs a hobby. Anything to take her focus off me so I can just vegetate sometimes."

"I sympathize, Dad," Dave said. "I'll have a talk with her."

"It won't do any good. She thinks she's keeping me from being sedentary. Sitting all day will kill you according to your mom. I don't want to sit all day, every day. But one day a week isn't asking too much, is it?"

"Absolutely not," Dave assured him.

Then his mother came from the kitchen and announced dinner was ready.

Afterward, his dad escaped to the den to watch sports while he and his mother went onto the front porch to have a chat.

They sat on the large, white, wooden swing, lined with comfortable cushions and suspended from chains.

His mother sighed as she visibly relaxed.

Dave sat back, his long legs stretched out before him. "Mamma," he began. She loved it when her children called her *mamma*, the Italian word for *mom*, as opposed to the Southern *momma*. She told him it reminded her of when she was growing up in Italy and when her own Mamma was alive. "Mamma," he repeated. "You've got to let Dad have at least one day a week to himself. He worked hard for over forty years. He should be able to do nothing if he wants to."

She turned toward him, shifting her hips on the swing. "I know I'm too hard on him sometimes. I'm working on it. I just remember my papa worked hard all his life, too. He retired and the next thing we knew, he was gone."

"Dad is not Grandpa Alberto."

"I know. Listen, I'll try my best to stop being a helicopter wife."

"A what?"

"You've got helicopter parents who hover over their children, and I hover over your father. I'll try to do better. I promise."

"Okay," Dave said, nodding. "Good. There's one more thing I want to talk to you about."

"Darla?" his mother asked with a humorous glint in her eye.

"Yes. Where did you hear that I'd asked her out?"

"Evie, of course. She and I talk about our children all the time. You scared the poor girl and she told her mother about it. Darla's skittish at this point, baby, so be patient with her."

Remembering that Darla had warned him his mother would probably warn him about getting involved with her, Dave gave his mother an incredulous look. "So, you're fine with my pursuing her?"

She laughed softly. "Why wouldn't I be? She's a lovely girl. I've always liked her. She's got a sweet soul. Everybody makes mistakes. Not everybody tries to correct those mistakes, which is what she's trying to do. So, I think she's worth the effort. Don't you?" And she gave him a coy look.

He laughed. "Mamma, you know I do. But she was really adamant about not dating anyone, not just me."

She sighed again. "You're young yet, so you might not realize this, but life has a way of working itself out. I'm sure she's beating herself up about abandoning her husband and child. However, give her time. She'll realize that there's more for her out there, and you'll be waiting. Like your father was waiting for me when I escaped from Italy and that old man my mamma wanted me to marry. After Papa died, she was just looking for security for me. But I would have rather starved than marry a man twenty years older than me. So I ran to America. Later, I heard he'd married another young woman and she gave him four more children. He already had six by his poor deceased wife. I dodged a bullet!"

Dave laughed. "Mamma, you're crazy."

"Crazy like a fox" was her confident reply.

His dad joined them on the porch at that moment and having heard his wife say she was crazy like a fox, he laughed as he sat down beside her on the swing. Dave got up so they could have the swing to themselves, the lovebirds.

"Now, now, Anna Margherita, you are a fox. But the only thing crazy about you is how you get more beautiful with every passing year. How do you do that?" his dad said while gazing lovingly at his mom.

"What flower wouldn't bloom under your care, you old Irish charmer?" she replied. And then they shared a quick kiss.

Dave laughed. "I think I'll give you two a little privacy. Thanks for dinner." And he hurried down the porch steps.

"Just make sure whomever you end up with thinks you're a charmer, too," his dad called after him.

CHAPTER FIVE

"I'M SORRY, BABY, I know there's no school for the students today, but I can't watch Bastian for you," said Darla's mom, Evie, with her hair sticking up and eyes watery and sleepy like she hadn't rested well last night. She sneezed into her pajama top's sleeve. "This cold sneaked up on me. I feel terrible. You'd better not let Bastian get near me."

It was six o'clock in the morning and Darla had to be at work in an hour. She wanted to go hug her mother and offer comfort but she was dressed in her nurse's uniform and she couldn't risk carrying her mother's germs over to her patient's place. Mr. Jenkins had Parkinson's disease and already had enough to contend with.

So she stood in the doorway and sympathized. "I understand, Mom. You just get your rest. I'll make sure a couple of sandwiches are in the refrigerator for you and before I leave,

I'll bring you a cup of that organic green tea you like."

Her mother smiled at her. "Thank you, sweetie. Maybe Sebastian and Marley can take him today."

"No, they went on a trip yesterday and won't be back until Saturday. Don't worry. I'll take him to work with me. I'm sure Mr. Jenkins won't mind. And Bastian will probably like a change of scenery."

She hoped she sounded optimistic. Inside, she was panicking.

"See you in a few minutes," she told her mother and closed the bedroom door.

She quickly walked down the hall to Bastian's bedroom and opened the door. Bastian was snoring loudly, one leg practically hanging over the side of the twin bed. He was a rough sleeper. She went to him and pulled him into her arms, sat down on the bed and whispered near his ear, "Bastian, Bastian, wake up." Although he was a deep sleeper, whenever he awoke he was instantly aware of what was going on around him.

He opened his brown eyes, so like her own, and frowned at her.

"Momma, where's Grandma?"

His grandmother usually got him out of bed when he didn't have to go to school because Darla left for work so early.

She smiled. "Your grandma isn't feeling well today. So you and I are going on an adventure. I want you to get up, go to the bathroom, wash your face and hands and brush your teeth, and by the time you're finished I will have picked out your outfit. And made breakfast sandwiches for us. You, young man, are going to work with me."

His face immediately lit up. "Really?" He sounded excited by the prospect.

She playfully tapped the tip of his nose with her forefinger. "Really! Now get moving." And she deposited him back onto the bed and left the room. She heard him bound off the bed and run to the bathroom only a few feet down the hall.

"No running!" she called, not looking back as she hurried downstairs to prepare their breakfast, put together those sandwiches she'd promised her mother and brew her green tea.

She had to smile when she walked into the modern kitchen with its white cabinets, top-of-the-line appliances and large island. Her mother loved large kitchens.

At the sink, she paused a moment and enjoyed the view from the window. The day had dawned with promise. The sunlight glinted through the leaves of the big oak tree in the backyard, and there was dew on the grass.

Look at me, she thought, *panicking but still handling my business. A few months ago, I would have doubted my ability to juggle work and care for Bastian. But today, I say bring it on!*

She found herself laughing at her thoughts as she turned around and went to the refrigerator to get the needed ingredients: ham, eggs, cheddar cheese and margarine.

She worked swiftly and proficiently, her kitchen skills honed from years of mentally taking notes while watching her mother in the kitchen. Her mother, like lots of mothers, didn't write down recipes. If you wanted to know how she made a dish, you had to pay attention and remember the ingredients and the instructions.

Ten minutes later, she'd prepared breakfast, made two ham-and-cheese sandwiches for her mother to nibble on throughout the day and brewed the organic green tea. She headed back upstairs, dropped off her mother's tea, wished her a good day and swift recovery from that nasty cold, then went to Bastian's room. Her son was in the midst of choosing his own outfit when she walked in.

He had a pile of clothing on the bed. He looked up at her when she entered. "I want to wear my pocket pants so I can put my soldiers in my pockets," he said.

What he meant was he wanted to wear his cargo pants. She'd forgotten he would need something to keep him occupied while he was on his best behavior today. She went and got the requested pants from the drawer and handed them to him. While he was putting them on, she quickly refolded the clothes he'd removed from the drawers and put them back.

Then she picked out a shirt, a pair of socks and some sneakers for him to complete his ensemble.

"If you're good, you can play with my tablet today."

Her son was adept at using electronics. She couldn't wait to see how he put his skills to good use over the years. "But only for an hour or so."

She went into his closet and retrieved a canvas bag. "Put a couple of your favorite books in this, and your soldiers. The ones that don't make noise. We're playing it by ear today. This will be the first time you meet Mr. Jenkins and we want to make a good first impression."

"Okay, Mommy," Bastian readily agreed. Sometimes he called her Momma and sometimes he called her Mommy. Either way, the term of endearment melted her heart.

In the car on the way to Mr. Jenkins's house, Bastian turned to her and said, "Joey says Mr. Jenkins is scary 'cuz he doesn't go anywhere."

Joey, Darla remembered, was a boy in Bastian's class.

"You've been talking about Mr. Jenkins to Joey?"

Bastian nodded.

Darla sighed. It was all her fault. Bastian had obviously overheard her talking to her mother about Mr. Theodore Jenkins and he had mentioned him to his friend at school. It was true that Mr. Jenkins was kind of a hermit. He never left his house for anything, except doctors' appointments, which she drove him to. He had groceries, and everything else he might need, delivered. He had a live-in housekeeper, Lily Johnson, who was her friend Kaye's aunt and, also, a good friend of her mother's. This was a small town and people talked. Nothing was more suspicious to some people than the thought of someone actually minding his own business and leaving other people's alone.

"Bastian, Mr. Jenkins likes his privacy, but there's nothing wrong with that. It's just a choice. That doesn't make him any scarier than anyone else. He's a nice man and has a perfectly good reason for behaving the way he does. So be kind and remember, he's just another human being trying his best to get along in the world. Like you and me."

"Okay, Mommy," Bastian said, smiling. He played with his soldiers the rest of the trip, providing his own low-volume sound effects.

Mr. Jenkins's Mediterranean-style, three-story home was made of white bricks with a red clay roof. There were ten acres surrounding it, and the grass of the well-tended grounds looked velvety soft and the flowering plants would make any florist envious. Lily told her that it was more than five thousand square feet, had five bedrooms, four and a half baths and three garages. Darla had yet to see every house in Port Domingo, but she was willing to bet this one was the most beautiful.

Every time she was driving up to it, admiring the spectacular yet somehow serene appearance of it, she would momentarily gasp in awe.

It seemed to have the same effect on Bastian, who was leaning forward in his seat, trying to take it all in. "That's a big house!" he exclaimed upon seeing it.

Darla parked her silver Toyota Corolla on the circular drive and turned off the engine. Turning to Bastian, she said, "Let's go."

They walked up to the front door and she pressed the push button of the doorbell. They heard the lilting notes of the chime and momentarily, Lily Johnson answered the door with a big smile on her face. She was in her mid-fifties, tall and plus-size. Her warm brown skin glowed, just like Kaye's. Her thick black hair was streaked with gray and she wore it in braids cascading down her back.

Dressed in her uniform of a white blouse and a black skirt with black athletic shoes, she gestured for them to enter.

"Well, what a lovely surprise," she said after closing the door. "Bastian!" She bent to meet his eyes. "I know you don't remember me, but I've known you since you were a tiny baby. What a handsome young man you are now."

Bastian smiled up at her. "Thank you, ma'am."

"And he's polite, too!" Lily beamed at him. "Come on through to the kitchen."

"I'm sorry for the surprise, Lily, but Mom's sick and there was no one else who could look after Bastian while I worked, and I didn't want to leave Mr. Jenkins high and dry today," Darla hastily explained as they walked through the foyer and the open-concept living area to the kitchen.

"Oh, honey, I understand. It was a long time ago, but I crossed that bridge a few times myself." She continued to smile at Bastian. "And I'd be happy to have Bastian's company today while you put Mr. Jenkins through his paces."

Darla breathed a sigh of relief. "Lily, you

are a lifesaver! So you don't think Mr. Jenkins will mind?"

Suddenly, from behind them, a familiar voice said, "Mind what?"

It was Mr. Jenkins, already dressed in his workout clothes, a gray sweatshirt and pants and a pair of pull-on black athletic shoes. He was using a cane, and his gait was slow and measured, as if he didn't quite have his balance, but was determined to keep going. She was used to that attitude. He fought through his physical challenges.

Darla hurried to him, pulled out a chair at the large round kitchen table and waited beside him until he was seated. He didn't like assistance unless he asked for it. And that didn't often happen because he was stubbornly independent. "I was just telling Lily that I had no choice but to bring my son, Bastian, with me today. I didn't want to miss our appointment."

Mr. Jenkins was in his sixties and of average height and weight. His brown skin had reddish undertones and his short, skillfully cut dark brown Afro was sprinkled with silver. He was handsome with a square jaw that was weathered but still attractive as though he used to spend a lot of time on the ocean, or maybe was a cowboy in his youth. Darla's imagination sometimes ran away with her. She liked Mr. Jenkins and wanted to believe that though he led a rather inactive life now, he used to be "the man" in his day.

Mr. Jenkins had a gruff expression on his face and she worried if Bastian's presence was causing it.

"Bastian, say hello to Mr. Jenkins."

"Hello, sir," Bastian said shyly.

Mr. Jenkins peered at Bastian from beneath his hooded eyes. Bastian was standing close to Darla, but didn't grasp her legs or otherwise try to hide behind her.

Mr. Jenkins said, "Hello, Bastian, I'm pleased to meet you. Come a little closer so I can get a good look at you."

Bastian didn't hesitate to walk forward. But he stopped when he was just out of reach of Mr. Jenkins. "Yes, sir?"

"How old are you?" asked Mr. Jenkins. His voice reminded Darla of James Earl Jones's: deep and cultured. She often wondered what Mr. Jenkins had done for a living before he moved to Port Domingo two years ago. He didn't talk about his personal life. Could he have been a stage actor? Because his voice was definitely compelling.

"I'm six," Bastian said. "And I'm in the first grade."

"Mmm," said Mr. Jenkins. "An educated man. I'm impressed. What would you say is your best subject in school?"

"Reading, sir. I love to read. And draw. I could draw you if you like."

"That I'd like to see," said Mr. Jenkins. His face was animated now. No frowns, only interest.

Bastian closed the space between them and went right up to Mr. Jenkins and said, "This is a big house. Do you have lots of kids?" And he looked around him as though he expected five or six kids around his age to come spilling into the room to play with him.

"I'm afraid I don't," said Mr. Jenkins with a smile. "I was never lucky enough to have any kids."

Bastian looked at him with sympathy in his big brown eyes. "We can pretend I'm your kid," Bastian said, smiling broadly.

Darla couldn't believe her eyes. Was that a tear rolling down Mr. Jenkins's cheek? She had to do something to neutralize the situation. She didn't want Mr. Jenkins to become unduly emotional. Sometimes people with Parkinson's disease suffered from depression because of the frustration they felt from having to live with physical limitations. She looked out for her patients' mental health as well as their physical health.

"Maybe later, sweetie," Darla gently said to Bastian. "Right now, Mr. Jenkins and I have to do our morning physical therapy."

"And you and I will make cookies," Lily brightly suggested, to Bastian's delight.

Mr. Jenkins smiled at Bastian. "Yes, we'll do that later, Bastian. Save me some cookies. I like oatmeal."

Darla firmly took Mr. Jenkins's arm as he rose from his chair and they began walking from the kitchen.

Darla looked back at Lily, who was guiding Bastian toward the pantry, where, Darla guessed, she was going to let him help her choose the ingredients for the cookies she'd promised him.

Darla whispered to Mr. Jenkins, "I promise you, this is a onetime occurrence."

"I hope it won't be," said Mr. Jenkins. "I like that young man."

In the gym, which was located at the back of the house near the laundry room, Darla had Mr. Jenkins sit on the professional massage table while she took his blood pressure. All the tools she needed as a nurse were in the room, including a blood pressure machine and a good stethoscope. She was wearing a watch with a second hand and peered down at it as the air was released from the cuff around his upper arm.

She noted the results. "Not bad, 134/80. Are you watching your salt intake?"

"Yes, ma'am," Mr. Jenkins said with a small smile. "So that's Bastian. I was wondering when I'd get to meet him. I suppose he's the spitting image of his father, because he only has your eyes."

Darla removed the cuff from his arm and stowed the blood pressure machine on its metal stand in the corner of the supply cabinet. Frankly, she was pleased he was showing interest in anyone. "Yes, he does look more like his father than me, but that's fine with me. His father's a good man."

Mr. Jenkins eyed her keenly. "Then there is no animosity between you and his father?"

"Somebody's been filling you in, I see," Darla said.

"Lily and I talk. Besides yourself, she's the only person I see on a regular basis. But don't worry, Lily is not a gossiper. She simply tells me what's going on in Port Domingo so I will be, in her own words, informed about the people who live around me. She couldn't be mean-spirited if her life depended on it. And I just want to see you happy. You do seem a bit happier than you used to be. Has something happened?"

Darla just pointed at the state-of-the-art treadmill. "Get on that for fifteen minutes and I might tell you what you want to know."

Mr. Jenkins gingerly climbed off the massage table and walked slowly over to step onto the treadmill. He had his balance now and apparently was ready to work. He programmed in the pace and started walking uphill. "I suppose you want to negotiate an exchange of information," he said as he climbed the imaginary hill. "Tired of my closed lips, are you?"

Darla laughed. "You bet I am. I've been working with you for months now and I don't know anything about you."

"You know I'm reliable," he said. "I'm always prepared when you get here in the morning. Dressed and ready to work out. And I pay you on time and I'm not stingy."

"Two qualities I totally appreciate," Darla allowed. "I just want to know where you're from and what you did for a living before moving here. You said you'd only been here for about two years. That's all I know about you. Forgive me, I'm nosy."

Mr. Jenkins chuckled. "Okay, I suppose enough time has passed. I will answer those two questions. But you have to promise me that when I reveal my answers, you will not insist on asking me anything else personal today. Just for today. If you want to ask something else, you'll have to wait until our next session. Do you accept those terms?"

Darla squinted at him. He was smart, this one.

She sighed. "All right. I accept your terms."

Continuing his stride, Mr. Jenkins calmly said, "I grew up right here in Port Domingo. And after that I was a professor of English literature at Harvard. Then, and this is a freebie, I retired and started writing novels. My pen name is…"

"Oh, my goodness, you're Charles Winchester!" Darla exclaimed before he could get the words out.

"Smart woman," Mr. Jenkins said with a smile in her direction. He continued to climb the treadmill. "That's one of the reasons I hired you."

CHAPTER SIX

THE FIRST DAY of Little League, the third Saturday of March, couldn't have fallen on a lovelier day. The sky was cloudless, the temperature was in the seventies and there was a cool breeze. Ideal, until Darla spotted her nemesis approaching. Her senses went on red alert. She and Bastian had gotten there early and were sitting in the stands with some other early birds when none other than Joyce Hines came strolling through the gates, a little cutie skipping ahead of her. Bastian, beside her, who until then seemed kind of subdued, perked right up and cried, "Skye!"

The little girl let out a screech of her own. "Bastian!"

Oh, oh, thought Darla, *this can't be good.*

Joyce didn't increase the speed of her leisurely pace as she languidly stepped onto the first rung of the stands and began climbing. Skye, meanwhile, was already at the top hugging Bastian.

"Who is this?" Darla asked. She couldn't help but smile. Skye was a little shorter than Bastian, with skin the color of toasted almonds, mounds of curly black hair pulled up in a ponytail, a bow mouth, dark brown eyes, a pert nose and a pleasantly plump physique. Darla had never seen such an adorable little girl. She looked at Joyce, then back at Skye. Yes, there was a resemblance. Then she remembered that Joyce had also been plump when they were in high school. Was her behavior, then, that of a vicious bully because she herself had been bullied because of her weight? Bullied people sometimes became bullies to protect themselves. It was food for thought.

"This is Skye, Mommy," Bastian said. "We used to be in kindergarten together."

"This your mom?" Skye asked, eyes sparkling. She had personality plus. And if Darla's instincts were correct, this little girl was quite sharp.

"My name is Darla," Darla answered, smiling. "And yes, I'm Bastian's mother."

"I didn't know Bastian had a mom," said

Skye thoughtfully. "I only met his dad, Big Bastian."

Darla chuckled at that nickname. But it was as good a way of remembering her friend's dad's name as any.

"Pleased to meet you, Skye," Darla said. Skye held out her tiny hand and Darla shook it.

"Pleased to meet you, Mrs. Contreras," Skye said.

"Miss Cramer," Darla provided. "I'm not married."

"Oh, cool," said Skye. "I'm not either."

Darla laughed. This tiny lady was hilarious.

Joyce had sat down a few rows below them. She turned to look back at Skye and said, "Skye, you can play with Bastian after practice. Get down here."

Skye, looking disappointed, grunted as she gave Bastian one last tight hug. "Gotta go," she said.

"See you later," said Bastian, also disappointed, by the tone of his voice.

Darla watched Skye carefully walk down a few rows on the stands and sit beside her mother. Joyce took off her sunglasses and glanced up at Darla, her eyes sending daggers in Darla's direction. Joyce didn't say anything, but she took a good long look at Darla and then turned her back on her. A second later several people in the stands started clapping and cheering, especially the kids, because their coach had arrived, carrying a huge bucket of white balls.

Darla tried to keep her expression blank behind her sunglasses but her face broke into a smile anyway. She hadn't seen Dave in about ten days and she hadn't realized until that moment how much she'd missed him. She reminded herself that she wasn't there to see Dave. She was there because her son wanted to join the team. And one of the stipulations that had come with Sebastian's okaying Bastian joining Little League was that she would be the one to bring him to the practice sessions. But now she had to admit that she'd been hoping all along that Bastian would say yes and she'd be rewarded with the bonus of being in the presence of the chief on a regular basis. She liked him in spite of the fact that getting involved with anyone right now scared her. However, she could not spend the rest of her life running.

He stopped at the bottom of the stands,

clipboard in hand, and regarded the parents and kids beaming at him. He was wearing a white polo shirt, a pair of black athletic shorts that came to just above the knee and a pair of black athletic sneakers. He removed his sunglasses and cleared his throat. The breeze ruffled his curly hair a bit and she finally took note of just how attractive he was.

His tanned skin looked so healthy. He was clean-shaven with a strong jawline. He was tall and fit, and his shirt molded over his biceps like a second skin. Gorgeous.

Then he started to speak, and she woke up out of her reverie. Daydreaming wasn't going to cut it if she didn't want to make a fool of herself. She was there to support Bastian. To run drills with him and help him find his love for the game. That was how Dave had put it when he'd phoned the other day to remind her of the first practice session. And that's what she planned to do.

"I'm so glad to see everybody here today," Dave said. "We're going to start drills today. We'll begin with basic throwing and catching. By hand at first with a soft ball. After you become good at catching with your hand, we're going to add gloves. Gloves can take a little getting used to. But don't worry, you'll get the hang of it." He ended with a big grin that went straight to Darla's heart. She glanced at the other women, all smiles and sultry looks. She wasn't the only one who was charmed by the chief.

"So come on down," said Dave as he gestured for them to get up and get busy. Darla took Bastian by the hand and they rose.

"Sounds like fun, huh?" she asked, peering down at him.

Bastian nodded, but he appeared a bit nervous to her.

"Just think, in a few weeks, you're going to be hitting the ball and running around those bases with the best of them."

He grinned. "Really, Mommy?"

"Really, really!" she assured him. And they slowly descended the steps, joining the other parents and kids on the red clay.

WHAT WAS I THINKING? Dave thought when he spotted Darla sitting in the stands with Bastian. He had rarely been nervous when he had to speak in public, but suddenly his brain was scrambling to remember why he was here. He hadn't seen her since they went for a coffee together. He'd spoken with her a couple of times, but those calls had hardly been long enough and perfunctory at best. His heart was racing. He inhaled and exhaled, then launched into his welcome speech. He'd been giving it to the new recruits for the past three years, so he shouldn't have had any trouble remembering what to say. But the presence of Darla made him feel like a tongue-tied novice.

He wished she'd take off her sunglasses so he could get a better look at her face. He wondered if she was using them to hide her nervousness. This thought strengthened his resolve to break down her walls.

After they were standing around him, waiting for his next instructions, a calm came over him. He looked into the faces of every child so he could familiarize himself with their unique features. Of course, some of them were already known to him because they were younger siblings of former Little Leaguers. He knew many of the parents but hadn't met all of the kids. In tee ball there were ten players on the team during each inning. Nine of them were position players and the tenth was an extra outfielder. So there were ten parents today and ten kids.

"Okay, I want the parents to line up here, and the kids to line up across from his or her parent. There's lots of room here to give each other space, so spread out."

After they had followed his directions, he walked down the line with the bucket of soft white balls, and each parent took several, palmed one of them and put what was left down by their feet for easy access.

When all the balls had been distributed, and the kids appeared eager to get started, Dave said, "You're going to start about three feet apart, and toss the ball back and forth. Nothing fancy, just concentrate on catching the ball and throwing it back. Get the feel for it."

He stepped aside and watched the parents toss the balls to their kids. Some of the children were old hands at catching, but a few of them were not as confident. As they improved in their efforts, he told them to put more space between themselves.

About twenty minutes into the drill, he moved on to the next. He held out the bucket for the kids to deposit the soft, white balls.

This done, Dave said, "Now I want you to grab your gloves while I go to my truck and replace these soft, spongy balls with regulation softballs. The softballs are a bit harder than these, but they're not as hard as the baseballs you'll eventually be playing with. So, off you go!"

The kids took this as a challenge and ran back to the stands where they'd left their gloves, with several of their parents reminding them not to run up the steps of the stands.

Dave turned to go to his truck, parked several yards away, just outside the fence of the enclosure.

"Hey, could you use some help?" he heard Darla ask from behind him.

"I'm not going to turn it down," he said easily.

Darla caught up with him. "That was fun," she told him. "I think Bastian enjoyed himself. He's pretty good at catching and throwing already because his dad plays touch football with him."

"I'm not surprised since his dad was quite the football player in his day. I'm glad Sebastian's not one of those fathers who insists his son follows in his footsteps and devotes himself only to football."

"Nah," Darla said as they walked toward the parking area. "Sebastian just wants Bastian to explore things he's interested in. Bastian likes football, too. I don't know, I think he might have taken pity on his poor mom and decided to do this to please me. He's highly sensitive to people's feelings. Despite my abandoning him," she winced, shame written all over her face, "he welcomed me with open arms the moment I came back."

It must have been hard for her to come back to her hometown after having left the way she did. She must have expected a lot of rejection, and not just from people like Joyce Hines, who enjoyed rubbing her face in her past mistakes. He couldn't believe it when Joyce had called him asking about signing her daughter up for Little League. Despite not wanting to deal with her mother, he couldn't bring himself to deprive the innocent little girl of a chance to be on the team. After all, Little League was for the children, not the parents. He just hoped Joyce behaved herself. Sometimes parents were way more trouble than the kids.

"He's an awesome kid," he said, smiling down at her.

They'd arrived at his pickup truck and he reached into the bed and pulled out another bucket, this one filled with softballs, and put the bucket with the soft balls in it back in the bed. There was also a cloth sack filled with various sizes of baseball mitts, just in case a kid had forgotten to bring his personal mitt with him today. The gloves weighed less, so he handed the sack to Darla.

As they made their way back to the others, he gave her his most winsome smile and asked, "So how am I doing so far?"

She chuckled. "I'd give you a B plus."

"A B plus! Then, I'm doing okay. But be warned, I plan on studying hard for the final exam. I'm going to get that A."

"We'll see," said Darla, her gorgeous brown eyes alight with humor. He was glad he'd put that spark in her eye.

AFTER THE KIDS had mastered using the mitts, or at least could catch and hold on to most of the balls, Dave announced they would let the parents take their leave as they were "old and needed their rest."

Some of the kids laughed, while the parents gratefully headed to the bleachers.

When Dave had the kids to himself, he bent forward as though he had a secret to tell them. Little faces were animated in anticipation of what their coach had to say. "Now for the real test of your abilities," he said in a low voice that they had to strain to hear. "I want you to pair off. Choose a partner you want to play catch with."

This was more of a social experiment to see how well they got along with others. He'd seen them with their parents, but their parents weren't going to be the ones on the field during the games, their teammates were.

Many of them were hesitant at first. But not Skye. She eagerly approached Bastian.

Dave smiled. Of course, Bastian accepted, although somewhat shyly. Then another little girl stepped up to Skye and said, "No, I want Bastian, shorty. You choose someone else."

Bastian surprised Dave by stepping in front of the other girl, thereby preventing her from getting closer to Skye, "Don't you say that," Bastian told the other girl. "That's not nice."

"Well, she's short," the girl said.

Dave had a zero-tolerance policy for bullying on his team, but this time he held back as he felt Bastian's words would affect the little girl better than anything he had to say.

"We all look different," Bastian said. He pointed at another kid, a little boy who wore glasses. "And Peter wears cool glasses. I like that we're all different. It means we're special. All of us. You don't have to be mean to be special, you just have to be you. And I like Skye."

He went and took Skye's hand. "Skye, you okay?"

Skye squared her shoulders and nodded.

By this time, the parents who had come down from the stands at the first sign of the drama were taking their children aside to see how the discussion between Bastian and Lissa (that was the girl's name, probably short for Melissa, Dave remembered now) had affected them.

A couple of the kids came and patted Bastian and Skye on their backs. Lissa's mother went to her and hugged her, whispering encouragingly to her. Lissa herself was crying softly. Her mother tried to walk away with her, but Lissa turned around and went back to Skye and Bastian.

"I didn't mean it," she said. "I'm sorry, Skye."

Dave had noticed Joyce hanging back, but there was a pained expression on her face as though she was fighting down anger and, he supposed, trying to figure out what her next move should be and how it might affect her daughter's psyche. In an instance like this, a parent wanted their children to be able to defend themselves. They wouldn't be there every minute of the day to run interference. To protect their child. It must have been agony for her to stand there and watch what her child's reaction would be in this moment. She hung back, though, her gaze moving between Skye and Bastian. And at one point, she looked toward the stands where Darla was sitting, with a somewhat puzzled expression on her face.

Skye looked at Lissa. Then she smiled at her. "I always liked you, Lissa."

Lissa burst into tears. "I like you, too, Skye."

Dave then saw an opportunity to lighten the mood and exclaimed, "Come on now, there's no crying in baseball! Hug it out."

To which everyone laughed, even Skye and Lissa, who wound up hugging one another. After which Joyce, who could no longer hold back, ran forward and took Skye into her arms.

Dave shook his head in wonder. Kids. Maybe the world was in good hands, after all.

DARLA COULDN'T HAVE been prouder of Bastian. What a little gentleman, coming to the defense of Skye like that. She wished she could take credit for his depth of feeling, but she was just getting to know him. The credit went to his father and Marley and her mother and Sebastian's parents, and so many others who had taken the time to teach Bastian to care about others. She felt like crying.

She didn't even notice Joyce until the woman said in her left ear, "I might have misjudged you. No one who has a kid like that can be half-bad. Welcome home, Darla."

Darla did start crying then.

Joyce just looked at her as if she thought she was crazy. "I'm not going to hug you. That's the best I can do in one day." And she walked off, leaving Darla laughing and crying at once.

A moment later, Dave was beside her. "You all right?"

Continuing to laugh, Darla said, "I'm fine." She looked over at the kids, who'd decided to organize themselves and had partnered off and were playing catch.

"How do you do this?" she asked Dave. "Children are complicated."

"No," Dave disagreed. "Children are honest. Their emotions are right on the surface and they say what's on their minds. And, it's been my experience that when they're wrong about something, they apologize and they're friends again. It's adults who are complicated."

"Well, I'm going to try to be less complicated from now on and listen to my inner child," she said, smiling up at him.

"Does that mean you're going to let down your guard and go out with me?"

"I'm working on it," she promised. "See you later. By the way, good job today."

"Thank you," he said, admiring the view as she strutted away.

THAT NIGHT, as Darla lay in bed, watching the ceiling fan rotate, she wondered if she would ever be able to respond to Dave. She occasionally felt like becoming a cloistered nun might be preferable to dating again. *Dating again*. Really, that wasn't the correct term. She hadn't dated J.J. She had moved in with him for the six months they were together. She'd made a foolish mistake in a moment of madness. A mere moment of madness, and six months to regret her decision. But was there any going back once she'd written that letter to Sebastian saying she simply didn't have it in her to be a wife and mother? No, she'd done the deed and she had to pay for it with her misery. She didn't deserve happiness after her actions. During phone calls to her mother to ease her worrying, her mother had tried to convince her time and time again that she should come home. She was loved. That people who love you forgive you, and that Sebastian would eventually forgive her and they would start over. Her mother had sent her photos of Bastian on a regular basis. She'd watched him age from infant to five years old, thanks to Evie Cramer.

She owed so much to her mother. Her constant pleas for her to come home had finally gotten through to her and she'd come back in spite of being terrified that Sebastian would never allow her to get close enough to Bastian to get to know him.

And yes, she'd gone to see Sebastian with a chip on her shoulder and been nearly thrown out of his office. If not for Marley's intervention, she didn't know how that day would have turned out. However, just as her mother predicted, Sebastian had calmed down enough to see that she was truly remorseful and he'd allowed her to share custody of Bastian. Now Bastian lived with his father and Marley during the week and came to her on the weekends and over the summer months.

She sighed and closed her eyes. The fan's rhythmic sound was finally lulling her to sleep. She reached over and was about to turn the TV mounted on the wall off when she saw J. J. Starr's face on the screen.

She turned the volume up a bit. "J. J. Starr," a beautiful anchor of an entertainment show, like *Entertainment Tonight*, said, "has released a new album of original songs and the critics are saying it's the best music he's ever produced."

Then the camera cut to J.J., who looked like a younger Lenny Kravitz, only without the dreadlocks. "J.J.," said the reporter, "you've been pretty quiet on the musical front for a while now. What inspired you to get back in the recording studio?"

J.J. smiled in that enigmatic way of his and said, "It was a woman, of course. A sweet woman who came into my life when I was at my lowest. I didn't appreciate what she did for me until I got sober and realized she was the only woman who ever truly loved me for myself. I've dedicated this album to her."

"Well, that sounds mysterious," the anchor cooed. "Care to tell us who this magnificent woman is?"

"No, Carol, that's going to remain private for the time being. You see, she's not in my life anymore and I've got to go find her."

Darla sat straight up in bed. J.J. had been with many women. He couldn't possibly be talking about her!

CHAPTER SEVEN

THE NEXT MORNING, Darla was up by six o'clock and in the kitchen preparing Sunday morning breakfast, when her mom, who was sitting at the island drinking a cup of coffee, said, "I've been thinking. You told me Joyce apologized to you at practice. I don't think Joyce Hines-Witherspoon ever hated you."

"Witherspoon?" asked Darla, momentarily taking her eyes off the pancake that was starting to bubble around the edges on the griddle.

"She married a guy named Raymond Witherspoon. I think he works for the electric company," Evie explained. "Anyway, I don't think she ever hated you. I think she was a bit envious of you and Kaye and Marley. You three were joined at the hip. I think Joyce had trouble making friends. And I'm pretty sure she got picked on for being overweight. Girls can be cruel to each other. And it's all out of fear and lack of confidence in themselves."

"Well, maybe she's over it now after all this time," Darla said. "But there's something else I need to tell you."

Evie's brows rose a bit, showing she had her undivided attention. "Yes?"

Darla went on to tell her about seeing J.J. on TV and his rather cryptic words at the end about looking for a lost love.

Her mother's eyes went wide. Apparently, the news alarmed her. "You don't think he's talking about you, do you?"

Darla had thought of little else the past few hours. In fact, she'd tossed and turned practically all night contemplating if he'd been referring to her.

"Nah," she said, hoping she sounded more convincing than she felt. The truth was, she had no idea. "Do you know how many women J.J. has known during his lifetime? I was a blip on his radar, believe me."

Her mother didn't look convinced. "You never know. You very well could be this mystery woman." She laughed. "But he did say he was on drugs. His memory probably isn't serving him well."

Darla turned the pancake on the griddle before it could burn.

"Momma, please, don't even tease me about J.J.," she said. "I want him to stay far away from me."

"Why?" her mother asked. "Think you might be tempted?"

That question startled Darla so much, she nearly poured batter on the countertop and floor instead of the griddle. "I don't think there were any real emotions between us. I was desperate to run away from my responsibilities and he was used to being worshipped by every woman he ran into. I came to my senses first and told him what I'd done. He thought I was just another groupie who'd latched onto a rock star. But I came clean and I actually apologized for using him. He gave me shelter, after all. We lived together for six months."

"So you don't think you're his one true love," her mother said, then finished off her coffee, got up and went to the sink to rinse the cup. She was standing right beside Darla now, who was busy flipping a pancake. Their eyes met, and her mother said, "Honey, we all make mistakes. There's no use in rehashing them twenty-four-seven. You've been doing so well. Bastian loves you. The whole family is behind you. Now you've got to decide what is, deep down to your core, most important to you and stick to it. That's all. So what's important to you?"

Darla didn't have to think long. "I'm at peace here, Momma. I love being Bastian's mom. I like working with Mr. Jenkins. This town is special to me. And there's a guy I'm starting to warm up to. I'm happy. I don't want what J.J. has to offer, if, in fact, I'm the woman he's supposedly looking for."

Her mother smiled. "Then you're no longer wishing you could have been a star? That's something he could offer you if you are the mysterious woman he's searching for."

"I'm already a star, Momma," Darla said with a short laugh, and meant it. "I'm singing in the choir better than I have in my entire life. I'm so glad I let Kaye talk me into it. I'm finally learning how to use my instrument. That means more to me than singing in front of a crowd. My growth as a singer is so satisfying. I know that if I work hard, I can do anything."

"That's my girl!" her mother exclaimed and wrapped her arms around her.

Leaning into her embrace, Darla chuckled. "Easy, Momma, you'll have pancake batter on you if you're not careful."

Her mother let her go and turned to leave. "I'll go get Bastian up. We have about an hour and a half before we need to be at church."

And she left the kitchen, humming happily to herself.

Darla went back to making the final two pancakes. Was she really certain that if J.J. showed up she'd be able to resist his charms? One of the reasons she'd been bold enough to throw herself at him back then was because he'd always been one of her favorite musical artists, and she'd had a crush on him for years. The other reason she'd done it was because she'd been desperate. J.J. had once told her that the two qualities he liked most in his women were beauty and desperation. She guessed she had passed his test.

However, she wasn't the same woman today that she'd been back then. She knew her own mind now. She was well aware that she couldn't possibly live with a man like J.J. Most of all, she wasn't willing now to part with her child. Nothing and no one was going to come between her and Bastian.

A few minutes later, she was enjoying a

pancakes-and-sausages breakfast with Bastian and her mother when her mother looked up and said, "I've been meaning to encourage you to start walking or running. You're in your early thirties and staying active is very important as you get older. Plus, you need stamina to keep up with that one." She smiled at Bastian, who was so intent on eating his pancakes he could barely smile around a mouthful of food. He appeared to still be a bit sleepy, as his eyelids had drooped a few times while they'd been eating, but he was definitely into his pancakes. She knew that by the time they walked into the church, he would be wide-awake and eager to see his friends.

"You're always welcome to join the church ladies and myself," her mother suggested with a humorous gleam in her eye.

Darla smiled. Her mother was up to something. She just didn't know what. "Mom, the youngest person in your group must be in her fifties."

"And she would leave you in her dust. You're fit now, but give yourself time. You'll thank me for my wise advice someday."

"I'm fine."

"A woman needs to be strong, have good muscle tone. You're a nurse. You know you've got to look out for your overall health. Walking is good for your heart."

"Are you saying my heart is flabby?"

"No, but wait a few years."

Laughing, Darla said, "Okay, I'll start walking a couple mornings a week if it'll stop you from cursing me with a flabby heart future. But I'm not joining the church ladies. I'll walk alone."

"Flabby heart future," her mom said, laughing, too. "That has an ominous ring to it."

"You writers are weird," Darla said lightly. She had been meaning to ask her mother how her writing was going. She'd published a few short stories in magazines but for years she had been talking about her novel in progress.

Her mother laughed harder. "You'll thank me later. However, one more thing. To stay safe, I suggest you walk on the high school's track. It's open to the public to use from five in the morning until eight. They don't like it when civilians are on campus when school is in session."

"Civilians?"

"That's what Eula Mae and I called anyone who wasn't part of the school's staff or the student body."

"Where did you two think you were, in the military?"

"Some of those students needed a firm hand," her mother joked. "And Eula Mae and I were up to the task, I tell you!"

Darla could imagine it. Her mother and Mrs. Eula Mae Syminette were OG schoolteachers. Old Guard. Tough but lovable.

"Okay," she agreed. "I'll try the high school's track starting Monday morning."

"Excellent," said her mother, satisfied. "I assure you, you'll be perfectly safe there."

DAVE WAS SERIOUS about working out. He arrived at the high school's track five o'clock in the morning, did his warm-ups: a combination of stretches, walking on his toes, neck rolls, torso rotations, knee rotations and ankle rotations. Running could be rough on the body, causing strained tendons, knee injuries. He even knew some runners who'd lost toenails because of their love of running. Warm-ups helped to prevent injuries.

After his five-minute warm-up, he began

jogging around the track at a slow pace, his speed increasing as he ran.

Usually, he tried to keep his thoughts off his upcoming day. Instead, he woolgathered about places he wanted to visit. His most current dream was to visit his mother's place of birth, Palermo, the capital of the Italian island of Sicily. Over the years his mother and father had traveled there several times to visit her mother. She never could persuade her mother to get on a plane. After her mother died, she stopped going. He, on the other hand, had never been to Italy. So he read books and watched videos online.

He daydreamed now of strolling through the streets of Palermo, an ancient city whose history dated back 2,700 years.

The United States was an infant compared to Palermo. He remembered his mother telling him how the people tried to preserve their history. It was a mixed heritage because even though Palermo was founded by the Phoenicians, it had subsequently been influenced by the Greeks. As Rome gained power, it was part of the Roman republic and later was controlled by the Byzantine Empire, Arabs and the Normans, who were originally pirates from Iceland, Norway and Denmark.

Learning this basically blew Dave's mind. A couple years ago he had taken a DNA test and discovered that besides being Italian and Irish he also had DNA from Denmark, Norway and Iceland, plus he had North African ancestry.

His mother in her own inimitable fashion had told him a story about an altercation she'd had with his grandfather, the one who had been chief of police of Port Domingo over half a century ago. She'd told him that his grandfather once asked her which part of Italy she'd come from.

You must come from the part of the boot that's close to Africa, his grandfather had said to her. *Because you are nearly as dark as some of the colored people around here.*

His mother had laughed at the old man. She told Dave, with hands on her hips, that she had stood up to him and said, *You're right. I'm part African. That means your grandchildren are going to be part Black. People stopped saying* colored *a long time ago in this country. I know that, and I wasn't even born here. Thank God your son is*

*nothing like you because I would never have
given him the time of day, let alone married
him if he had been!*

Then, she told Dave, *He grabbed his heart
and collapsed. Dead as a doornail.*

Even as a boy, Dave knew his mother had
been pulling his leg. His grandfather had
died in the hospital after a long illness.

But his mother liked to embellish her stories and he let her.

Suddenly, he heard the creaky gate open
in the aluminum fence that surrounded the
track. Day was dawning and he could make
out the figure of a woman approaching. Her
silhouette was shapely and she had a bag
slung over her shoulder. He kept running.
She stopped walking just before she stepped
onto the track.

At that moment, the sun peeked over the
horizon illuminating Darla, dressed in workout togs. Excitement coursed through him.

"I thought that was your truck parked in
the lot," she said.

He was rounding the bend in the track and
kept moving. He only had around half a lap
to go before he had his five miles in. He was
glad he was healthy because her sudden ap-

pearance like this might have been the death of a lesser man.

"I'll be with you in a minute," he called to her breathlessly. *Lord, don't let me smell,* he thought. *And let me be patient when I have a little talk with my mother later, because I know she's behind this.*

After he'd finished his lap, Darla joined him, keeping pace, as he continued walking to cool down. He took a quick drink from his water bottle and put it back in his pack he wore around his waist.

"I guess you know this isn't coincidental," she said. "Evie Cramer. That's what I call her when I'm mad at her. Evie Cramer insisted that I needed to start walking to stay in shape. And not just anywhere, at the high school track. Early in the morning. No wonder she told me I'd be safe here. She knew you would be here."

"Our mothers must be stopped," Dave said, enjoying the cool morning air in his lungs. He was sweating and grabbed the hand towel he kept in the band of his shorts to wipe his face. Then he placed it around his neck.

"It's good to see you, even if it is a set-up," he told her. "How've you been? I only

see you when you bring Bastian to practice. I heard you were in the Saint Domingo
Catholic Church choir. I've got to come to
hear you sing."

She laughed. She smelled of honeysuckle,
clean and fresh, and her voice was musical,
or maybe that was because he loved hearing her talk.

"They haven't given me any solos yet. I
don't think you'd be able to distinguish my
voice from the other sopranos."

"Are you enjoying yourself?"

"I am, very much so," she said. "How've
you been? Catch any hardened criminals
lately?"

"Not lately, but we do get our share of serious crimes. In a small town, the crimes are
often personal because everyone knows everyone else. Whereas in the city, you might
have somebody get attacked by a perfect
stranger, in a small town it's Joe from down
the street whose Weed Wacker you bor-
rowed and didn't return in a timely manner.

"But don't get me wrong," he continued,
"There are problems here like there are in
big cities. We've got people hooked on drugs,
selling them. There are domestic violence

cases, which are often not prosecuted because oftentimes the victim refuses to cooperate."

"I'm sorry I made light of your work," she told him seriously.

"It's okay," he told her. "You can ask me anything."

They stopped walking and simply gazed into each other's eyes.

He could have stood there all day long, just taking her in. She was looking at him as though she were seeing him clearly for the first time. And the thought made her nervous, especially since they were the only two people out here.

A slew of emotions crossed her pretty face before she abruptly turned away. "Well, I'd better start walking. I told Evie Cramer I would walk at least a mile today."

"You need to stretch first," he advised, moving around her so that he could keep her face in view. He was amused by the way her nose wrinkled at just the mention of a warm-up.

"I'm lazy," she admitted with a short laugh. "I figure I get enough exercise on the job and running after Bastian. But okay. Do you have time to show me some easy stretches?"

Her asking for his help surprised him since he thought she wanted to put some distance between them.

"I do," he answered immediately, pleased she'd asked.

"None of that football stuff you probably learned when you were a fullback in high school," she said.

"You know which position I played? I was under the impression you didn't even remember me from high school."

"I'll be honest," she said. "I looked you up in my yearbook. I'm sorry, I didn't pay attention to who was on the football team in high school. Sebastian played, and that's all I remember about it. That's not to say I didn't notice you. You and Sebastian hung out together. You dated a cheerleader."

"Half the guys on the football team dated cheerleaders. That was one of the perks of playing high school football."

"So, she wasn't your steady girlfriend, huh?"

"I didn't have a steady. I was pretty clueless when it came to girls. Still am, actually."

She laughed. "I don't know. I, for one, think you're pretty charming."

"You do?" he asked playfully. "Even standing here this early in the morning, dripping with sweat? Maybe you'd like a squirt from my water bottle to cool you off." And he took his water bottle from his pack and squirted some water in her direction.

Darla giggled, ducked and, stifling a scream, ran away from him. He followed her, calling out, "You're already moving pretty well for a lazy person."

"Stay away, or I'll tell your mother on you."

"My mother would be happy we're in the same place at the same time. She planned this, after all."

Darla tossed her bag onto the grass next to the track and picked up speed.

"Is this the warm-up?" She laughed.

"It's working," he said. She'd claimed that she was lazy, but she actually had pretty good form. But he was a seasoned athlete and soon caught up with her. He reached out for her arm. She jerked away, lost her balance and nearly went sprawling on the track.

He caught her just in time. An intake of breath, a sigh of relief later, she was fully in his arms and he could breathe regularly again.

"I'm so sorry, I shouldn't have let things get out of hand like that. I would never want you to get hurt."

She should have pulled away, but kept her left ear pressed to his chest. His heart was beating fast. He felt the pulse in his neck. He felt her tremble.

"Are you okay?" he asked softly.

She breathed deeply, then looked up into his eyes. "I almost forgot how it felt for a man to hold me like this."

"I'm not at my sartorial best," he joked as he smiled in gratitude that she wasn't angry with him.

She pushed away, and he let go of her even though he didn't want to at that moment.

She stood with her hands on her hips, her gaze never leaving his face. "I like you, Dave. Which is why I don't think I should come here again. You know how I feel about getting involved with anyone. I don't know exactly what it is about you that I can't ignore. But since I can't ignore it, especially when we're alone together, then the solution is not to be alone with you."

Dave remembered his mother's advice to take things slowly with Darla, but decided to follow his own mind and told her, "Maybe you're right because when I held you I realized what I've been missing. Take that any way you want to."

He turned to leave. "I've got to get to work. I'm usually here by five and gone by five fifty-five. Have a good day, darlin', I mean, Darla."

He faced her once more and smiled.

She just stood there watching him with longing in her eyes, which made him feel ten feet tall. Today was going to be a good day.

CHAPTER EIGHT

WHEN DARLA CAME through the back door, following her brisk walk around the high school track her mom, still dressed in pajamas, was standing at the counter in the kitchen pouring coffee into a mug.

"Good morning, Mom," Darla called as she closed the door behind her.

"Good morning, baby." Her mother yawned.

Darla placed her bag on the bench near the back door.

"I'd love some of that coffee," Darla said and hurried over to the coffee maker on the counter. Her mother moved aside to give her access. But it was clear to Darla, by the intensity with which her mother was regarding her, that she was about to burst from curiosity. Her eyes were animated as though she was in expectation of exciting news.

Darla calmly poured herself a cup of Colombian coffee. She took a tiny sip, smiling at her mom all the while.

Her mom continued to observe her and, even though Darla knew her to be a seasoned busybody, she wasn't capable of maintaining a straight face.

She finally gave in to her curiosity, grinned at Darla and asked, "How was your walk?"

Darla was ready for her. She went and sat down at the table before answering, "Oh, uneventful. No one else was around. It was still kind of dark when I got there. It was sort of spooky, actually. They really need security lights. How could you think I'd feel safe there?"

"What!" Her mom looked confused. "That's odd. You're teasing me, right?"

"Mmm, no," said Darla. She sipped her coffee. "This is good. But I'd better get moving. It's already six fifteen. Mr. Jenkins is very punctual and I don't want to be late."

She took another quick sip of her coffee, rose and left her cup on the table. "I'm going to finish that later, so please don't pour it out." She walked over and gave her mom a kiss on the cheek. "You look fabulous. That beauty sleep is working."

Her mother stared at her with her mouth partially open. "I can't believe no one else was out there. I was sure someone else would be there. At that time of morning, I mean."

Darla was by the back stairs now. She put her left foot on the first step and looked back at her mother. "I think I might have glimpsed a lawn maintenance guy from a distance."

She ran upstairs, smiling to herself. She wasn't giving her mother an inch, which would, hopefully, help to put an end to her matchmaking attempts. It was worth a try.

"THINGS ARE GETTER weirder and weirder at Joy Henderson's store," Laraine reported to Dave when he walked through the double doors of the Port Domingo Police Department building. The lobby was two stories tall with a glass front. About four people were sitting on the padded chairs in the waiting area, probably hoping a loved one would be released from custody soon. One woman had two small children with her. She had a black eye, and one of the kids, no older than a year old, was asleep in her arms, while the other one, maybe four, was sitting quietly next to her. Probably wasn't his first time at a police station. Poor little guy.

Laraine cleared her throat to regain his attention. She was the front desk sergeant. They had a dispatcher, but when the dispatcher wasn't on duty, Laraine sometimes handled those duties, too. Dave, who was wearing his uniform and his Braves cap— the Stetson had been too high maintenance for his tastes—said, "Good morning, Laraine. Thank you."

She was handing him a piece of paper with the notes she'd taken over the phone on it. "Says the thief actually returned the merchandise and left a regretful message, typewritten of course, saying he was sorry. You want to check it out yourself or send someone else to take her statement?"

"I'll go," said Dave. After his encounter with Darla, he wanted to stay extremely busy today so he wouldn't keep rehashing it in his mind. No use dwelling on whether his last move was a mistake or not. It was done. He'd told her exactly how he felt about her. The ball was in her court now.

He did have a couple of administrative tasks that needed his attention today, though.

This was a small town police department and while he made the decisions around here and Laraine often issued the orders for him. "Make sure to remind Josh and Rosie that they're due for training, and no excuses."

All officers were required to annually complete a medical exam, physical exam and continuing education regarding changes in laws.

"Don't worry, Chief, I've got you covered," Laraine assured him. Dave smiled at her. If anyone had his back in this department, it was Laraine.

"I'm heading over to Miss Henderson's shop, then."

But before he could make it back out the door, Rob Conrad and Josh Plummer came in with a handcuffed man who wasn't being cooperative. He wasn't surprised to see it was Raff Chandler, a late-forties alcoholic who'd been arrested at least three times last year. He was quite belligerent when he was drunk, and generally a terrible human being.

He was not only resisting the officers, he was calling them every vile epithet in his vocabulary.

Raff Chandler reeked of alcohol. He was

sweaty and his thin mousy brown hair was plastered to his head.

"Calm down, Raff," Dave said, walking forward and then taking the prisoner firmly by his left arm. No wonder, because Raff had spotted the mother with the two children, who was Black. Raff was a known racist, and he started saying vile things about Black people.

Rob's wife was Black. They had two children and one was on the way.

"I've got him, Officer," Dave said. He met Josh's eyes and jerked his head to the left, which was the direction the holding cell where they took the intoxicated detainees was located. He and Josh carried on while Rob went somewhere to cool off.

Raff continued to put up a fight. Even after he and Josh got him through the door of the cell, which had tile on the walls and floor for easy cleanup, Raff twisted and turned in an effort to wriggle loose.

Dave firmly pushed Raff down onto the blue plastic-covered cot. Raff instantly stopped fighting. He was at his destination and probably saw no reason to.

"Looks like you're going to do time, Raff."

From his perch on the cot, Raff looked up at

Dave. "I bet you think you're something, don't you, Dave? Remember, I knew you when you were a snotty-nosed kid. The apple doesn't fall far from the tree. Your granddaddy knew the score, and you need to wake up and smell the coffee."

Dave briefly wondered if Raff had any more idioms, metaphors or common sayings to share with him. Truth was, he was tired of this reprehensible man, with whom he had a history. But Raff's goading wasn't going to make him forget he was an officer of the law and thus bound by his pledge to serve and protect.

When nothing he said got a rise out of him, Raff gave Josh, who was also Black, a disgusted look. "You've got more Blacks working here than any other color. What are you trying to prove?"

"You can go, Officer," Dave said to Josh. Josh left the holding cell.

Dave unlocked Raff's handcuffs. "We're going to let you settle down, then you'll get your phone call."

"I don't need a phone call," Raff said. "I'm the richest man in this one-horse town and

you're going to let me out on my own recon-
naissance!"

"The word you're looking for is recogni-
zance," Dave told him. "And no, you need a
lawyer this time."

Dave detested privileged people who got
off with just a slap on the wrist. He hoped
that this time Raff Chandler was going to
get the punishment he so richly deserved.
Even if he was the son of a Florida Supreme
Court justice.

"Well…" Raff began, but something was
wrong and he couldn't continue. He gagged,
and the next thing Dave knew he was rushing to the nearby toilet.

Dave walked out of the holding cell, making sure the door was secure. Then he watched
from the other side until Raff finished throwing up and dragged himself back over to the
cot. Dave stood there a few moments, just to
make sure that Raff was all right. He watched
as Raff curled up on his side and laid his head
on a pillow. Finally, he left. He would send
someone to check on him in fifteen minutes
or so to make sure he hadn't vomited again.
If he had, they would make sure he got medical care.

COMPARED TO HIS experience with Raff Chandler, taking Joy Henderson's statement a few minutes later was a breath of fresh air.

Joy was animated this morning, and her white hair, in its customary spiky style, reminded Dave of a cartoon character who had stuck their finger in an electric socket.

The store was open and a couple patrons were browsing while she and Dave had a conversation at the checkout counter.

"I'm beginning to think I should get cameras," Joy was saying as she handed him the evidence she'd told Laraine about over the phone. "I need to help nip this in the bud. Not that I feel threatened or anything. I've been lucky. I have the nicest customers. Repeat customers. Mothers bring their daughters in. Over the years, the same daughters bring their own little ones in. I'm only keeping you informed about the goings-on because I'm curious as to who's responsible. If anything, this is a mystery, and I love mysteries. Do you have any idea who could be doing it?"

"It must be someone who's in here often. Someone who is aware of your movements. They would have to be to be able to steal items while you're not looking. You are here every day. And you only have one employee, am I right?"

Joy smiled as she nodded. "She gave birth to you."

Dave laughed shortly. "Everyone's a suspect until I catch the culprit."

Joy laughed now. "I can't imagine Margherita doing something like this. Why would she?"

"I have no idea what her motive might be," Dave said. "I don't think she's a kleptomaniac."

"You don't know your own mother?" Joy asked, still laughing.

While Dave would have liked to take this situation as lightly as Joy, he was an officer of the law and he had to be fair and unbiased in his dealings with everyone. Therefore, his mother wasn't exempt from suspicion.

"Everybody has the persona they show to the world and the one they keep secret," Dave told her. "So no, I don't know how my mother thinks. And she doesn't know I think."

Joy considered this. "Yes, you're right. We never truly know everything about anyone."

"If you're serious about getting cameras

put in, I would suggest you hire someone who can install hidden cameras. And don't tell anyone you're doing it. Then we'll get to the bottom of this mystery. Deal?"

Joy had stopped smiling. She met Dave's eyes. "Deal."

"YOU SEEM MORE loose-limbed today," Darla observed. She was walking alongside Mr. Jenkins on the south lawn of his estate.

"I'm grateful that I didn't have to use the lift to get out of bed this morning," Mr. Jenkins said, a contemplative expression on his face. "Parkinson's is such a tease. One day you can barely get out of bed, and the next day you almost feel normal. Then the shoe drops and you're once again a prisoner in your own body. Unable to control the ticks, the stiffness and, God forbid, the hallucinations that some of us have. Yesterday, I thought I saw my dear, sweet mother sitting in the home theater watching an episode of *Scandal*. My mother wasn't even alive when that show was on television."

The grass still had dew on it at this time of morning, but it was a pleasant walk nonetheless. Since she had brought Bastian for a surprise visit, her patient had been down-right chatty.

"So, you watched *Scandal*," Darla said, trying to keep things light. "Who was your favorite character? Olivia Pope? Or maybe Poppa Pope? That's what I called Joe Morton's character. That was one scary man."

"Scary?" returned Mr. Jenkins with a laugh. "Huck was the one who was scary. You just never knew what he would do. Now, that's suspense."

"You should know," she said. She noticed that he wasn't breathing hard and they had been walking a good twenty minutes. Also, since she'd begun walking three days a week, she had more stamina. Her mother had been right about that. "You write some of the most tension-filled scenes. Sometimes I find myself holding my breath when I'm reading one of your books."

"You don't have to flatter me, Darla. I don't have an ego when it comes to my writing. I learned a long time ago to simply write for my own pleasure and not worry about what other people think of my work. You save yourself a lot of unnecessary pain that way. I know my books won't be everybody's cup of tea."

Darla sighed. "That could be the reason my mom has never tried to publish any of the books I know she has stashed around the house somewhere."

Mr. Jenkins stopped walking and turned to face Darla. "Your mother is still writing?"

"What do you mean, still writing? How did you know she's a writer? I never mentioned it."

He momentarily glanced away, then faced her again while running a hand over his head. "I knew your mother in high school. We were in the same English class. Our teacher would have us write short stories and read them aloud in class. She used to write the most beautiful stories. At least, I thought so. They were wasted on the rest of the class, as were my stories. But she and I were rapt listeners of each other's work. I felt like an outcast most of the time. Except for when Evelyn and I were in English class."

"Evie," Darla told him. "Everyone calls her Evie."

"Evie." He tried the name out and smiled.

"So, Evelyn got married and had how many children?"

"Just my brother, Jerald, and me," Darla told him. "We call him Jerry."

"And your father?"

"He died when I was ten. She never got close to anyone else. She always said Jerry and I were all she needed. She was an English teacher herself. Retired now and devoting herself to the church and a charity she founded with some other women in town."

"Oh? What's the name of the charity?"

"Silver Seniors," Darla answered. "Mom said the members are all women of a certain age serving neighbors who are also seniors. The group makes sure they have plenty of food and a decent place to live."

"Sounds like a worthy cause," said Mr. Jenkins.

"Oh, it's great. The ladies are warmhearted but practical and like generals when there's work to be done. I've been 'volunteered' a few times by Mom, so I know what I'm talking about. I learned how to paint houses, decorate them and I once even assisted a carpenter in building a new front porch."

"Then you're handy with a hammer."

"And a saw and a drill," she proudly replied.

"Those are good skills to have."

"Thank you." Her mind raced with romantic, perhaps unrealistic, what-ifs. What if Mr. Jenkins was the man her mother had been waiting all these years to meet? What if her mother was the woman who could convince Mr. Jenkins to rejoin society?

You're almost as bad as Evie Cramer, she silently accused herself. *You're thinking about matchmaking your mom and Mr. Jenkins. Perish the thought!*

"Evie was quite the athlete in high school, too," Mr. Jenkins reminisced. "She was on the track team and the girls' basketball team. She wasn't very tall, but she was tough. Is she still into sports?"

Darla told herself she would answer Mr. Jenkins's questions, but that was all. She would not try to get him and her mother together.

"She walks a lot," she told him. "In fact, she made me start walking recently. She told me I might have a flabby heart future if I didn't."

Mr. Jenkins found that as hilarious as her mother had. They walked for at least two more minutes before his laughter subsided. "Sounds like she's as delightful as she used to be," he said, smiling at the memory.

That statement touched her heart.

"I could bring her over one day and you can see for yourself."

Mr. Jenkins's demeanor immediately changed. He stopped smiling and looked her dead in the eyes.

"I forbid it, Darla. I can't meet Evie under any circumstances."

"But why?"

"Look at me. I'm a shell of what I used to be. I have nothing to offer your mother. Not my friendship, and definitely not anything more serious."

"What are you talking about? You're a very accomplished man. You're kind, you're intelligent. You write wonderful books. Anyone would be honored to meet you. Or, in Mom's case, rekindle a friendship with you."

He laughed, but with no humor. "Maybe a few years ago, but I'm not worth knowing now, Darla. Promise me you won't surprise me with a visit from Evie. I'm asking you to respect my wishes."

"Of course," she said softly. "If that's how you feel about it."

"That's how I feel about it," he confirmed.

They resumed their walk in silence.

"CHIEF, WE'RE AHEAD of him now, and he's slowing down," said officer Luke Confino.

Dave was behind him and his partner, Jimmy Delgado, in his police-issued vehicle, a black Dodge Charger.

The speeding suspect was sixteen-year-old Damien Spivey, whose mother, Teresa, had reported her car stolen a few hours ago. Now, Dave realized Teresa had done that to teach her son a lesson. He watched as Damien pulled off onto the shoulder.

Officer Confino and Delgado stopped behind Damien, and Dave pulled in front of Teresa Spivey's battered Honda Civic.

Dave exited the car and after getting the boy's attention, gestured for him to do the same.

Damien got out and immediately held his hands up. "Is my mom mad at me?" he asked.

"What do you think?" Dave replied. He took his cuffs off his utility belt and readied them with a little shake as he walked toward Damien. When he got to Damien, he turned him around and snapped the cuffs onto his wrists. "Shoplifting. Now a stolen car. What's next for you, Damien?"

Damien laughed nervously. "Mom's mad now, but she isn't going to send me to jail. She loves me."

"That depends on how tired she is of you," Dave told him. "And she sounds like she's fed up with you. She's the one who reported the car missing."

Damien looked crestfallen. "I thought you stopped me because I was driving too fast."

"You were driving too fast, and you stole your mother's car. Now you're ours."

By the time Dave had Damien handcuffed, and had read him his rights, Officers Confino and Delgado were there to put him in the back of their cruiser for transport to the police station.

"But I didn't mean it," Damien called to Dave as he was walked to the cruiser. "I just wanted to have a little fun."

"This isn't going to be fun for anybody," Dave said regretfully. He returned to his own car. He hated scaring Damien. But sometimes, a kid like Damien needed scaring. Plus, Dave believed Damien would be a good candidate for a youth program his department had recently started.

CHAPTER NINE

IT WAS LATE MAY, and Darla was starting to feel more confident in herself and her ability to redeem herself, or at least change the effects of her absence on the people she had abandoned five years ago. Bastian was at the top of her list, and on that score she felt she was doing pretty well. He was a happy, well-adjusted kid. She was just grateful to be allowed in his world. Her mother, too, appeared really pleased to have her back. A little too pleased since she and Miss Margherita were apparently in cahoots in their efforts to get her and Dave together.

But there were others whom her actions had affected, too. Like her brother, Jerry, who, she had been told by her mother, was diagnosed with depression during her absence. She didn't think she was the cause of his depression, but she felt she should make it clear to him that she loved him and was glad to be in his life again. Of course, they had spoken over the phone while she'd been away, but it was not like being there for him.

Therefore, when Jerry's birthday came around on May fifth, Cinco de Mayo, a holiday in Mexico and the United States that was celebrated in honor of the military victory in 1862 over Napolean's forces, she remembered that Jerry loved Mexican food, and she planned a surprise party for him at her mom's place.

She and her mom joined forces in preparing for the party. Her mother promised to invite around twenty of Jerry's friends. She knew whom he was close to and would want to attend. Darla would do the cooking and the decorating.

It was also her job to get Jerry to drop by their mom's house at 8:00 p.m. Jerry's after-work hours were devoted to "me time." He hated being disturbed then.

She called his cell phone at a quarter to six, knowing he would probably be lounging in front of the TV watching football. She suspected he wasn't going to answer. Such was his devotion to the NFL. She left a quick message. "Hi, Jerry. I'm sorry for having to ask you to do this, but I've got to go into work. And Mom has already gone out with some of the church ladies. Mr. Jenkins slipped and fell and is in some pain and I need to go work with him for a couple hours. Of course, Lily is with him now, but some physical therapy would do him a world of good. I wouldn't ask you to watch Bastian for me if I didn't really need you. So please be here by eight, I'm in a bind. Call me back soon. Love you!"

Her plea had worked because Jerry phoned her back in under five minutes. And she'd picked up immediately.

"Oh, thank you for calling me back, Jerry."

"Hey, sis. Okay, I'll be there. You owe me one, though. Making me miss even a minute of my game." But he hadn't sounded put out at all. That was Jerry. He supported his family.

She'd breathed a sigh of relief. "Oh, thank you. Mom has a TV, too, you know. Did you get my card?"

He laughed. "Black Panther?"

The birthday card she'd sent had a Black Panther theme. "You're the only person I know who read the comic books. You know you loved it."

"I did. It made me laugh out loud. It reminded me of all the times we used to argue when you got into my comics collection."

"I loved them, too."

"You could at least have asked my permission."

"You weren't always home."

He laughed again. "As much as I'd love to continue this argument, and win it, I'm missing the game. That doesn't mean I don't love you. I'll see you at eight."

"Okay, and thanks again."

"No problema, mi hermana," he said. "You know, it's Cinco de Mayo today, too."

"I do," she said, smiling to herself. "Okay, see you soon."

She hit the off button and went back to what she'd been doing before the phone call, whipping up a variety of Mexican dishes. So far she'd made chicken quesadillas with corn tortillas, Jerry's favorite; carne asada tacos; and chorizo tortilla pizzas. Plenty of guacamole, other dips, corn chips and drinks were on the table from which the guests could help themselves; and for dessert, there were homemade churros. She'd been making them for her family from the time she was about sixteen and had gotten the recipe from her Spanish teacher, Mrs. Serrano. She knew from experience they would be gone in a flash because they were so irresistible.

The guests began arriving at seven thirty. They'd been asked to park down the street to throw Jerry off the scent. Her mother had phoned neighbors to get their permission for strange cars to park in front of their houses, and had issued invitations to the party if they would like to attend.

Bastian was with his father and Marley, so she knew he was safe and sound. So when the doorbell rang, her mother, who was already dressed, hurried to answer it. Darla heard the doorbell from upstairs in her bedroom, where she was putting the final touches on her look for the night. It wasn't as if she had a closet full of designer outfits. But she owned a few nice dresses that she wore to church. The rest of her wardrobe consisted of mostly jeans or slacks and T-shirts. She wasn't much of a clotheshorse. Not a shoe girl, either.

A few minutes before the doorbell rang,

her mother had been in the bedroom with her while she was choosing what she was going to wear. She pulled out a nice pair of jeans and a colorful blouse.

Her mother wrinkled her nose in distaste. "Honey, you wear jeans all the time. Put on a dress. Something that emphasizes your best feature, those gorgeous legs. Which, I might add, look even better since you've been walking regularly."

Darla glanced down at her legs. "You think so?" She was flattered in spite of her suspicions about her mother's motives. And lately had started feeling bad about lying to her about her encounter with Dave at the high school track. Her mother hadn't done any matchmaking since then. And Darla hadn't seen Dave except at a couple of Little League practices, during which they had only exchanged greetings. She had found herself daydreaming about being in his arms again. Seemed she was unable to turn off her attraction to him. She felt like a hypocrite for distrusting her mother's motives when she didn't even trust her own where Dave was concerned. When it came down to it, she refused to give him a chance because she simply didn't want to break another good man's heart. She was already living with the guilt of breaking Sebastian's heart. She let herself slide when she judged herself on her behavior with J.J. because J.J. had also used her. They were, in essence, equally in the wrong, which canceled out the blame. Or at least that was her reasoning.

She quite often found herself thinking about Dave. And she'd swear she could feel his emotions whenever they were together, as though she was becoming attuned to him. Was that weird or what?

She wound up wearing a sheer dot mesh swing dress in blush, a soft pink pastel, whose hem fell about two inches above her knees. The soft material floated about her body. The top of the dress ended just above the bustline, and the short sleeves were made of sheer material. Solid material covered her chest and the rest of her body, so the dress was modest but sexy at the same time. She put her long, wavy black hair up in a loose knot and wore minimal makeup. A pair of leather sandals with three-inch heels in the same color as the dress were on her feet. Even her toenails were matching.

She turned this way and that in front of a full-length mirror. She wouldn't scare small children and animals. She smirked at her reflection. This was a date outfit. Her mother had encouraged her to dress up as though she were going on a date. Gotten again by Evie Cramer!

She got downstairs at a quarter to eight. Her computer-savvy, comic-book-collecting brother prided himself on being prompt. That meant they had fifteen minutes to hide all of the guests.

She hoped they'd all arrived by now. Hellos greeted her when she entered the open-concept great room. The guests were gathered in groups, looking fashionable in their party attire, enjoying each other's company already. She knew a few of the men and woman, all in their twenties and thirties, but there were several she hadn't met yet. She looked for her mother, who was nowhere to be seen. A handsome man she knew was grinning as he approached her. Lance Baker. She was immediately swept up in a hug by Jerry's best friend, whom she hadn't seen since she'd returned home.

Lance was a tall, fit man with dark brown

skin, dark brown eyes, a proud African nose, full lips and a square chin. He wore his black natural hair shorn close to the scalp of his well-shaped head and he had a daddy moustache, the kind that helped make veteran actor Tom Selleck famous. Lance's eyes danced and that delightful smile of his produced dimples in both cheeks.

"Look at you," he said happily. "As gorgeous as ever."

"And you still don't wear your glasses, I see," she joked.

He hugged her a bit tighter and then let her go.

"Seriously, you've never looked better. We've missed you."

She smiled gratefully up at him. "Thank you." She glanced around them. "You didn't bring a date?"

He cocked his head to their left, indicating a lovely Hispanic woman wearing a short, white sleeveless dress and a pair of platforms with straps around her ankles, also in white. She had mounds of wavy dark brown hair with golden highlights that fell down her back. "You haven't lost your touch," Darla commented, looking at Lance once more. "She's beautiful."

"Beautiful and sweet, and we just got engaged," Lance said proudly.

Darla gasped. "Congratulations! I'm so happy for you." She'd known Lance since she was a little girl and thought he'd be a confirmed bachelor for the rest of his life due to the way he attracted women but never appeared serious about any of them.

"Have you set a wedding date yet?"

"A year from now," Lance said. "Sofia wants time to relocate before the nuptials."

She didn't get the chance to respond to Lance's last statement because her mother came rushing into the great room, Dave right behind her looking suave in all black. A tailored black shirt, dress slacks, highly polished black leather oxfords on his feet. His curly hair was even tamed and combed back from his forehead. Now she knew why her mother had wanted her to dress nicely.

"Come on, everyone," her mother said excitedly. "Jerry's going to be here any minute now. Everyone in the kitchen, as close to the back door as you can get. Darla is going to answer the door. As soon as you hear her say

Jerry's name, go to the great room and yell *surprise*."

Everyone started walking toward the back of the house, which gave Darla time to get in a few words with Dave. She glanced up at the clock on the wall: 7:58 p.m. She had two minutes to spare.

Dave moved closer to her. "Your mother invited me. Hope you don't mind."

She had to talk quickly. "I didn't know you and Jerry were friends."

"Yeah, he helped us out when we were hacked. Cleared the problem right up and installed safeguards so it wouldn't happen again. We got to be friends after that. We have common interests, like we're both cutthroat board game players."

"Well, you definitely clean up well."

His eyes held an amused expression as his gaze moved over her face. "And you're just plain beautiful."

To say she melted would be an understatement. There was no time to bask in a compliment from a man she was attracted to, though.

The doorbell rang. Jerry was prompt, as usual. Darla pointed in the direction of the kitchen. Dave took the cue and hurried to join the other guests.

When Darla opened the door, Jerry took one look at her and said, "You're not dressed for going to give Mr. Jenkins a rubdown to relieve his suffering."

"Jerry!" Darla yelled.

Jerry stepped into the house. "Why are you being so loud?"

Then pandemonium erupted and twenty-one people, including his mom, came rushing into the living room, shouting, "Happy birthday, Jerry!"

"Gotcha!" Darla said and was the first one to hug her brother. She was moved aside by her mother, who tried to squeeze the life out of the poor guy.

Jerry was grinning from ear to ear. "You guys!" He looked across the room at his best friend, Lance. "No wonder you were so agreeable when I said I was going to spend a quiet night at home and not go somewhere to celebrate."

And so it went, with Jerry hugging all of his closest friends, and Darla looking on with affection. Jerry hadn't always had it easy in life. She enjoyed seeing him surrounded by people he loved.

"I'm going to bring the food out shortly," she called before disappearing into the kitchen. She wasn't alone, though. Dave followed.

"Can I help?" he asked. "I know my way around a kitchen."

The food that needed to be kept warm was in the oven. The cold foods were displayed on the huge island, and on another table were drinks in buckets of ice.

Bending to retrieve large aluminum pans covered with foil from the oven, Darla said, "I'm just going to set these—" she gestured at three pans "—over there." She nodded her head in the direction of the island, where protective heating pads were laid out. "You can look in that drawer next to the stove and get serving spoons."

She already had put the napkins, utensils, and paper plates and cups on the table with the drinks. The buffet was self-serve.

After she had transferred the hot food to the island, she turned off the oven and put the churros inside. The residual heat was just enough to ensure the churros stayed warm until she was ready to serve them. Dave inhaled deeply when the pan with the churros passed close to him. "I'm not a donut man, but those smell delicious."

They had been deep-fried and dusted with mouthwatering cinnamon sugar.

"Maybe you ought to have one now," Darla said. She'd tested one earlier and it had melted in her mouth. She was quite proud of how they'd turned out.

Dave bit into the churro. He might have been exaggerating, but his eyes rolled back in his head and he moaned his pleasure. He looked at her as he munched on the churro. "You know they used to have these at the county fair when we were kids, but they never tasted like this."

Darla took the compliment in stride. Or so she hoped it appeared as though she was taking it in stride. In her mind, she was throwing herself into his arms and kissing him.

"You're sweet, Chief," she said as she placed the rest of the churros into the warm oven. Straightening back up, she left Dave in the kitchen and went and announced that everyone could eat. Her mom insisted on a quick prayer beforehand, and Jerry did the honors.

For the next hour, Jerry enjoyed himself

while eating and conversing with some of the most important people in his life.

He even took a moment and pulled Darla aside to thank her for preparing the delicious food. "You made all my favorites."

Darla pulled him into a hug. "You deserve it, Jerry. I'm so glad you stayed with Mom as long as you did. I know she would have been lonely without you. Thanks for looking out for her while I was away."

Jerry laughed. "We comforted each other. But now you're back. Don't ever leave us again, sis."

And she knew by the sincere expression in his eyes that he meant every word.

Shortly after their conversation, Jerry announced, "Who wants to work off some calories?"

His boy, Lance, who worked as a DJ part-time, was ready to supply the beats with just his cell phone and speakers with Bluetooth. Lance had them all dancing to hip-hop with some soul, reggae and standards thrown in out of respect for Miss Evie, his best pal's mom.

As the evening was winding down, Darla became bold and took Dave by the hand and led him outside to the back porch, where they could talk in private.

The night air was a little cool. May was hot during the day but the temperatures lowered to around sixty-five degrees at night in that part of Northwest Florida.

When they were alone, she peered up into his warm brown eyes.

They were mere inches apart and she could feel the heat emanating from his body. She remembered the last time he'd held her and she wanted more of that, but she was scared.

However, if she didn't take a chance, she would miss out on a lot in her life, and she didn't want to live like that. She wanted to make brave choices. She wanted to feel fully alive.

She thought about Mr. Jenkins and how he wouldn't see her mother because of his Parkinson's and his belief that he wasn't good enough for her. When she instinctively felt her mother wasn't the kind of woman to pass up a good man because he had certain physical limitations.

And here she was passing up a good man because she herself was hampered by self-doubt and didn't think she was good enough for him.

She peered deeply into his eyes and smiled at him. He returned her smile with a mega-watt grin of his own, which encouraged her to finally say, "Kiss me, Dave."

CHAPTER TEN

"KISS ME, DAVE," Darla whispered, smiling at him.

He swallowed hard. Good thing he'd popped some breath mints after eating that delicious Mexican food she'd made.

He lowered his head and met her mouth. She went up onto her toes and wrapped her arms around his neck. Their bodies pressed closer, and the rest came naturally.

She tasted sweeter than he'd imagined, and his imagination was pretty over-the-top. The wonderful smell of her warm skin, the softness of her hair, the firmness of her shapely body all combined to make this moment worth the wait. He gently broke off the kiss and took a step away from her. They looked into each other's eyes.

In hers he saw wonder, and a little bit of fear. He was certain her asking him to kiss her had not been something she'd planned.

No, not Darla. She had seemed pretty adamant about not getting involved with him. So what had changed?

He smiled at her. "Not what you expected, huh?"

She smiled back. "On the contrary, I knew I'd like your kisses. That's why I've been trying to avoid them."

"Then why did you ask me to kiss you?"

"I'm tired of being scared to take chances. I don't want to be one of those people who dies with a lot of regrets. And I would have regretted it if I never kissed you."

He nodded his understanding, then said, "So what comes next?"

"An official date, if you're still interested. But know that I'm still figuring out some things."

"I wouldn't have kissed you if I weren't still interested. What kind of guy do you think I am?"

She laughed shortly. "I think you're kind of nutty, but I like that about you."

He pulled her back into his arms and she cozied up to him and laid her head on his chest. "I could get used to this," she murmured.

"I'll see that you do," he promised.

They heard a noise from behind them and both turned to look at the back door. The curtain covering the window at the top of the wooden door was fluttering back into place. "Your mother?" he asked.

"Probably," Darla answered. "Do you ever feel like our mothers missed their calling?"

"Yeah," he said. "They should have been spies."

"I bet Evie Cramer is on the phone right now giving Miss Margherita an update on Operation Get Darla and Dave Together," Darla joked.

Dave didn't reply, though he felt she was probably right. All he wanted to do now was hold her in his arms. They had a lot of time to make up for.

THE NEXT DAY was Saturday, Little League practice day. Darla and Bastian were at the field by 10:45 a.m. Practice began at eleven o'clock.

It was a typical day in May, with temperatures in the high seventies, clear blue skies, a slight breeze and plenty of Florida sunshine. Darla joined the parents in the stands. The kids were playing tag and Bastian was waved over by Skye, who was right beside Lissa. The girls had been inseparable, Darla noticed, since that incident weeks ago.

She wished she and Joyce were as innocent as kids. After Joyce had told her she must not be too bad if she had a kid like Bastian, the two of them hadn't exchanged many words. Joyce was no longer shooting daggers at her with her eyes, but they definitely were not pals.

When the kids started cheering, she knew Dave had arrived. She wondered if the star treatment was getting to his head. But no, he was his goofy self, she saw, when he pulled off his jacket and revealed the T-shirt underneath. On the front of it was I Coach Little League. No, I'm Not Crazy.

The kids cracked up after seeing it because there was a cartoon coach on the front of it hitting his head with a baseball bat while his eyes comically bulged out.

"Is he nuts?" she heard one of the mothers ask no one in particular. The other parents laughed. But Darla didn't find the question particularly funny.

"'He's no nuts. He's crazy!'" Darla heard

Joyce say. Then she laughed, too. That line was from *Indiana Jones and the Temple of Doom*, said by Short Round, who was portrayed by actor Ke Huy Quan. It was one of her favorite movies.

After that, Dave called the parents down off the stands and they began hitting drills using the tee, not a pitcher.

"Parents, I want you in the field to retrieve balls. I'm going to be here with the kids showing them how to hold the bat. Everybody finds their own method as they learn how to play. Kids, each of you will come up here and hit the ball. After hitting, I want you to run to first base and stay there. After another batter hits, you run to the next base and so forth until everyone has had his or her turn at bat. Okay, let's get started!"

Hitting drills began. The parents were in the outfield, spread out, waiting for their little ballplayers to hit one out to them. Darla and Joyce stood a few feet apart in the outfield in their athletic clothes and shoes and holding leather mitts at the ready.

"When I signed up for this," Joyce said, "I didn't know I was going to be playing ball, too."

Darla's eyes were on Dave and the kids at home base. Looked like the action was about to start. "Neither did I," she hurriedly said to Joyce. "Batter's up."

She and Joyce turned their attention to home base.

First up to bat was a little boy named Jeremy. He was small for his age but feisty, Darla had noticed. He was consistently optimistic even when he kept dropping the ball or failed to catch it. The other kids encouraged him to keep trying.

Dave showed Jeremy how to grip his bat and the proper stance for swinging the bat.

Jeremy's face reflected his determination to hit the ball. He swung and connected. The ball went straight down the middle of the field. Parents scrambled to grab the ball as it rolled across the field. Jeremy was grinning and running to first base. He jumped up and down a couple of times on base when he reached it. The kids cheered for him.

Darla could see their encouragement was paying off. Jeremy had never looked happier.

The parents, she thought, looked like participants in a comedy sketch, running all over the field vying with each other to collect the ball Jeremy had hit. One of the mothers claimed it and jumped up and down like she'd won a prize. Everyone was having fun.

All of the children had their turn at bat, and Dave patiently guided each one, telling them to relax and enjoy themselves. When Bastian came up to bat, Darla felt a little tension in her belly. She wanted him to do well, yes, but most of all, she wanted him to do this for himself. And to have fun doing it.

"Go, Bastian!" she yelled.

Her son looked up and grinned at her. Then he walloped that ball. It flew high into the air parallel with third base. A father was in left field backing up, ready to catch it. But he missed and the ball bounced out of his glove. Darla cheered. Bastian made it to first base, not even looking to see where his ball had been heading.

An hour later, they were all enjoying snacks and talking about the wonderful hitting drills. The parents had brought snacks for their children that Dave had suggested. Not sweets or chips or sodas but fresh fruit and vegetables, and juice without added sugar in it. Plus water, arguably the most important thing to have on hand for them.

Dave was eating a Granny Smith apple and chatting with one of the fathers when Darla walked up to the two men. "Good practice, Coach," she said.

"Thank you, Darla," Dave said. "A few more of these and we're going to play a real game against a team from Pensacola. I've already arranged it with their coach. I was just telling Peter Senior here." Darla knew Peter Sr. was the father of Peter, the little boy who wore glasses.

"That's great," said Darla. She looked around. She always liked to know where Bastian was. Foremost in her Mommy Mind was the memory of that incident months ago when he'd disappeared for hours and they didn't know where he was.

Bastian was playing tag with the other kids only a few feet away from her. How much energy did they have to spare?

"We're having a cook-out later on," Peter Sr. was saying when she focused back on the two men. "You're both invited."

"I'm sorry, I've already got plans," Dave told him regretfully.

"If I had known earlier, I might have been able to get away," Darla said. "But I have other plans, too. Thanks for the invitation, though."

She smiled at them both. "Bastian and I had better go. See you next time!"

"Sure, Darla," said Peter Sr. He turned back around to Dave, and Darla walked away, but not without one more glance at Dave. She caught him watching her. The expression in his gorgeous eyes told her he was as excited as she was about their date tonight.

DAVE DROPPED BY the police station on the way home from practice. Even if it wasn't a workday, he liked showing up just to make sure things were running smoothly. He knew he should be able to put the job aside in favor of a personal life, but to be honest, he was a policeman through and through. He didn't live and breathe the job, but it was an intrinsic part of who he was.

He liked keeping people safe. Maybe it was an attitude that had been inculcated in him in the military.

As he strode through the double doors of the police station, he overheard Laraine talking to someone on the phone and exclaim, "That's ridiculous. I know you're just doing your job. But even you know that man should go to rehab or prison before he kills someone!"

She looked up and saw him approaching and said, "Hold on, the chief just walked in. You wanna talk with him?"

Dave was right across from her by now, eyeing her with interest.

"Raff Chandler's lawyer," she whispered to him.

She listened a while longer, and the attorney must have said he would like to speak with Dave, so she handed him the receiver.

"Aaron?" Aaron Hammond had represented the Chandler family for decades. He was a good man who tried to give them wise counsel. However, the privileged always thought they knew best, and deserved the best. So, although they didn't always take Aaron Hammond's advice, they retained him because he was the best lawyer to be had around here. At least that was Dave's theory.

"Dave, I'm sorry to have to inform you that Raff Chandler is suing you for negligence. He says you just watched him vomit. He could have choked to death and you didn't do anything to help him."

"I made sure he was all right before I left him alone. I followed procedure, Aaron. I made sure he was okay before I left and another officer checked on him later. He was fine. You know Raff is doing this only to take the attention off himself. He's an out-of-control drunk and he isn't doing anything about his addiction."

"Off the record, I agree with you," Aaron said with a resigned sigh. "I told him he had no case. He insists he does. At the very least I think he hopes to taint your reputation as a law officer. I don't know why he has it in for you."

"I know why," Dave said. "Because he's a spoiled Daddy's boy who has never earned a dime of his own. And his father is enabling him and one day last year I happened to be at a social gathering where he showed up and started talking about the 'race problem' in this town, as he termed it. No one around us would say a word contrary to the hatred he was spewing, but I did. I told him he was a fool and people like him are, thankfully, dying out. This is a new world. A world in which everybody, no matter their color, has the right to a good life. He's hated my guts ever since. And he knows whenever he gets arrested for drunk driving, his father is going to save him. This last arrest was the third time in a year. So he got his license revoked this time and still no jail time. Suing me is his way of at least getting some satisfaction."

"Well, I thought you should know," Aaron said. "I won't be representing him. I told him he had to find another attorney. I'm retiring. I'm too old to kowtow to their foolishness anymore."

"Congrats, Aaron," Dave said sincerely. "I don't know how you put up with it as long as you did."

"Neither do I," Aaron said.

"Enjoy your retirement, Aaron."

After he hung up the phone, Laraine said, "You've got friends in this town, and he's one of them. He didn't have to call to warn you."

"Yeah," Dave said contemplatively. He forced a smile as he regarded Laraine. "Let's keep this quiet for a while, shall we? I need time to figure out my next move."

"You've got it," said Laraine, her smile forced, too, he knew. In addition to being a very competent police officer, Laraine also wore her heart on her sleeve, and she was very devoted to people she cared about. Dave was grateful to be on that list.

"Don't you worry, now," he said. "Everything's going to be all right."

"I'll try not to," she promised.

The phone rang and Laraine answered with her usual flair. "Port Domingo Police Department. How can I help you?"

"I'm out," Dave said over his shoulder to her as he turned to go. Finding out he was going to be sued was quite enough for one day. He'd leave other problems, if they existed, for another day. Besides, he had a date tonight.

Raff Chandler could go straight to... But then he stopped himself. Raff Chandler was sick. His thinking was warped and his excessive drinking didn't help matters. If only he could figure out some way to get Chandler to go to rehab and truly make an effort to get sober. This would not only help Chandler but keep the rest of Port Domingo safe from his drunk driving and vitriol.

He sighed as he stepped back outside into the bright sunshine. He would not let this ruin his happiness. He was going to plan and execute the best date of his and Darla's lives. Armed with a fresh perspective, he walked swiftly to his waiting truck, got in and drove home.

"RESERVATIONS, FOR TONIGHT, SIR? On such short notice? I'm afraid we're completely booked until next September."

Okay, Dave silently admitted. That was a slight exaggeration. All of his calls to so-called good restaurants in Pensacola in his quest to dazzle Darla on their date tonight weren't answered by snooty hosts or hostesses who made you feel common over the phone.

He was, however, unable to get a reservation at any of the restaurants he was considering. Then he thought about what Darla had said when he'd asked her where she wanted to go tonight.

Someplace with good food but without pretensions, she'd said. So he chose a restaurant on Pensacola Beach he'd gone to on a few occasions that had wonderful food, a relaxed atmosphere and was accessible to the beach.

He texted Darla: Dress casually and bring some sandals for walking on the beach.

DARLA READ THE text twice, then put her phone in the back pocket of her jeans. She'd just gotten home from driving Bastian to his dad's house.

When she walked through the back door, her mom was in the kitchen putting away groceries.

She turned around at the sound of Darla coming in. "Oh, Darla, you scared me."

Darla had yet to ask her mom if she had indeed been spying on her and Dave last night. She hadn't figured out how to phrase it without sounding accusatory. She knew their mothers had their best interests at heart.

But she was still annoyed with her and hadn't told her that she and Miss Margherita could abandon their matchmaking mission since their mission was accomplished. She was going out with Dave.

She decided to tell her now. "Mom," she began, walking around the door of the open refrigerator. Her mother was placing a half gallon of milk inside.

Her mom closed the refrigerator door and looked up at her. "Yes, sweetie?"

"I have a date tonight. Bastian is spending the night with his dad and Marley."

Her mother pulled the reusable shopping bag that was sitting atop the island toward her so she could see what was inside of it. "Mmm, huh," she said absently. "Margherita already told me you and Dave were finally going on a date."

"Seriously, Mom?" Darla said sharply. Anger flared up just like that. She was livid. "How did she know?"

"Honey, Dave talks to his mother. Unlike you. You prefer to keep your business to yourself." Her mom huffed and put down the box of cereal she'd removed from the bag. Turning to look Darla in the eyes, she said, "You wouldn't ask me for help before you ran away. You kept things bottled up and I was useless to you. Useless as a mother. I might have been able to help you, honey. If I'd only known. I'm sorry if I've been so nosy lately. Both Margherita and I are sorry if we've overstepped in our attempts to try to see that our two children, the two who haven't been lucky in love, wind up together. But you know it never would have worked if you weren't attracted to each other. You two had something to do with the success of our plan. Now, though, we've decided that since you have found common ground and you're going to give each other a chance, we're going to step aside. No more games. You're on your own. And we wish you the best."

Her mother took a deep breath, let it out and smiled at her.

After that speech, Darla felt incredibly ashamed of herself. She knew she'd hurt her mother when she'd ran off with J.J. However, she hadn't known that her actions had caused her mother to believe she had failed her.

She went and pulled the shorter woman into her arms. "You didn't fail me, Mom. You're a wonderful mother. The best! I just hope to be half the mom you are one day."

"Oh, baby, you're a good mother. I always knew you would be. You just didn't give yourself a chance. And I read up on it—postpartum depression has been part of the reason why mothers abandon their children all over the world. You weren't the only one. Some mothers left their children at fire stations. On doorsteps. Even dumpsters. You left Bastian with his father. With people who loved him when you couldn't. And you came back. I wish you could forgive yourself now and realize you have a home here with people who love you. And Dave could love you, too. You deserve to be cherished."

Darla was crying as she said, "I'll try to remember that."

Her mother gently shook her as though she were trying to shake some sense into her. "You do that!"

They parted and Darla wiped her tears away. "I've got to stop crying all the time."

"Let it out, honey," her mother told her, wiping away her own tears. "Crying releases stress. It's good for you."

Darla smiled at her and gave her a quick kiss on the cheek. "I'd better get upstairs and find something to wear tonight."

"Oh," said her mother excitedly. "Wear a pretty dress!"

"Mother!"

"Wear whatever you want. See if I care."

Darla paused on the stairs, then looked back at her mother. "On second thought, maybe I could use some help."

Her mother grinned and raced her up the stairs.

CHAPTER ELEVEN

"It doesn't look like much. But the food's good," Dave said as he and Darla entered the unpretentious restaurant on Pensacola Beach that night. The restaurant was close to the water and had a weathered clapboard look to it. A wooden walkway led to the restaurant's entrance, and beside the door stood a pirate with a peg leg. Inside the high-ceilinged main eating area, various novelty items associated with piracy on the high seas were on display. There was one incongruous item Dave couldn't figure out: a replica of the Tin Man from *The Wizard of Oz*. Like the other pieces, it was suspended from the ceiling by a string.

Darla looked around them. "I like it," she said.

The place was packed. The aromas coming from the kitchen made Dave's mouth water. They'd only been looking the place over a couple of minutes before an enthusiastic hostess approached them with a big smile on her brown face. "Welcome to Peg Leg Pete's," she said. "We've got a table by the window, if you like."

Dave demurred to Darla. She nodded in agreement. "Sounds good."

They followed the hostess between full tables until they arrived at theirs. Dave pulled Darla's chair out for her and after she was seated, he sat down across from her. He hadn't been able to stop marveling at the fact that they were together tonight. Alone. Without any expectations, on his part, except to get to know one another better. After several weeks of Little League practice, he felt he knew her a little. He knew she was kind and patient. He knew that she could make concessions and give someone another chance. He'd noticed her and Joyce Hines laughing together. Talking like friends instead of enemies. So she had a forgiving heart.

While he'd been thinking all of that, the hostess had given them both menus and promised to send a server to take their orders as quickly as possible.

Darla was smiling at him as if she'd caught

him off in his own world, which she probably had.

"What are you thinking?" she asked.

She was wearing a white, cotton, sleeveless summer dress and white low-heeled sandals. The starkness of the white accentuated the smooth reddish-brown tone of her skin. She'd worn her hair down tonight. It fell halfway down her back in loose curls. Black and luxurious and shiny. It framed her heart-shaped face perfectly. Just sitting across from her made him smile.

"I'm wondering what would have happened if I'd asked you out in high school. Before you and Sebastian started dating. Would you have gone out with me then?"

Darla thought for a moment. "I don't know. I was an impressionable teen. Interracial dating wasn't that popular at our school, don't you remember? Unless I'm mistaken, I think Kaye and Miguel were the only mixed couple at our school at the time."

"So, you might have said no."

"I might have. Who knows?" Then she asked, "Why didn't you ask me out before I started dating Sebastian?"

"I didn't know you then. I only noticed

you after you started dating Sebastian, and the cardinal rule is you don't try to steal your friend's girlfriend."

She tilted her head to the side and gave him a slow smile.

"So this what-if scenario wouldn't have happened in real life, anyway. Because you didn't notice me until I was already with Sebastian. Now I don't feel so bad about not knowing that much about you when we were in high school."

He laughed softly. "That's the problem with 'what might have been.'"

"Let's live in the here and now," Darla suggested. She looked down at the menu. "You've obviously been here before. What's really good?"

"Fresh seafood is what they do, so you're safe ordering just about any seafood on the menu."

As if on cue, their server, another cheery individual whose name was Jefe, according to his lanyard, walked up to their table with pen poised. "Good evening, I'm Jefe, and I'll be your server. Have you decided what you want to start with?"

They decided to begin with the fried calamari, and for their entrées, Darla ordered the pan-seared grouper, while Dave ordered the grilled Gulf shrimp. Both came with two side dishes.

The waiter asked for their drink orders.

Dave said, "Water's fine."

Darla said, "Water's fine for me, too."

After the waiter had gone, Dave asked, "You don't drink alcohol?"

"No, I never developed a taste for it. And you?"

"Yes, but sparingly. And I don't drink and drive."

She smiled and looked at him like she was trying to figure him out. Two minutes later, Dave was beginning to feel uncomfortable sitting there with her studying him. He decided to break the silence.

"Just say it, Darla," he finally encouraged her. He mentally prepared himself for what would come next. His luck hadn't been good today, and he really couldn't take any more bad news.

"What's wrong with you?" she asked softly, a frown creasing her brows. "Every other time I've been alone with you, I've been able to feel your emotions. You're sure of yourself. You go after life, full throttle. You didn't give up on me, but now when we're finally on a date, I'm getting negative vibes. Am I wrong? Tell me if I'm wrong."

Dave was so relieved, he let out a short laugh and a long sigh. "You're not wrong. I was told today, by the attorney of a person we recently arrested, that he's going to sue me for negligence. He was put in the holding cell and threw up while there and said I just stood there and did nothing to help him."

Darla's brows shot up in a questioning gesture. "What were you supposed to do?" Then she sat up straighter in her chair and gave him a serious look. "I'm going to take this from a medical professional's point of view. You said he was in the drunk tank. Therefore, I'm assuming he threw up because that's what some drunk people do when their systems can't take anymore alcohol and the body flushes it out."

Dave nodded. "It wasn't the first time he's thrown up while in his cell."

"What is the protocol for that sort of thing?"

"If the prisoner appears to be fine, he's left to his own devices. Which this guy appeared to be. We regularly check on intoxicated people for that very reason. By all reports, he didn't have a second incident. If he had, we would have gotten him to a hospital or called EMTs. We don't want prisoners dying on us."

"Of course not," she said, her gaze never leaving his face.

Dave started to feel more comfortable. His mind had been a bit unsettled since learning Raff Chandler meant to make his life miserable. He hadn't been entirely surprised that Chandler had it in him to be so vindictive, though. The man's heart was full of hate.

Darla's eyes held a contemplative expression in their depths. "He's obviously lying. But you know him and the court system. Do you think he could win a lawsuit against you?"

Dave smiled slowly. "Wait. How are you so certain he's lying?"

"Because you'd never willfully neglect anyone, Dave. You are the epitome of a hero. I've heard about your military service. I know you don't like talking about it. But your mother does, and she regaled us with stories of your bravery while in Afghanistan."

Dave looked anywhere except into her

eyes after she mentioned his military service. He didn't like thinking about it, let alone talking about it. He'd done what he'd had to do to save his fellow soldiers. They called him a hero for doing it. But in his opinion, he hadn't done enough. Good friends died on the mission for which he'd been praised as a hero. In fact, his best friend, Cameron, had died. That was not something he'd ever get over.

Darla must have noticed the change in him, because she reached across the table and clasped both his hands in hers. "Sorry I brought it up. I feel you. I don't know if I'll ever be normal again. Or the normal that I used to be. But I've got to believe that who I am now, and what I'm doing to make up for my past, will one day outweigh what I did, and once again, the scales will tip in my favor."

He peered into her eyes then, because she did get him. She did feel him. "Maybe one day I'll tell you about it. But not until we're old and gray."

She laughed softly. "See? There's that optimism I love so much."

At that moment, the waiter arrived with

their food. Darla let go of his hands, and they sat back in their chairs, allowing the waiter to place their food on the table.

After they'd thanked the waiter, and he'd gone, they bowed their heads and Dave said a soft prayer of thanks.

"Home training," Darla quipped afterward, referring to their silent agreement to pray before beginning their meals.

"That's right," Dave said. "Our mothers go to the same church."

"That's how they met," Darla told him. "It was in the early 1980s, I'm told. Your mother was relatively new to the United States. My mother was an English teacher. One morning, they attended the same Mass service and, afterward, started talking. My mom, who can't resist teaching, became attached to your mother just like that. Your mother taught mine to cook Italian food. My mother taught yours to speak Southern English." She ended with a laugh, and Dave marveled at how beautiful she was when her eyes lit up with merriment.

They were quiet for a few minutes as they tucked into their meals. Dave watched Darla's face for any indication the food was bad, but her expression was pleasant as she ate. She also seemed to be enjoying the ambience, such as it was. People around them were talking and laughing and chowing down. There was country music playing in the background. It was a bit loud but altogether enjoyable.

"Good food," Darla said, smiling at him. "And this place is so warm and welcoming. Thank you for bringing me here."

Dave really relaxed then. Their first date was going okay, so far.

"Tell me what you like to do in your free time," he said.

Darla had to ruminate on the request while she chewed another forkful of food and washed it down with a drink of water.

"I like to cook. I like to sing. I'm a voracious reader."

"Oh, what kinds of books?"

"All kinds of books," she answered. "My mother is a retired English teacher, remember? She wasn't going to allow her children to hate reading. She introduced Jerry and me to books as soon as we were born. When I was a kid, I slept with a book in my arms, not a teddy bear. And you?"

"I fish, watch sports. I'm building a house…"

Hearing about his house obviously piqued her interest. She set down her fork and gave him her undivided attention. "You're building a house?"

"Dad was in construction before he retired. I've been building things since I was old enough and strong enough to lift a hammer. So I'm building my dream house. It's on the outskirts of Port Domingo on two acres. I don't even have any close neighbors. It's quiet out there. And you can see the sunset from my back porch. Would you like to see it?"

"I didn't mention my obsession with decorating," she said with a grin. "Well, that's what my relatives call it, anyway. Yes, I'd love to see your house. In fact, let's skip the beach and head back to Port Domingo after dinner."

Dave laughed with delight. "No sand between your toes tonight, huh?"

"Are you kidding me? When you've seen one beach on the Emerald Coast, you've seen them all. They're all beautiful. But in my opinion, they don't compare to a house under construction. I'm stoked!"

"I think I'm beginning to know the real you," Dave said.

He gave her the side-eye. "Or are you just taking pity on me because I may be dragged through court by a vengeful man?"

She literally waved that suggestion off by flicking her dainty wrist at him. "I'm not worried about you, Dave. That dude, who-ever he is, doesn't have a leg to stand on. He's going to need witnesses to testify that his interpretation of what happened is true. And no one will back him up."

She smiled at him after saying that, looked over at his plate and asked, "Are you going to eat those fries?" She then proceeded to spear a couple with her fork and relished eat-ing them.

Dave just smiled.

DARLA HADN'T KNOWN what to expect when Dave told her about his house. But seeing as how he was a public servant, and an honest one, she hadn't expected this huge two-story farmhouse-style house.

They got out of his truck and began walk-ing toward the covered front porch. The light was on. There were tall windows across the entire front of the house. The exterior was painted white with black trim. It had a steep-pitched gable roof and dormers on either side. The wide porch extended to the south side of the house.

"What kind of roof did you put on?" Darla asked.

Dave was unlocking the front door and answered, "Metal. It's more durable and I built this house to withstand hurricane-force winds, this being Florida."

"Solid choice," she agreed. "Windows?"

"Double-hung, two-over-two," Dave said. "Top and bottom operable. Which means there are…"

"There are four windowpanes in each window. Two on the top, two on the bottom." Darla picked up where he had left off. "Energy-saving."

They stepped into the foyer, and Darla admired the exposed beams on the vaulted ceiling.

Dave saw her looking and said, "They're made from reclaimed pinewood, recycled from an old theater in Tallahassee. The guy who is helping me build it knows a guy."

"When you said you were building a house,

I thought you were just putting it up, but it looks like you have the exterior done and you're finishing the interior."

"That's about the size of it." Dave confirmed that her observation was correct.

The hardwood floors were gorgeous, although it looked as if he hadn't gotten around to painting the inside yet. There was no furniture in the huge living room, but when they walked farther into the house, she saw that the kitchen was pretty much finished.

He then took her on a tour of the remainder of the house. There were four bedrooms, two and a half baths, and an extra room upstairs he was thinking of turning into a theater. Back downstairs, the laundry room was off the kitchen, as well as a mudroom. French doors in the kitchen opened onto a huge deck. Looking outward, Darla could barely see the backyard.

"How many acres did you say?"

"Two, mostly untamed woods." He gestured to the west, where he'd earlier told her you could see the sunset in the evenings. "I've got the area around the house fenced in because of critters."

"Critters?"

"I've seen possums, rabbits, even a coyote. Did you know Florida has coyotes?"

"Yes, I've heard about them, but I've never seen one," she answered.

They returned to the kitchen.

"So, you have an operable kitchen, bath and bedroom. All the things required for living, and you're slowly finishing everything else," Darla concluded from their tour of the house.

"Exactly," Dave said as he walked over to the kitchen counter, where a Bose Wave music system sat. He tapped a few buttons and Nina Simone's full-throated voice came floating through the air.

"May I have this dance?" he asked Darla, standing before her with a smile on his face.

Darla went into his open arms. She had been wondering how it'd feel to lay her head on his chest with his arms wrapped around her. He seemed to be a man who loved his monochromatic colors. Last night it had been all black. Tonight, all blue. Shirt, trousers, even dark blue suede shoes. He made the outfit work, though. With that thick, dark brown hair, so wavy that she wanted to run her fingers through it just to test its resiliency. Would the waves fall right back into place if she tousled them? And he smelled good, too.

She was so nervous, her thoughts were rambling.

They danced in silence as Nina serenaded them with "I Put a Spell on You."

He was smiling down at her. She tried to maintain the gaze, but being in his arms reminded her of how long it'd been since she'd dated anyone, and the last time hadn't ended well. In this day and age, there were so many expectations people had of each other when it came to a relationship. She'd only been in relationships with two men in her lifetime. One, she'd married. The other had been a mistake. What did she have to bring to the table? She was notorious in this town for running off with a rock musician who'd been with famous actresses, singers and fashion models. Why had he chosen her? they were probably asking themselves. And did it mean she was now a different person with different values since she'd lived in the rock star's world for a while?

When Dave bent down with the intention

of kissing her, she froze. She suddenly realized that Dave might have gotten the wrong impression when she'd been so eager to see his house tonight. Which was the furthest thing from the truth. Blast her interior decorating obsession!

His mouth was on hers now, and she wasn't responding.

He raised his head and peered down at her. "Have I done something wrong?"

"No, no," she assured him.

He continued to regard her with a confused expression on his face. Then he drew a big hand through his wavy hair and took a step backward. "Oh, I think I understand. You're afraid I expect more from you since we're alone in my house. But remember, I invited you. I asked if you'd like to see it. Believe me, *mia amata*, you are safe with me. I don't expect anything from you that you're not ready to give."

Darla supposed she didn't appear convinced, so he pulled her into his arms again and gently rocked her within them. "We'll take things slowly."

Darla couldn't help it, she laughed. "Mom

always said my love of decorating would get me in trouble someday."

"I understood that you couldn't possibly be ready for that," Dave said. "It took me months to get you to go out with me. I'm just happy to have you here in my house. Listening to Nina and, perhaps, stealing a few kisses. I've waited a long time to get this far. I'm not going to mess it up by trying to convince you to do something you're not ready for. Are we clear on that?"

"We are clear," Darla said.

Nina was now singing "Feeling Good" and it was the appropriate song because Dave had allayed her fears and she was now relaxed enough to enjoy the moment.

They danced until midnight there in his spare, almost finished, house. They talked about life and what they hoped the future would bring them. Dave said he just wanted a family to fill this house up with. She said she wanted to feel good in her skin again. And to feel worthy of being loved.

"You are worthy of being loved. We all are," he told her as they danced with his hand at the small of her back and her head on his chest.

"Now I just have to convince myself," she said. "That's the hard part."

"Take it one day at a time. You'll get there," he said, his voice a soothing balm to her heart.

CHAPTER TWELVE

"MOM, WHAT ARE you doing here?" Darla asked her mother. She glanced around nervously to make sure Mr. Jenkins wasn't within earshot.

Lily had opened the door when the bell rang, and she was now ushering her mother into the house. Lily looked as surprised to see her mom as she was.

Her mom was stylishly turned out, as always. She was wearing a pastel yellow sundress with a pair of beige espadrilles. Her shoulder bag was also beige. Her short salt-and-pepper Afro was perfectly coiffed. She walked into the house with her mouth slightly ajar. "I've driven by this house dozens of times but never imagined I'd be inside of it. So this is where you come every weekday."

Darla gave Lily an apologetic look.

Lily shrugged and turned to leave. "I'll go get Mr. Jenkins."

Darla rushed to Lily's side. "Hold that

thought. Let me see what this is about first. You know how he can be."

Lily seemed pleased to have the problem taken off her shoulders. She shrugged again. "All right. See you later, Evie."

"Okay, thank you, Lily, dear," said her mother pleasantly. Darla remembered Lily and her mother were old friends. Her mother had lived here all her life. It stood to reason she would know quite a few people.

Now that they were alone, Darla asked her mom, "What are you doing here? Is something the matter with Bastian? Someone else in the family?"

Her mother calmly set her shoulder bag in one of the padded chairs at the kitchen table. "I'm not here because of you, sweetie. I'm here to see a Theodore Jenkins." She rummaged in her bag and removed a letter-size sheet of paper. She handed it to Darla. "Read this."

Darla took the sheet of paper. She couldn't believe her eyes. An anonymous benefactor had donated a hundred thousand dollars to Silver Seniors, her mother's charitable organization. The donation amount was unprecedented.

She looked at her mother. "That's wonderful. I'm happy for Silver Seniors. But this says the donation was anonymous. What are you doing here?"

"Because I sweetly asked Stewart who the anonymous benefactor was. And, in his own way, he gave me the information."

Darla knew that Stewart McInnis was the bank manager at her mother's bank. He was also one of her ex-students.

"You strong-armed poor Stewart? What if he loses his job because he gave you privileged information?"

"I'll never tell," her mother said, still excitedly looking around them. "I'm here because I have a theory. I know it's a longshot, but the name Theodore Jenkins sounds vaguely familiar to me. But the Jenkins I knew a long time ago was known as Teddy to me. Teddy can be short for Theodore, though, can't it? Theodore Roosevelt, Teddy Roosevelt. Get me?"

"I can't believe Stewart gave you the identity of an anonymous benefactor," Darla said, outraged.

"He didn't," her mother calmly informed

her. "He stepped out of the room and I saw it on his computer's screen."

"Mother, you have gone too far!"

"Darla, I'm too old to live life at a sedate pace. Now, go get your employer. I'd like to speak with him."

"I will not," Darla said stubbornly.

"You don't have to. I'm right here," said Mr. Jenkins as he walked into the kitchen. "And don't be angry with your mother. I told McInnis that if a nosy woman by the name of Evelyn Crammer came asking about me that it was okay for him to give her the information she requested. I think he was having a little fun with her when he let her have a look at his computer's screen."

At this time of the day, Darla had already helped him with his exercises. When her mother had rang the doorbell earlier, he'd been in his suite changing out of his sweats and showering.

Now he was dressed in his usual sartorial style for staying home. He wore a white long-sleeved dress shirt, black slacks and black oxfords, all of the very best quality. His hair was neatly trimmed because his barber had come to the house just yesterday.

Her mother stood frozen, her gaze on Mr. Jenkins. Darla held her breath and then remembered to exhale.

"Evelyn," Mr. Jenkins said with a warm smile. "You are as lovely as ever."

Darla's mother seemed at a loss for words. Which, Darla thought, was a miracle. Her pushy, loud, opinionated and altogether impossible mother just stood there blushing. And the blush was evident on her cheeks because Evie Cramer had honey-colored brown skin, and it showed her emotions all the time. Angry or embarrassed, you could see it on her face. What was she feeling now?

"Teddy!" her mother exclaimed. The next thing Darla knew, her mother was in Mr. Jenkins's arms and the two of them were hugging fiercely.

"I knew it was you," her mother said through tears.

Mr. Jenkins's eyes were misty, too. "I wasn't sure you'd find me, but I was hoping you would."

"If I had known you were the Theodore Jenkins Darla was working for, I would've been over here long before now."

"How could you have known?" he said

soothingly. "We haven't seen one another in half a century!"

Darla turned to give them their privacy by leaving the room, but Mr. Jenkins called her back. "Darla!"

"We'll talk later," Mr. Jenkins told her. "For now, just know that I'm happy to see your mother again. She never could resist a mystery."

Darla realized, then, that Mr. Jenkins was no longer satisfied with watching life from the sidelines. He'd risked it all to see his Evelyn again. Score one for Mr. Jenkins!

Happy to know her job was safe, Darla left the room but not before taking one last glance at the happy couple. They were beaming with pleasure at seeing one another again.

IT HAD BEEN three weeks since Dave got that phone call from Aaron stating that his former client intended to sue him for neglect. Dave had begun to believe that Raff Chandler had made the threat while on a drunken tirade and had subsequently forgotten all about it.

But one afternoon, while he was in his office going over the monthly budget, as any administrator had to do, there was a knock on the door.

"Come in," he called.

It was Laraine. "Sorry, Chief," she said just before a brash young man in a dark suit walked into the room and thrust an envelope at him. *Process server*, Dave thought.

"Chief David Harrison?" he asked.

"Yeah," said Dave as he took the envelope.

"You've been served," said the young man, and he immediately turned and left.

Laraine stood there in the doorway, her hand on the doorknob.

"Want me to phone Eugene Pryor for you?"

Eugene Pryor was the best defense attorney in the county, Dave knew, but he was the one who should make the phone call.

It was time he became proactive. "Thanks, Laraine. I'll do it."

Laraine gave him a sympathetic look and pulled the door closed. In her absence, Dave took out his cell phone and googled Eugene Pryor. He certainly didn't have the attorney in his contacts. He'd never needed a lawyer before.

He located the phone number and dialed.

He got a machine, of course. He sure wasn't in the mood to listen to a menu before he finally got a human being on the phone. But he patiently waited until a woman who wasn't a machine answered and he made an appointment to see Eugene Pryor. Eugene Pryor and only Eugene. He didn't want to be passed to a junior partner.

Appointment made, he ended the call and sat back in his brown leather swivel chair.

So it begins, he thought.

THE DAY OF the big Little League game arrived bright and shiny and full of promise, or so Darla thought. She and Marley and Sebastian, her mother and—oh my God!—Mr. Jenkins, and Jerry, who had found cheerleaders' pompoms from somewhere and had brought enough for everyone, were sitting in the stands enjoying themselves. Perhaps a tad too much. She thought Bastian was either going to feel supremely supported by his loved ones or slightly embarrassed by them.

The kids looked adorable in their new baseball uniforms. They were white with royal blue stripes on them with matching royal blue helmets. Most of the kids wore white athletic shoes. They were now officially known as The Dolphins. As soon as the kids learned they were to be called The Dolphins, many of them began making squeaking sounds like dolphins during the games and to cheer each other on. Bastian and Skye were particularly good at it.

The Dolphins were playing The Gators, a team from the neighboring city of Pensacola. Dave had told her his nephew, Ben, was on the team since that was where his sister, Maria, and her husband, Grant, lived with their two children, Benjamin and their youngest, Sadie.

Darla was pleased that Sebastian had agreed to come to the game. She still wasn't entirely sure of his opinion of her since her return. However, he was always civil, and he and Marley made a wonderful couple. Was she jealous of their happiness? Did she have any regrets that she wasn't the one sharing a life with Bastian's father? She had to admit that she still had affection for Sebastian. However, it was the sort of affection that meant she wanted only good things for him. He'd been kind to her by being willing to share Bastian. He could have fought her to the bitter end. No, she wasn't still in love with him. She sometimes wondered if their love had ever been the lasting kind. High school sweethearts. Had either of them known what real love was? Sebastian was always intent on following in his father's footsteps and taking over the fishing company. He'd made it the most successful business in town. He was the reliable type of man who never let his family down. And Marley was his perfect match because she was a true friend and put family first. Darla now agreed with her mom that sometimes life turned out for the best. Marley and Sebastian were meant to be.

Cheers rose around her as Skye got a solid hit and began running to first base. The bases were loaded, and Peter was up to bat next. He adjusted his glasses and narrowed his eyes. Darla leaned forward, hoping that he followed Skye's example and took his time. During their last game, Peter had had trouble connecting with the ball. He'd hit the tee ball stand. He'd swung too low.

But today, he hit the ball and it went straight down the center of the field. He took off running to first base, his legs pumping. Skye, smiling, ran to second base. And the two players who had been on second base and third ran home. The score was now 4–3 in favor of The Dolphins.

The spectators on the home team's side cheered. In her section of the stands, Darla and everyone else stood up and waved their pompoms, cheering, "Go, Dolphins!"

She peeked to her left, wondering how her star patient, Mr. Jenkins, was faring. He didn't like crowds. He was afraid he might have an episode of "freezing," a symptom of his Parkinson's. His brain would fail to send a signal for his limbs to work and he would freeze in place. But they'd been working on that, and he had learned to watch for signs that an episode was coming. He seemed to be doing well today. He was having fun. Her mother was very protective of him, and Darla was sure that she would react appropriately should Mr. Jenkins actually have an episode. She'd had a long talk with her mother about his condition and he'd also explained to her what to expect. This openness between them encouraged Darla to believe they would become good friends.

Her mother had plenty of friends, but Mr. Jenkins could use a loyal one.

"Nephew's turn," Darla heard Jerry say, and she returned her attention to the game.

Bastian was at bat. She was nervous, but not as much as the last time when her stomach muscles had constricted painfully. She knew her son was there to have fun. His life didn't depend on the game, and he didn't have anything to prove to anyone, least of all his parents, who would love him no matter what.

Bastian took his time. Got into the batter's stance that Dave had taught him and swung that bat, connecting with the ball immediately and sending it flying into right field. He dropped the bat and ran hard, his face a mask of glee. Skye was jumping up and down, cheering him on.

"Run, Skye!" Joyce shouted, reminding her daughter to run to the next base. She was below them on the stands sitting beside a tall, muscular guy Darla assumed was her husband, Raymond. Her mom had told her he was a lineman for the local electric company.

"Run, Skye!" Darla yelled, too. Joyce looked back at her and gave her a thumbs-up.

Now Skye was on third base, and Bastian was on first. If the next kid up to bat got a solid hit and brought in Skye, The Dolphins would win the game, 5–3.

Lissa came up to bat, her blond hair in a ponytail beneath her batting helmet. After she'd picked up her bat, she wiggled her hips a bit as if loosening up. She assumed the batter's stance. Dave moved forward and placed the ball atop the tee.

Lissa's face contorted into a fierce grimace. She didn't mean to show any mercy to that ball. She swung and hit the tee instead. "Aww," moaned the crowd in the Port Domingo stands.

"You can do it, Lissa," shouted Lissa's mother.

Lissa took the stance once more, painted an even more determined expression on her face and hit the ball as hard as she could. It was a ground ball, but it had quite a bit of power behind it and rolled past three kids in the field before one of them went to one knee with his glove held out before him and finally stopped it. By that time, Skye was home as well as Bastian. Lissa made it all the way to second base.

The Dolphins had won their first game. Pandemonium erupted in the stands of both teams.

Later, everyone gathered on the field and the teams shook hands, some hugging, sealing their status as comrades instead of bitter rivals. Darla looked on with a lump in her throat.

There was a mini party before the other team got back on the road for home. The Dolphins' parents had brought snacks for all to share. Darla was in charge of passing out the juice boxes.

They had plenty, but the juice boxes were disappearing rapidly. She was looking down at the sweet face of a toddler who wanted a grape juice when she saw the legs of an adult step up to her table.

She handed the little girl the last juice box. The toddler thanked her and went to join a teen who was waiting for her a few feet away.

Darla raised her eyes to meet Dave's. His thighs and legs were toned from all that running he did.

She smiled at him. "You're out of luck if you want a juice box."

"I'd prefer something much sweeter than

that," he said and the look in his eyes told her what he wanted had nothing to do with refreshments.

Darla was glad that no one else was within earshot, or eyesight for that matter, because she was blushing so hard her face was hot and it wasn't that warm out today.

"Pick me up at seven?" she asked shyly. They had a date tonight.

"I will not be late," he promised just as one of The Dolphins' fathers grabbed him by the hand to shake it. "Great job, Dave!"

Dave gave Darla a regretful look she understood entirely. She picked up the empty cardboard box from the juice boxes and left him to his fans. She went to find Bastian and the rest of her gang.

CHAPTER THIRTEEN

DAVE HAD MET Eugene Pryor a couple of times, so he recognized the short, muscular lawyer on sight when he was ushered into his office.

Pryor's assistant left shortly afterward and Pryor invited him to take a seat.

Eugene was a Black man in his late thirties. He had dark skin and wore his dark brown hair in dreadlocks that hung to the back of his neck.

He wore a dark blue suit, white shirt and red tie. Dave had worn a suit today, as well. His was also dark blue, and he wore a light blue shirt and a royal blue tie with it.

"Dave, welcome," said Eugene. "We've been doing some research on your case, and I personally don't believe Raff Chandler has a leg to stand on. You have an exemplary record as a law officer. He has a terrible reputation as a human being. There were four adults, Officers Conrad and Plummer, Officer Winston, and a Mrs. Jefferson, who was sitting in the waiting room at the time, who are willing to testify that Chandler's behavior that day when your officers brought him in was reprehensible. Also, thanks to the fact that your officers wear body cams, we have footage of how hard he fought them during the initial arrest and continued fighting them once he was brought to the police station."

"But there is no footage of the incident," Dave reminded him. "No one was in the cell when he threw up except Raff and myself."

"This is a question of credibility, Dave. We're pitting your reputation against his reputation. Whom will the jury believe? Oh, wait, I'm getting ahead of myself because I'm at heart a trial attorney. This may not even go to trial. We'll try to get this tossed out at the pretrial hearing." He picked up a piece of paper from his desk. "The pretrial hearing is when both sides present their cases. If the judge rules that the petitioner, Raff Chandler, has a legitimate reason to sue you, then we go to trial. If he doesn't think you, the respondent, deserve to be sued, he'll dismiss the case. Are there any questions?"

Dave had plenty of questions. Would this

case ruin his reputation? Was it possible for Chandler to bribe the jury if they did go to trial? Because he was fairly confident that what Eugene had just said was true—if they stacked up his past behavior against Raff's, he'd come out the winner. However, life had a way of kicking you in the gut when you least expected it. He didn't want to get gut-kicked. He was thinking about his future now. He was more optimistic than ever that his dreams of having a deep and abiding love with the right woman and subsequently building a family together had a great chance of coming true. What chance did he have if he became known as a chief of police who stood and watched his prisoners be sick and didn't lift a finger to help them? He certainly didn't want to go down in history being compared with his racist grandfather. And ever since his best friend, Cameron, had died, he'd taken it upon himself to somehow live a good life in tribute to him. He wouldn't be keeping his promise if his reputation were ruined by this accusation.

However, he and Eugene represented different aspects of the law. Eugene was the ex-pert trial attorney, while he was a law officer who tried to bring order to their town. After he arrested someone, the jurisprudence system took over.

"Having never been sued before, I have plenty of questions, Eugene. But you're good at your job and I'm sure you would tell me if you thought Raff had a good case. I'm not rich and will probably never be. In the course of my career, I've seen the rich get away with things your average person could never get away with. So yes, I have worries. But I'm going to try to put them aside and trust in your capabilities."

Eugene smiled, and when he did, Dave found himself relaxing a little. In Eugene's eyes he saw confidence and honesty. He saw that Eugene genuinely wanted to defend his good name.

"We can do this," Eugene said, standing.

Dave rose, too, and they shook hands.

"He doesn't have a case," Eugene reiterated, continuing to smile. "You're going to be okay, Dave."

"Thanks, Eugene," Dave said. But he wouldn't begin to truly relax until he heard the judge say he was throwing out the case.

Dᴀʀʟᴀ, Mᴀʀʟᴇʏ ᴀɴᴅ Kᴀʏᴇ were having lunch at Kaye's café in downtown Port Domingo. They had a booth in the back where they had their privacy and Kaye had ordered for the three of them, knowing exactly what Darla and Marley liked.

Marley had suggested they get together and she'd sweetened the invitation with a promise of a major announcement. Darla had been wondering what the announcement would be since Marley's text yesterday asking if she were available to lunch with her and Kaye. Her best guess was Marley was expecting a baby. She knew Marley wanted a child. She'd heard about Marley's attempt to adopt Chrissie, a sweetheart of a little girl whom she'd met when Chrissie came from Pensacola for a playdate with Bastian. However, Chrissie, who'd been in the foster care system, had been fortunate when Marley had been key in locating her birth father. Now Chrissie was living with her father and grandmother, but Marley had been asked to be Chrissie's godmother, which Marley took very seriously. She doted on Chrissie.

"Mmm, girl, what do you put in this gumbo, magic?" Marley asked Kaye as she finished her bowl of gumbo over rice. She patted her flat belly.

Darla looked down at her stomach. *That big bowl of gumbo didn't even do anything to enlarge that belly.*

"No, I put *l-o-v-e* in it," Kaye said with a chuckle. "And stop prolonging the announcement. Tell us why we're here."

Marley smiled at Kaye, then she turned her attention on Darla. "You know the Seafood and Music Festival is coming up soon. Two weeks from now. So I know you've heard about it. Well, I had an idea that I wanted to float by you."

"That's not an announcement," Kaye protested. "An announcement is when you tell us about something that's happening in your life. Something big."

"This could be big," Marley said excitedly. She had her thick black hair in braids that fell to the middle of her back, and her brown skin was glowing.

Maybe she is pregnant after all, thought Darla.

"I want you two to sing with me at the festival," Marley said in a rush, as though one of them would stop her if she weren't quick about it.

Kaye frowned. "You know I only sing gospel in the church."

"You sang at my wedding in the park," Marley disagreed nicely.

"That was a favor for a friend. I sing for the Lord. You know that."

"I don't think the Lord would mind. The song is 'Sparrow' by Emeli Sandé. It's a heartfelt anthem. It's like gospel and it's very inspirational."

Kaye didn't dispute her opinion of the song, which, Darla saw, made Marley smile even wider.

Marley now looked at her. "You haven't said anything. Are you game? The three of us singing together in public again after nearly twenty years?"

"We sang in the church's parking lot," Darla said. "Wasn't that enough?"

Marley shook her head. "No, it wasn't."

Then it occurred to Darla that maybe this was a test. Was Marley trying to find out if she was still starstruck? This sort of thing was definitely in Marley's wheelhouse. She was the type of friend who wanted to help you fight your demons. And one of the reasons she'd ran away with J. J. Starr was the thought that maybe it was her chance to sing onstage with an established entertainer. She had already been at the emotionally weakest point in her life. With doubts swirling around in her head due to the postpartum depression, there had also been this crazy notion that stardom was within her reach. Could she now get up on that stage without succumbing to the pull of the enticing drug that feeling like a star was? Many people were incapable of resisting it.

Marley was sitting directly across from her in the booth. Darla looked her squarely in the eyes and said accusingly, "You think I'm still weak-willed and I'm going to run away again."

Marley's eyes went wide in alarm and hurt. "Is that what you think of me?"

Darla hadn't meant to blurt out what she'd been thinking, but there was no taking it back once the words left her mouth. "Marley, you took care of my child when I couldn't. You were there when Sebastian needed you. Don't tell me your protective instincts haven't been in full force since I've been back home. You're worried that I might skip town again, and Bastian would be psychologically affected by my abandoning him. The first time, he was a baby and you all surrounded him with love. He had no memories of me. This time, though, I've been home for months and he's grown to love me. I understand where you're coming from. Don't you think I live with doubts every single day of my life? I worry that no one will ever think I can be trusted. It's something I have to live with. I will take your challenge, though, and gladly sing at the festival. I'm home for good and if it takes singing in front of the whole town to prove it, I will."

"If Darla's going to do it, I will, too," said Kaye. Kaye and Darla turned their gazes on Marley. Marley sat with a stunned expression on her face. Then she smiled slowly. "Well, I didn't expect to be vilified and put on notice for asking you two to sing with me, but so be it. By the way, I'm pregnant."

Darla and Kaye simply stared at the grinning Marley for a beat or two, then they jumped out of their seats and started screaming with joy.

They got out of the booth and all three

of them wrapped their arms around one another. Other diners stared at them as though they'd taken leave of their senses, then started laughing at their antics.

"I'm so happy for you!" Darla exclaimed, and she was. "You're going to be the best momma!"

"Yeah," said Kaye, the crier of the group.

Marley whispered in Darla's ear while they were close, "I don't believe you're weak-willed and I know you're here to stay and that's why I want the whole town to see you up there on that stage. I love you, girl."

Darla burst into tears. *Darn*, she thought, *and it's been weeks since I cried.*

They calmed down and reclaimed their seats in the booth. Marley regarded Darla. "Okay, tell us what's got you so stressed-out. Because, honey, you handed me my butt on a platter. But then, what are friends for?"

Darla wiped her tears with a paper napkin and blew her nose in it, as well. She took a deep breath. "I'm worried about Dave. He's being sued for negligence. A man he had in custody said he could have choked on his vomit while Dave just stood there and watched. The preliminary hearing is Wednesday."

"What?" Marley said, seemingly shocked by the news.

"That's a lie and we all know it," Kaye emphatically stated. "If there's one good cop in the world, it's Dave Harrison."

"We'll march on this town if they try to fire Dave," Marley promised Darla. "When you hear about police on the news, it's usually about a bad cop. Here we have a good chief of police and somebody's suing him! Wait until I tell Sebastian. We'll all go to that hearing."

"Calm down, Sojourner Truth," Kaye told Marley. "The only one Dave needs at that hearing is Darla."

Darla was glad to hear that because she'd already planned to be there even if spectators weren't allowed. She'd be waiting in the corridor when Dave left the hearing.

"I'm going to be there," she told her friends.

Marley and Kaye both looked pleased by her statement. In fact, they were smiling knowingly at her.

"What?" she asked. She was immediately suspicious of their rather smug expressions.

Did they think they knew something that she didn't?

"I'm remembering that night we ambushed you in the church's parking lot," Kaye said. "Marley here was saying you all had to get along for the sake of Bastian, and all of the future children who would eventually show up in your extended family, and you said you were never going to have another child."

"And the gist of your little speech was that you'd never find a man you wanted to have children with," Marley put in. "And I said you never know what's going to happen."

"Then Dave happened," Kaye said, taking up the narrative.

Darla shook her head in exasperation at her two oldest friends. "Just because I care whether or not Dave's reputation is tarnished or not doesn't mean I want to have his babies."

"No, it doesn't," Marley said. "What it means is that your heart is open to the possibility of love. And that's enough for now, my sister."

"Don't freak out," Kaye told her.

Darla supposed Kaye had noticed the frightened expression on her face. Was she falling in love with Dave?

"No, I'll freak out for you," Marley said. "You think your mom and his mom have been sticking their noses in your business now, just wait. Should you and Dave actually fall in love, they will then want to rush you into an engagement, then a wedding, then into having a baby as soon as possible."

"You know you love it," Kaye told Marley.

"I'm a little nutty," Marley admitted. "Yes, I love it now, but while it was happening I didn't appreciate it. What I'm trying to say is they do it because they love you and they want you to be happy. Also, they want more grandkids to spoil."

"True," Kaye said. "My mother doesn't have any grandchildren yet and she reminds me all the time. I told her I had some of my eggs frozen so she'd get off my back."

"Did you?" Darla asked. If so, it was the first she'd heard of it.

"Nah," said Kaye. "But what she doesn't know won't hurt her. Such are the trials thirtysomethings go through nowadays."

They laughed. Darla's phone pinged. She checked to see who had texted her. "Dave," she murmured, smiling. Even reading a text from him made her feel mellow and excited at the same time.

She sensed her friends' gazes on her and glanced up at them.

"Go ahead," she told them. "Tell me I'm in love."

"You're in love, girl!" Marley and Kaye said in unison.

ON THE DAY of the hearing, The judge wasn't allowing anyone in her courtroom except the petitioner, the respondent, their lawyers and witnesses, and courtroom personnel such as the bailiff. Dave was disappointed because Darla had expressed interest in being there to support him. Her presence would have made things more bearable. However, there was nothing he could do about it, so he texted her with the news.

She texted back saying she wouldn't be far away. What she'd meant by that, he didn't find out because his lawyer told him that the hearing was about to begin and to silence his cell phone. Judges were notoriously unforgiving when interrupted by devices.

The bailiff entered, told everyone to rise

and then announced the judge. The judge was a woman in her fifties with light brown hair styled in a choppy pixie cut. She wore half-frame glasses and minimal makeup. She did not smile when she entered the courtroom wearing a robe.

After she was seated on the bench, everyone else sat also.

"Good morning, we're here to adjudicate the case of Raphael Paul Chandler and David James Harrison the third, in which Mr. Chandler claims that Mr. Harrison, an officer of the law, did willfully neglect to attend to his needs when he was incapacitated while a detainee in the city of Port Domingo's jail."

Raphael, Dave thought. Raff is named after an angel, or one of the most talented Italian painters of all time?

He glanced Raff's way. Raff glowered at him.

"I will hear the petitioner's accusations first, followed by the respondent's rebuttal. Should I deem it necessary, I will then hear testimony from the witnesses. Shall we begin?" the judge concluded.

Raff's attorney, Ezra Benson, a middle-aged gentleman of average size and height and with gray at his temples, was wearing an impeccable gray suit. He rose and spoke from his present position, at his appointed table right beside his client. "Mr. Chandler was arrested for drinking while driving on May 17 of this year. He does not dispute the charges. He is an alcoholic who has sought help numerous times, to no avail. However, he is still trying. Mr. Chandler also does not deny that he was in a rather rambunctious mindset the day he was arrested. He is nothing like that when he is sober."

That's not true, Dave thought. *He's generally a pain in the butt whether sober or intoxicated. I've seen him in both states.*

"What Mr. Chandler is upset about is the fact that after he had been taken to his cell in what is known as the drunk tank, he became violently sick and went to his knees in front of a toilet in the throes of that illness. He barely made it back to his cot. But when he did, he looked over and saw Mr. Harrison watching him. Mr. Harrison stood there and didn't do a thing to help him. He didn't ask if he were okay. He simply walked away."

There was a pause, and the judge asked, "Do you have any witnesses to attest that Mr.

Chandler's memory as to the events of that day in the drunk tank is accurate? One could suggest that he was drunk and people who use alcohol to excess aren't known to have good memories."

"I can only trust that my client is telling the truth, Your Honor," answered Mr. Benson.

The judge directed her next question to Raff. "Tell me, Mr. Chandler, why do you think Mr. Harrison should have inquired as to your health when it was apparent that you reacted as so many other detainees in the drunk tank react? You threw up. According to notes I received from Mr. Harrison's attorney, all of the other times you were arrested and spent time in the drunk tank, you threw up. The policy of the police department is, if a detainee shows signs of further illness after the initial episode, they get him/her medical attention. Records show you did not have another episode, nor did you ask for help. Why is that, Mr. Chandler?"

"I fell asleep after the first time, and I was fine the rest of the night. But, Your Honor, I thought I was going to choke during the first episode. I was very frightened for my life.

And he just stood there watching my misery the whole time."

"How was Mr. Harrison to know you were miserable when you didn't say anything, Mr. Chandler?"

Raff turned to look at Dave. He seethed with hatred. His attorney placed a hand on his arm, perhaps as a cautionary measure or a reminder to be on his best behavior in the judge's presence. Dave couldn't be sure. However, Raff calmed himself.

By that time, though, the judge, who was quite an observant person herself, had come to a conclusion. "You don't like Mr. Harrison, do you, Mr. Chandler? Would you please tell us why?"

"I have nothing personal against Mr. Harrison, Your Honor. He is supposed to serve and protect. And I don't feel as though he served and protected me!"

"I find your response to my question wholly unsatisfactory, Mr. Chandler," Judge Evergreen stated. "And I think there is something you're not telling me. But, you've had your chance." Her gaze settled on Eugene.

"Mr. Pryor, I would like to hear from you

and your client now. Why do you believe Mr. Chandler has brought this suit?"

Eugene stood, and Dave could feel the confidence coming off his attorney. It was as if Eugene were in his natural element. Mere mortals breathed air. Eugene lived for conflict and the opportunity to conquer it.

"Your Honor, I have witnesses who were present at a social event some months ago. During that event, Mr. Harrison and Mr. Chandler had words. Mr. Chandler was on a political tirade that devolved into a racially motivated indictment of every person of color. Mr. Harrison challenged him, and Mr. Chandler didn't like it. Mr. Harrison believes Mr. Chandler was publicly embarrassed that night because of the ugliness he was spewing, vile racial epithets that he repeated at the time of his arrest at the police station, I might add. Since then Mr. Chandler has had a vendetta against Mr. Harrison."

"Bring forward your witnesses, Mr. Pryor. I would like to hear what they have to say," Judge Evergreen said.

Dave looked around the courtroom. He was in as much suspense as everyone else.

Eugene had informed him he had a couple of surprise witnesses lined up and then told him not to worry about it, he had this. Dave, feeling a bit shell-shocked at that point, had put his trust in his attorney.

From the back of the courtroom walked the mayor of Port Domingo, Tom Steadman, and his wife, Bette. Tom was tall and well-built and dressed in a suit. His wife, Bette, was petite with beautiful brown skin and hair the color of a raven's wing. She wore a lovely business suit in navy blue with matching pumps. The mayor allowed his wife to precede him as they approached the bench.

The judge smiled down at them. "Well, you two need no introduction. Mr. Mayor, Mrs. Mayor. It's a delight to have you both in my courtroom. Would you please enlighten us as to the altercation Mr. Chandler and Mr. Harrison were engaged in on that fateful evening? I take it you were guests at that social event?"

The mayor deferred to his wife, Bette, gesturing for her to go first.

Bette seemed to gird herself for her speech, pulling herself up to her full height of five foot one, Dave guessed.

"Oh, it was awful, the words coming out of that man's mouth, Your Honor," said Bette in her high-pitched voice. She reminded Dave of the actress Bernadette Peters, who was very feminine and petite, only Bette had brown skin.

Tom put his hand on the small of his wife's back in support while Bette recounted the conversation she'd overheard while attending dinner at the home of Florida Supreme Court judge Branford Chandler, who was the father of Raff Chandler. "Of course at parties of that size it's normal for cliques to form. People who think similarly tend to gravitate toward one another. Well, Tom and I were standing behind the group that Raff had joined. He began to explain why, in his opinion, the country was no longer as strong as it used to be. Apparently, it was the fault of Black and brown people. The racial epithets he used were offensive, to say the least. Dave was passing by and stopped and listened for a moment, and then he told Raff exactly how he felt about his opinions. No one else in that group had refuted a word Raff said, but Dave told him his theories were ugly and demoralizing and he would be glad when people stopped espousing his particular racist views. The world would be a better place." Bette gave a huge sigh and smiled in Dave's direction. "He was splendid. Tom and I would have gone over and backed him up but just as we started walking in that direction, Judge Chandler made an announcement and asked Tom to come up and support him. Where Raff gets his racist ideas from, I don't know. His father is a lovely man. Lovely, but maybe a bit soft on his son. But you can't tell a parent how to rear their children."

"No," agreed Judge Evergreen. "You certainly can't. Mr. Mayor, have you anything to add?"

"Just that I've known Dave since he was a teenager, and I've never known a more upright person. He served his country and came back to his hometown to serve his community. He could have done anything, anywhere, but he came back home. And I, for one, am glad he did."

Dave didn't know how to feel. He was touched by Bette's and Tom's testimonies. He didn't think he deserved all the accolades, though.

"Thank you, Mayor, Mrs. Steadman," Judge Evergreen said. She turned her gaze on Eugene. "I'd like to hear from a witness who was there when Mr. Chandler was brought into the police station that day."

Eugene smiled. "Your Honor, I call Mrs. Emily Jefferson."

Dave remembered Mrs. Jefferson as the mother with the two small children who had been in the waiting room when Raff had been brought in. The look of horror on her face as she tried to prevent her children from hearing Raff's barrage of hate-fueled profanity aimed at Black people was etched into his memory.

She was a tall, slender African American woman in her twenties. She wore slacks and a blouse with a jacket over it and low-heeled black pumps. She looked nervous as she stood before the judge today.

Judge Evergreen smiled down at her. "Good morning, Mrs. Jefferson."

"Good morning, Your Honor," she answered softly.

"You were in the waiting room that day with your children. How old are they?"

"My son, Eric Junior, is four, and my daughter, Tiffany, is almost one," Mrs. Jefferson answered.

"Tell me, what did you witness that day?"

Mrs. Jefferson cleared her throat. "Mr. Chandler was brought into the station by two officers. He was wriggling, trying his best to get loose. And he was insulting them all the while. Then he looked over and saw me with my children and he grinned. That's when he started saying awful things about Black people. Things I had never heard and I'm twenty-seven. Seriously, Your Honor, these were things I don't want to repeat, they were so horrible. I tried to cover my son's ears while holding my baby girl. I saw the chief go over and relieve one of his officers right away and then he and the other officer pulled Mr. Chandler out of there. I've never been so glad to see someone go."

"I'm not going to ask you to repeat the words that he said, Mrs. Jefferson. I'm sure you've be traumatized enough. Thank you. You may sit down."

Judge Evergreen peered at Raff Chandler, her eyes narrowed.

Dave waited anxiously for the next words out of Judge Evergreen's mouth. He didn't have to wait long. Before speaking, though, the judge took a few seconds to look over the courtroom. Then she returned her attention to Raff Chandler. "Mr. Chandler, I urge you to get help for your alcoholism, and although I have never known anyone who shares your particular racist agenda to change their minds, I am hopeful that the possibility exists. As far as I'm concerned, you are the one who has been neglectful. Firstly, you are neglectful as a son. Your father has a fine reputation, and your behavior undoubtedly reflects on him. And you are neglectful of yourself. Imagine what your life would be like if you got control of your drinking? You can go to rehab for that. Where you'd go to lose your racist agenda, I have no idea."

And then she said the magic words, "Case dismissed."

Dave shot out of his chair. "Thank you, Your Honor!"

"You're welcome, Mr. Harrison. Have a good life." The Honorable Constance Evergreen took her leave. The bailiff announced that the hearing was at an end. And Raff Chandler leaped for Dave's throat.

"Raff, do you want to go back to jail?" Ezra Benson shouted at his client, trying his best to restrain him. He couldn't, though. Raff fought to get his hands around Dave's throat, but Dave, much younger and stronger than Raff, easily held Raff off until his lawyer could talk some sense into him and get him to leave the courtroom with a modicum of dignity.

Dave adjusted his suit, and he and Eugene stayed at their table as they watched Raff and his attorney walk out.

"Wow," Eugene said. "If that man doesn't get help soon, he's going to explode."

Dave smiled and offered Eugene his hand. "Thank you, Eugene. You're an awesome attorney."

Eugene returned his smile. "Your anxiety notwithstanding, I enjoyed it. It's always thrilling when the right person wins."

Tom and Bette Steadman also offered their congratulations, and by the time Dave left the courtroom, he was on cloud nine. The Steadmans hurried in Eugene's wake and Dave took his time exiting. When he finally stepped into the corridor outside of the courtroom, he looked up and saw Darla sitting on a bench directly across from the courtroom's double doors. She got up and ran into his arms. "There you are," she cried. "I was beginning to worry."

Dave held her tightly. "No need to worry, darlin', the judge saw the truth of the matter and the case was dismissed."

Their eyes met and held. People walked around them as they stood in the corridor. Dave was aware of the others, but his attention was on Darla. Relief was mirrored in her eyes and then warmth and caring. He couldn't have been happier. Could she be falling in love with him? Or were those emotions he saw only concern for a friend?

There was one way to find out. "Darla," he whispered. "I love you. I'm putting it out there because I'm a simple man and I know what I want and I don't play games…" He had more to say, but she'd cut him off by grabbing him and leading him to a more secluded spot, out of the way of other visitors walking in the courthouse's corridors. Then, on tiptoes, she threw her arms around his neck and kissed him passionately.

When they came up for air, the look on his face must have revealed his confusion, because she said with a warm smile, "I love you, too. I think I've been in love with you since our first date."

He grinned down at her. "I was hoping that would work in my favor." By silent consensus, they began walking toward the exit, their arms about each other's waists. "Mamma told me you had a thing for decorating. I thought, if the house doesn't get her to fall for me, nothing will."

Darla laughed heartily. "It wasn't the house, you nut. It was the care and love that you put into everything. Here is, I thought to myself, a man who wants to nurture and protect. And he's not bad-looking, either."

"Well, whatever it was, I couldn't be happier. When are you going to marry me?"

"Slow down, Chief. Loving you is one thing, getting married is quite another. Let's enjoy the love part awhile longer, okay?"

"I won't rush you," he promised. "But I will nudge you from time to time. So be forewarned."

"Nudge all you want. But this girl is not budging until she knows that marriage is the best thing for you, and for me. Loving you comes with some perks, Dave. One of them is, your heart is now mine to protect at all costs. And that means from yours truly, as well."

Dave sighed inwardly. His Darla had come a long way in the months they'd gotten to know one another. But she was still doubting herself. And, God bless her, she didn't want to break his heart in the end.

CHAPTER FOURTEEN

Two WEEKS LATER, Darla was standing backstage with Kaye and Marley, or more specifically, behind the biggest pavilion in the public park in Port Domingo, waiting to be announced by the annual Seafood & Music Festival's master of ceremonies, Father Rodriguez.

She and her friends had practiced their selection until the song was a part of them. Kaye's big gospel voice, Marley's soulful alto and her pop soprano merged together to produce a harmony that she believed was their best work ever.

She just hoped that, tonight, she didn't let her nerves get the best of her. She had the least working experience as a performer, after all. Kaye performed regularly as a soloist in the church choir. Marley never let her skills as a singer and guitarist lose their beauty through lack of use. She was also one of the founders of the festival and performed in front of thousands every year. Darla was the only one of them who had stopped singing publicly for a number of years.

She observed her friends. Kaye, dressed in a beautiful white dress and matching summer sandals, was cool as a cucumber. Marley, in a denim jumpsuit studded with crystals, appeared ready to give her all on that stage. Her electric guitar was strapped across her chest. She had a guitar solo. Even the high school band member who would be accompanying them, Josiah Walsh, a tall, skinny kid with spiky natural hair and skin the color of burnt caramel, looked collected, as if this were a common occurrence for him. He was wearing his band uniform, and his snare drum was suspended from a shoulder harness. His beats would accentuate the anthem theme of the song.

Darla looked down at her feet. The three-inch heels of her wedge heel sandals were designed to add height but were still comfortable and walkable. She had visions of tripping on the stage. And her simple, sleeveless, royal blue cotton dress's material was thick and, most importantly, not see-through.

She didn't want the bright lights to inadvertently give the audience more of show than they'd come here for tonight.

Marley cleared her throat and said, "Okay, everyone, let's hold hands. Josiah, get over here."

Josiah joined them, awkwardly lumbering toward them. "Yes, ma'am," he said.

"Don't call me ma'am, I'm not that much older than you," Marley said, smiling at him.

They held hands. "Kaye, you're good with God. Say a little prayer," Marley insisted.

Kaye, as though she were prepared for the request, said a brief prayer, and then Marley said, "Now, there's no need for fear because we know this song. We love it, and we're going to share that love with the audience. That's all we're doing, sharing the love."

"Sharing the love," Josiah said, grinning. "I can dig it."

"Sing from your heart," Kaye told them. She looked directly into Darla's eyes. "You've got this, sis."

Darla instantly felt better. Kaye had never lied to her about her ability as a singer. If you hit a bad note around her, she told you about it, and how to improve.

Marley smiled at her. "I second that. You've never sounded better."

"Don't make me cry before I even sing a note," Darla warned them.

Suddenly, Father Rodriguez's booming bass voice announced, "Ladies and gentlemen, please welcome three ladies who started singing together when they were fifteen years old. Many of you remember them as Sweet Harmony."

Darla was shocked to hear the crowd cheer with abandon after their high school moniker was announced. But then, there were family members and friends among the five thousand or so festivalgoers out there.

"Welcome, Marley, Kaye and Darla. And accompanying them on the snare drum is high school senior Josiah!"

The four of them took the stage amid more applause and cheering. After Marley plugged in her electric guitar, she and Josiah began playing their instruments, and Kaye sang the beautiful first line of the song, "'I got wind beneath my wings…'"

Kaye's voice demanded attention. The audience went quiet and reflective as soon as the words issued from her throat. Darla could feel the timbre in the pit of her stomach.

The song's lyrics spoke of struggles and how you can personally ease the trials of others by reaching down and offering them a hand up . Together, we could move mountains.

The notes of Marley's guitar reverberated on the night air. Darla had never been this close to her while she was playing her Stratocaster. It was electrifying.

All of this combined to build up the desire in her to express her own emotions, and when her turn to sing came, she gave it everything she had. She sang for all of the people she loved, and how grateful she was to have them in her life. And yes, she felt a little like she was having an out-of-body experience. Outside of herself, looking on. When she got to the part in the song that she had been struggling with during rehearsals, she subconsciously told herself to shoot for the stars, and her vocal chords supported the aspirations. Was that her voice? Astonishingly enough, it was. She was so happy.

Euphoria. Now she knew what the word meant. The excitement was so intense, she lived in the moment.

However, as she and her best friends and Josiah finished the song to thunderous applause, she knew that this was enough. This occasional waltz in the spotlight. Yes, it was a glorious feeling. But as her eyes grew more accustomed to the spotlight and she could make out Dave standing down front with Sebastian and Miguel, she knew that this wasn't real. This feeling was intoxicating like a drug, but you couldn't exist on drugs alone. Loving someone and sharing a life with that person, having children and participating in the lives of your family and having good friends… Those enduring things were much more appealing to her than this kind of temporary high.

All four of them stood together onstage after their performance and bowed. The audience continued to show their appreciation with enthusiastic applause. And roses were being tossed onstage by their men, Dave, Sebastian and Miguel.

Then she saw a man standing behind the row in which Dave and the other guys were. He looked eerily familiar. He was wearing dark sunglasses even at night. Plus, he was wearing a black cap pulled down low, further obscuring his features. Yet, it was a wide silver band on his right wrist that identified him for her. J.J. wore that wristlet all the time. The band was more than an inch thick in width and it was engraved with a stallion on its hind legs. This guy was standing with his right wrist crossed over his left, as if he wanted her to see the distinctive piece of jewelry.

She suddenly felt chilled to the bone.

She was glad when Kaye gently grabbed her by the upper arm and said, "Time to leave the ball, Cinderella," and pulled her offstage with her.

Behind the pavilion, after Marley had stood her guitar against a post by its neck, the three of them hugged, and Josiah got kisses on his cheek from all of them. "That was great," he said. "Thanks for asking me to play, ma'am— I mean, Marley," he added shyly.

"No, thank *you*," Marley said.

"Well, I'd better go. I was invited to a party tonight."

"Thanks, Josiah," Darla and Kaye chorused.

With a final wave in their direction, Josiah sauntered off.

Now that they were alone, Darla said, "Kaye, you rescued me. I froze out there."

"I noticed," Kaye said. "And after the performance was over. You did great, by the way."

"You did, too," Darla said, talking fast. She looked at Marley. "You both were great. But either I'm losing it or I just saw J.J. in the audience."

"Here?" Marley asked doubtfully.

"He was here five years ago, remember?" Kaye said drolly. "He knows the way to Port Domingo."

"But why would he be here?" Marley asked. Then her expression changed to one of deep concern. "You don't think he's here for you, do you?"

She and Kaye stared at Darla.

Darla hadn't told anyone about that strange interview of J.J.'s she'd seen on TV except for her mother, and they hadn't talked about it since. To her, that would be giving it importance, lending it credence and believability. She didn't want to believe that she was the woman J.J. had said was the love of his life. The woman he was searching for.

Now she told her best friends about the interview.

"It's been more than four years since I've seen him," she said after sharing the story. "I can't imagine having to explain this to Dave should J.J. really be in town to find me."

"Did I hear my name mentioned?" Dave asked good-naturedly as he strode around the back of the pavilion, with Sebastian and Miguel right behind him.

The women went to meet them. They exchanged hugs and the fellas told them how much they had enjoyed their performance.

Darla, although she was still upset after spotting J.J. in the audience, was nonetheless happy with the state of her present life. Here she was, after just performing a song with Marley and Kaye, and the men in their lives were showing their love and support. What was more, their situation was quite unusual. What they had here was due to a series of events that might have turned out negatively if they hadn't been the kind and forgiving people that they were.

Marley was married to her ex-husband and expecting his child. Kaye and Miguel had been high school sweethearts, but he'd dropped her for a cheerleader and they'd lived separate lives for nearly twenty years. She'd recently forgiven him and now he was hinting about marriage. Kaye, however, wanted to be very sure he wasn't going to pull another vanishing act before she committed to him. She was a cautious girl. And Darla was in love with a guy who was a friend of her ex's. Sebastian and Dave had known one another since high school and were still friends.

Dave had her fully in his embrace, and the other couples were following suit, she noticed out of the corner of her eye.

"Are you ready to go have a bite to eat, and then maybe go dancing?" he asked softly.

"I would like nothing better," she said.

She wasn't going to spoil his plans for them with talk about J.J. It could wait. She promised herself she would tell Dave everything at the end of the night.

"Well, good night, you guys. Sebastian and I promised Bastian we'd let him stay up late tonight and watch his favorite movie," Marley announced. She and Sebastian walked away after Darla, Kaye and Marley shared quick kisses on their cheeks.

Kaye and Miguel also left, holding hands. "See you in church," Kaye called with a wave.

"Good night, Kaye, thanks again for having my back when I froze onstage."

"No biggie," Kaye said, and she and Miguel took their leave.

Now it was just her and Dave. The night air was pleasant, and with the park being near the water, the ocean breeze helped to alleviate the heat that had built up during the day.

A few people were milling about behind the pavilion. Darla nervously looked around her, wondering if that person she could have sworn was J.J. would make another appearance.

Dave, ever the observant police officer, noticed she was checking out the pedestrians and asked, "What's the matter? You seem a little jumpy."

Darla stared up at him, her conscience warring with her. Why didn't she just tell him now instead of drawing out the discussion until her nerves were stretched so taut that she'd probably lose her ability to be calm and rational?

Maybe the man she'd seen wasn't even J.J. and after discussing things with Dave, she could relax and chalk the sighting up to an overactive imagination.

"Dave, I thought I saw J.J. in the crowd tonight. It was just after we'd finished our song. He was standing behind you and Sebastian and Miguel. If it wasn't him, it was someone who was a dead ringer for him. He was wearing dark glasses and a cap to hide his face, but in the past I saw him use that disguise so many times that I can see through it."

Dave went still. He pulled her back into his arms and kissed the top of her head. "Let's take this step by step. Babe, why do you think J. J. Starr would be here? If that was really him, there must be a reasonable explanation for his being here."

She had never told him about the TV interview. She hadn't had a reason to. Odds were she wasn't the woman J.J. was supposedly on a quest to find.

Now, however, she felt he needed to know about it. "Months ago, I saw J.J. on an entertainment show on TV. He was talking about his drug addiction and how he's been clean for some time now, and a part of his recovery was to thank the people who had been there for him. He talked about a woman he considers to have been the only woman who truly cared about him. He said he was looking for her."

"Did he say who she was?"

"No, he became cryptic and said he wouldn't name her because he had to go find her. Which made the anchorwoman swoon as if that were the most romantic thing she'd ever heard."

Dave was nodding as he took everything in. "That was months ago, and he's just getting to town? He knew Port Domingo was where you two met. Why do you think it took him so long to get here?"

"I wouldn't know," Darla said. "I'm just telling you the facts, Officer." His tone had been a bit sharp for her liking.

He sighed. "I'm sorry. Look, let's go. No need to stand out here and discuss this when we could do it in the privacy of the truck on the way to the restaurant. That is, if you still want to go."

"Actually," said Darla, "I'd rather go home."

"*Home* home?" Dave asked. "Or to my place?"

"My mother's house," Darla said. "It's empty. She's spending the night with a friend.

I can make us something and we can talk there."

"All right," Dave said and took her hand.

DAVE WAS JUST trying to stay positive. The probability of the man in the audience being J. J. Starr was not high, in his opinion. And Darla was plainly upset about the prospect of J.J. being in her hometown. On the ride through town to her mother's house, Darla was quiet. Thinking, he figured, about the possibility of seeing J. J. Starr again. He wished she'd talk to him.

"Penny for your thoughts," he said.

"I just can't imagine what he's thinking, if he is here to see me. It's been over four years since we've seen one another. He can't think I'd be interested in getting back with him. He's a smart man. Wrapped up in his music, yes. Self-centered. Arrogant. Not unkind, but not really interested in anyone but himself."

"If he is here, maybe that's why," Dave suggested. "To apologize to you for not treating you the way you deserved to be treated. You said he was making amends after going through rehab."

"That's a possibility," Darla agreed. Then she fell silent again.

He made a right turn. The car directly behind them also turned right. A couple blocks later, he made a left. The car behind them also turned left. Were they being followed? Nah, he was just being a bit paranoid. Given their recent conversation, there was no wonder he was feeling suspicious.

They arrived at Miss Evie's house and he parked on the street in front of it. The car behind them kept going. He made sure to note the tag. It was a Florida tag. But that didn't tell him anything. Even if Starr had flown here and rented a car, rental cars usually had regular tags on them. You might look for a license plate framed with a placard advertising the rental company, but other than that, even he couldn't tell a rental from a privately owned vehicle.

Once they were in the house, Darla told him to make himself comfortable while she ran upstairs and changed her clothes.

He took a seat in the living room. The color scheme was gray and various shades of brown, from light to dark. Darla had told him since she'd been back home, she'd redone the floors in engineered white oak. It was not only durable, she said, but beautiful and never lost its luster.

He had to admit, she did have a flair for design. The big light gray leather sectional he was sitting on was extremely comfortable. He would have to get her input when he started furnishing the rest of his house. But oh, wait—if he lost her to J. J. Starr, she wouldn't be around to decorate the house he'd hoped the two of them might one day live in together.

He mentally shook himself. *Stop thinking negatively. She said she loved you.* Macy had said she loved him, too, and she'd still left him…

Okay, Dave. Snap out of it! You're a good catch. You're not perfect, but you have always tried to do right by everyone. You fought for your country and won medals for bravery. Now you serve your community. You love children and animals and… God, what was he thinking? He sounded like the most boring man in the world, at least he would to women who gravitated toward men of another sort.

Was Darla one of those women? Perhaps

she used to be. But he had to remember that Darla was not the same woman she had been when she'd run off with J. J. Starr. He had to believe that she had truly changed. He resolved that he would do that, and when he set his mind to something, he did it without fail.

The next thing he knew, Darla was bouncing back into the great room wearing a pair of jeans, a bright orange T-shirt and a pair of white Chucks. She seemed more relaxed. Relaxed and ready to talk. She went to him, bent and planted a kiss on his lips. "Let's go to the kitchen. We can talk while I make us salads with chunks of turkey, ham and cheddar. Is that all right with you?"

"Sounds good," he said with a smile, rising to follow her. "I can help."

So she put him to work washing the vegetables while she prepared the meats and cheese. They worked side by side at the counter next to the farmhouse sink. A few minutes later, they were nearly finished making the salad.

"Some date, huh?" she joked. "Sorry, I felt too preoccupied to go out. I thought it best to tell you what was going on. If he is here in Port Domingo looking for me, I didn't want you to find out from anyone but me. People can get things so misconstrued. I just wanted you to know that I don't want anything J.J. might be offering. My mom is the only person I'd told about the interview, besides Marley and Kaye. And the only reason I told them about it was because I froze tonight after spotting someone who looked like him in the audience. Kaye grabbed me and led me offstage, I was so stunned. They asked what was wrong, and I told them. Now I've told you about it."

"What if it isn't him at all?" Dave asked as he dried the cucumbers, tomatoes and radishes on paper towels. "What if you just imagined it?"

"That would be great," Darla said without hesitation. "Because then I wouldn't have to speak with him at all. But I believe it's him." She went on to tell him that the guy in the audience had been wearing a silver band, the same as J.J. always wore. And try as she might to forget it, she knew the angles of his face.

"Why do you want to forget his face?" he asked her.

"Because J.J. is a reminder of how low I sank," she said softly. "Of the worst time of my life. No one wants to be reminded of their failings."

Dave understood that. All too well. Because try as he might, more than ten years ago, in the heat of battle, he'd failed to save the life of his best friend, Cameron. "I do know how you feel," he told Darla now. "During my last hitch in Afghanistan, we were there to transfer the training of their troops to Afghan Special Forces units. We were not supposed to be involved in fighting insurgents. Cameron and I were getting ready to get out of there and never go back. But we were attacked in Kunduz and returned fire. Three of our soldiers were wounded. I was able to lay down fire while the others got to safety, and reinforcements arrived and took out the rest of our attackers. All of us had survived, I thought, until I couldn't find Cameron. He'd been shot at the beginning of the skirmish. I'll never forget that. It was selfish of me, I know. But the one person I wanted to save above all the rest because he was a personal friend was the one person who died. I still feel bad thinking like that."

"It's only human," Darla said, stopping what she was doing to put her arms around him. "We want the people we care about to be safe. That doesn't mean you didn't value the lives of the other soldiers."

"Logically, I know that," Dave said. "But I still feel bad about not being able to save him. He had a wife and a son."

"How are they?" she wanted to know.

"His wife is happily remarried now, with two more children. But I'm sure it wasn't easy for her to move on. That's what we have to do, though, keep living."

"That's a lesson I recently learned," Darla said. She inhaled deeply and let it out. Then she tilted her head up to meet his eyes. "I want you to know that you have nothing to worry about. I am your girl, Dave Harrison. Heart and soul."

She playfully kissed his chin. "Keep trying," he said.

She kissed the tip of his nose. "You're almost there," he said with a laugh.

This time, she kissed his mouth and lingered for a while.

That kiss did a lot to chase away the negative thoughts that had taken up space in his head.

"Come on, let's eat," she said, her smile bright again, as well as the light in her eyes. He hoped that meant she had stopped being afraid of an encounter with J. J. Starr.

As for him, he was sticking to his faith in her and their future together.

"You sounded fantastic tonight," he said as they walked over to the island to sit down and enjoy their meals. "You and Marley and Kaye could be a professional singing group. If J.J. was in the audience tonight, he's going to really put up a good fight for you."

"Oh, you!" Darla cried. She had reached the island and grabbed a sleeve of saltine crackers from its top and threw it at him.

Dave caught the crackers, sat down across from her and grinned. "No playing with your food, young lady."

She threw her head back in laughter. When she stopped laughing, she smiled at him. Her lovely dark brown eyes held his gaze. "You make even a rough night bearable. I thought I'd spend the rest of my life alone. Then came you, and you convinced me to trust again.

That's major. I hope you can feel how much I love you for that, and many more reasons."

This touched Dave so deeply, all he could do was take her hand, turn it over and kiss the palm in gratitude.

"Ditto," he said sincerely.

CHAPTER FIFTEEN

It was Sunday afternoon and Darla was curled up on her bed reading a good novel. Earlier she and her mother had gone to church together, where, afterward, they'd spent a few minutes chatting with friends and family. She'd gotten the chance to hug Bastian, who was enjoying his weekend with his dad and Marley. She was able to get in a word or two alone with Marley and Kaye also, to tell them that she and Dave had discussed the J. J. Starr matter and both of them were of the opinion that it probably wasn't J.J., but if it was they'd handle it together. Dave had told her that when he was driving her home last night, he'd thought they were being followed, but nothing had come of that suspicion.

She sighed as she continued to read. There was nothing more enjoyable than curling up with a good book on a lazy Sunday, with her favorite drink within reach. She took a sip of her lemon iced tea with honey.

Just as she placed her glass back down, the doorbell rang.

Her mother had gone out for a brisk walk, so she was the only one at home.

"This had better be good," she grumbled as she put on her slides. She was wearing a comfortable top and leggings lounge set in emerald green.

Her hair was piled on top of her head in a loose knot. She'd made sure she was presentable because Dave said he might drop by later with a plant her mother had hinted around about but was finding it difficult to locate: coral honeysuckle. Her mother wanted to plant it near the back and hoped that the vines of the plant would climb the fence.

The doorbell rang again before Darla could make it downstairs. "I'm coming."

She hoped it was Dave. After their long talk last night, she was feeling exceptionally mellow. Like a huge weight had been lifted off her shoulders. The J.J. question had been addressed and put to rest. By the time Dave went home last night, she was certain they were fully committed to one another.

She was confident in his love for her. He'd also seemed convinced that her heart belonged to him.

It appeared that the universe was on their side, as well, because she had not heard from J.J. all day. If he were in Port Domingo, what was taking him so long to show up?

It was now 5:15 p.m., and it had been around 8:30 last night when she'd seen the J.J. lookalike. The J.J. she'd known had been too impatient to draw out a surprise, and this would be a huge surprise. Although, he had enjoyed making a grand entrance.

That was the thought that was running through her head when she took a peek through the front door's peephole and saw J.J.'s face. He was smiling broadly. And confidently.

She opened the door and before she could utter a word, he'd swept her off her feet and into his arms.

"Hey, beautiful! Surprised?"

"Not so much, actually," she said irritably as she wriggled to be put down.

He laughed and continued to hold her captive.

She'd forgotten what a magnetic presence

J.J. had, and how strong he was. Imagine a man whose eyes held an almost hypnotic gaze that made the average woman's legs turn to jelly.

Add to that a powerfully built body, skin the color of toasted pecans, soft curly hair he wore a little too long, with a dusting of gray that only added to his appeal. And a voice so melodic that you would gladly listen to him read a physics textbook. Plus, he smelled heavenly. J.J. was all of that, and more.

Yet, what she felt right now was not physical attraction to him but vexation. How dare he walk in and assume he'd be so welcome that she wouldn't mind being manhandled by him?

"Put me down," she seethed.

J.J. set her down. He took a step back, a confused expression causing his thick brows to meet in the center of his forehead. He dug both hands in his jeans pockets, a nervous habit, she recalled. His jean shirt was open several buttons to reveal a muscular chest. He had on his silver wristband, and the buckle on his belt also had a rearing horse embossed on it.

"I'm beginning to think you aren't pleased

to see me," he said. He looked hurt, or at least he wanted her to think her attitude had stung him.

Darla took the opportunity to put a couple feet between them.

He looked around him. "Nice digs. You live here by yourself?"

"My living arrangements are none of your business," Darla said, her eyes never leaving him for one second. It wasn't that she thought she wasn't physically safe with him. It was because J.J.'s behavior was unpredictable. It was true that he'd never done drugs in her presence. But now she realized his erratic behavior and mercurial moods might not have been caused by an artistic soul but by drugs.

He slowly walked around the great room, his black motorcycle boots' heels tapping the hard floor. "I was at your performance last night. I didn't know you were that good. If I had, I might have taken you more seriously and let you sing with the band. Those two chicks with you were good, too."

Darla left the door wide open. Her cell phone was upstairs, or she would have phoned Dave by now to get over here. The main topic of their conversation last night was standing in her living room, acting like he'd never been in a "regular" house before. Regular as in real people lived in it, not rock stars.

"I saw you," she told him. "I saw you and I almost convinced myself I hadn't. Why didn't you just come up and say something to me last night? What's with the skulking around like a…"

"Stalker?" he suggested with a smile as he turned to concentrate on her once more.

"You said it."

He sighed. "This isn't turning out the way I imagined it would."

She stood with her arms crossed over her chest, waiting to hear something that sounded rational.

"Because you didn't show up the right way," she told him. "You don't surprise someone you haven't seen in over four years. You give them the courtesy of phoning first to ask if it's okay for you to drop by. Not this… this…ambush!"

"Girl, you know me. I'm not like everyone else" was his explanation. He began walking toward her, which made her back away from him farther.

"Okay, here's the deal," he said with a conciliatory half smile. "I'm clean now and one of the things my therapist told me I needed to do was make amends to anyone I believe I'd slighted in some way. You're on that list. I'm here to say I'm sorry for the crappy way I reacted after you told me why you latched onto me. You were sweet enough to confess what you'd done and apologize to me. I felt I owed you that much."

Darla felt relieved he hadn't mentioned anything about her being his "one true love." She could live with simply being on his list of people to apologize to. However, the thought that he might consider her his soul mate was uncomfortable and sad, too. A six-month-long relationship with a stranger should not be considered eternal love.

She dropped her defensive stance and relaxed somewhat.

J.J. stood smiling at her. "I'm sorry if I spooked you, Sweet Cakes."

Oh, no, not that nickname, Darla thought. Whenever he called her that it made her feel like a nonentity. She was just a sweet thing, not a person with feelings.

"Okay," she said, walking over to the door

and then grasping the doorknob. "Thank you for the apology. I'm glad you're clean and sober and congrats on your new album."

J.J. jumped at the opportunity to prolong the conversation when she mentioned his album.

Grinning, he said, "I have you to thank for that."

Alarm bells clanged in Darla's head. He'd said in the interview that the woman he was searching for had encouraged him to write his own music. She had done that.

She stood straight and tall as she directed her next words to him. "You're not here just to apologize. I'm the woman you were talking about in that interview."

He smiled slowly. "You were always smart."

He began pacing the room again. "I'm here to make you an offer. Come back to me and I'll do everything within my power to get your career off the ground."

He didn't look her in the eyes. It was as if he were suddenly unsure of himself. Or it was a clever ruse to get her to lower her defenses. Which she wasn't about to do.

"I'm older now, Darla, and since I got sober I've had time to think about my life,

such as it is. I don't have a family, per se.
A woman I can feel safe with. Safe in the
knowledge that she loves me for who I am.
Maybe it was your innocence. Maybe it was
your desperation. I don't know. But I remember that you actually cared about me. You
cooked healthy meals for me. You told me
stories that helped me drift off to sleep when
I was keyed up."

"You're describing a good mother, not a
woman you want to spend the rest of your
life with," Darla told him. "I have a son, J.J.
He's six years old and he's the most important person in my life."

"I like kids," J.J. said. "I'd be a great step-
dad."

"And I'm in love with someone," Darla
hastily added. "He's special. He helped me
to realize that even after I did what I did, I
deserved a second chance at happiness. I'm
whole now, J.J. I won't go back to you. I
never loved you. You didn't love me, either.
Like you said, you were on drugs. Those
memories of me may not even be real. Maybe
you just want them to be real. Which I can
understand because there are lots of memo-

ries I have that I would love to edit and make them pleasant ones instead of awful ones."

Here I go again, she thought as tears welled in her eyes and dripped onto her cheeks. "We've all been hurt in some way by life, J.J. But we can survive the hurt as long as we're willing to fight for happiness. I fought, and I won. And I wish the same thing for you."

To her utter shock and surprise, tears were in J.J.'s eyes, too. He walked toward her, and this time she didn't move away. He didn't try to pull her into his arms, though. He simply met her eyes and said, "I guess I'm too late, huh? I should have gotten sober and come looking for you before you fell in love with someone else. He's a lucky guy, whoever he is."

"I'm the lucky one," Darla said.

J.J. cleared his throat and continued looking her in the eyes. "Look, I know you're with someone else now, but when my album drops, I'd sure like to send you a vinyl copy. You inspired the songs, and I'd like you to hear them. Plus, there's a nice dedication. I hope that's not an embarrassing prospect for you now that things have turned out this way."

"Embarrassing?" Darla said with a laugh. "I'm honored to have been your muse. At least for a little while. Now I want you to go out there and find a more permanent muse."

He handed her his cell phone. "If you could put your mailing address in my contacts, I'd appreciate it."

Darla took the phone and quickly granted his request. She was handing the phone back to him when Dave walked through the still-open front door carrying a potted plant that she assumed was the coral honeysuckle her mother had hinted around about. He spoiled that woman.

His handsome face crinkled in a frown when he walked in and saw J.J. there. She naturally smiled at him, she was so happy to see him. Dave set the plant on the floor beside the hall table.

She walked over to him, took his hand and then introduced him to J.J. "This is David Harrison, our police chief," she said, "and the man I was just telling you about."

She felt Dave's release of tension. Of course, he'd immediately recognized J.J.

What her reaction to J.J. had been before he'd gotten there was a mystery to him, though. Now he knew J.J. did not pose a threat to their happiness.

Dave laughed softly. "As I live and breathe, J. J. Starr. I'm a fan."

He and J.J. shook hands. J.J. didn't disguise his interest in Dave. He sized him up with his eyes. Darla thought the handshake went on a bit too long. And from the slight wince on Dave's face, J.J. had squeezed his hand too hard, too.

Dave was a couple inches taller than J.J. and just as fit.

No displays of male dominance today, she prayed. *Let's all chill.*

The handshake over, J.J. said, "I know this is a quaint town, but cops deliver flowers around here?"

"They do if they want to impress their girlfriend's mom," Dave said. Darla loved his ability to roll with the moment.

He was going to let that show of machismo in the form of a painful handshake, slide. After all, he'd been declared the victor.

"Well," she said, thinking it was time she showed J.J. the door, "thanks for dropping by. I hope the album's a huge hit for you."

Dave stood with his arm about her shoulders. J.J. whispered as he walked past her, "Sorry, the big dog came out of me there for a second. My territory and all that. He's just so young and good-looking, and he's a cop, too? This just hasn't been my day."

She nodded in the direction of the door. J.J. left without another word. She and Dave went onto the porch to watch him leave. As he hurried to his waiting car, her mother came jogging down the sidewalk. She passed J.J. and did a double take. Darla smiled. She knew her mother had recognized him.

Just then, Dave pulled her into his arms. "I won the fair maiden?"

"You're not getting rid of me that easily," she verified.

Her mother stomped onto the porch, her breathing labored more from surprise at seeing a rock star walking out of her house than from the exertion of walking, Darla figured.

"Was that who I thought it was?" asked her mom.

But she got no reply because she and Dave were busy kissing.

"Never mind," said Evie Cramer and continued walking.

By August Dave was seriously considering ordering shorts for him and his officers to wear as part of their uniforms. It wouldn't be unheard of among Florida police departments.

One morning, during the assignments meeting, he asked his officers how they felt about them.

Rob Conrad was the first to protest. Rob was of average height and muscular with dark brown hair and blue eyes and he had a year-round tan. "Nah, Chief. There are too many guys here who aren't blessed with great legs like mine. I don't want to see that."

"I wouldn't mind," said Laraine. "But the hem has to come just above the knee. This isn't *Reno 911.*"

Dave laughed because *Reno 911* was a sitcom about cops and one of the lead characters wore uniform shorts that could only be described as hot pants. "No," he assured Laraine. "We stay dignified or we don't wear them."

She nodded. "Then they're okay with me."

Seeing that time was running out and his officers needed to get to their assignments, Dave said, "Laraine, please put a box on the front desk. You all write *nay* or *yay* on a slip of paper and I'll tally the votes next week, this time. You're dismissed."

Before Rob filed out with the rest of the officers, he walked up to Dave and said, "You got time this afternoon for a little target practice?"

Dave did have a couple hours free that afternoon, so he agreed right away. Rob was one of his closest friends on the force and sometimes they discussed personal matters while getting in some target practice at a local gun range.

"Meet you there at six?" Rob asked.

"Sure," said Dave, wondering what was up with Rob. His wife, Kayla, was expecting their third child. Maybe Rob wanted extended leave to help with the baby.

Later, though, he found out the talk Rob wanted to have with him had nothing to do with babies. It was about him and Darla.

They had been at the range for half an hour, and while Dave had been doing pretty well, Rob's aim was off. Dave felt Rob wasn't concentrating. He was a much better shot than he was demonstrating today.

Both men had on noise-reduction headphones. Dave pulled his off after Rob had gone through his ammunition and gestured for Rob to join him a few feet away from the shooting area.

Rob did, and Dave asked him what was on his mind.

Rob grimaced as though he really didn't want to say what he was about to say. "Dave, people who grew up around here know your grandfather had a reputation as a racist. I know you want to distance yourself from that legacy as much as possible, but are you only dating Darla to prove something?"

Dave was genuinely taken aback by this accusation. Rob was married to a Black woman. Where had this come from? Rob must have seen how shocked he was, so he began talking quickly.

"I know, my wife is Black and I love her to death. But, Dave, you're a true friend, so that's why I feel like I need to have this conversation with you. It's about your intentions. Are you dating Darla because she's exotic to you? Something different? Because I'm telling you, Black women are unique. They're individuals like every other woman in this world. But they're not interchangeable. It's not like every Black woman is the same as any other Black woman. They are their own persons with their own dreams and aspirations. And should be treated with the utmost kindness and respect."

He paused, for emphasis, Dave assumed. "Dave, I've never known you to date a Black woman before."

"That's just it, Rob. I didn't want to date just any Black woman. I wanted Darla. And until recently, she wasn't available. I've been half in love with her since high school. Now that I have the opportunity to have her in my life, I'm not going to let it pass me by."

Rob laughed, relieved. "I'm glad to hear that because, although things have changed for the better here in the South, interracial couples still come up against some challenges. Kayla and I have had to be a united front. We just want you to know that you and Darla have our support, that's all."

"Thanks, I appreciate that" said Dave. "You and Kayla have each other's backs. You are one. I can see that, Rob."

"Truer words were never spoken," Rob said happily. Then they went back to target shooting, and Rob's scores escalated mightily.

CHAPTER SIXTEEN

"I FINALLY TOOK your advice and had hidden cameras installed, Chief Harrison," Joy Henderson said as Dave walked into her jewelry store on Main Street one morning in early September.

Joy was in her usual bohemian-style attire. A long, flowy tiered dress, sandals and lots of her own jewelry as accessories.

By contrast, he was wearing his uniform today. He was usually in plain clothes, but he was going to a graduation later this afternoon and he wore full uniform when he attended public events.

Dave was surprised to hear Joy had installed cameras. He'd given her that advice several months ago. He'd figured she had solved her missing-jewelry case on her own and had decided not to involve him and his department.

He noticed his mother was several feet

away, dusting shelves. She was dressed casually and appeared industrious and was pretending she wasn't at all interested in the reason he'd put in an appearance at her workplace today. He knew she was listening to every word.

Several customers, male and female, were perusing the merchandise, earrings, necklaces, ankle bracelets and various other items made from gemstones.

Joy came around the counter to meet him, holding her cell phone in one hand while tapping on the screen with the fingers of her other hand. When they were close enough, she said in a low voice, "Look, I have a video of the person who has been stealing from me. It took weeks before she struck again, but I have it all here for the whole world to see."

Then she handed him her cell phone, and he watched the video she'd indicated.

Without making a comment as to what he'd just viewed, he handed the phone back to Joy. "I see," he said. "Might I have a word with you outside, Miss Henderson?"

Joy smiled at him. "Of course, Chief." Then, "Margherita, I'm stepping outside for a moment!"

"I'll hold down the fort," his mother assured her friend and employer.

Once outside, where they wouldn't be overheard, Joy looked up at him. Dave was confused by the mirth in her eyes. It was as if she could barely contain her laughter.

"I knew it was her all along," she said. "What kind of thief brings the stolen items back with a nice note of apology? But I want to teach her a lesson for trying to control me. I told her I didn't want to put cameras up and she insisted that I do. It was a bone of contention between us. Now she's got her wish. The cameras are up, and they caught her red-handed!"

"My mother, the jewelry thief," Dave said, and he did laugh.

"I figured she was the culprit, but I wanted to see just how far she would go to get her way. What do you propose we do to teach her that lesson?"

Joy gave him a conspiratorial look. Then she told him what she wanted to do.

The two of them went back inside of the jewelry store. Now his mother was behind the counter at the register ringing up purchases for a customer. She smiled at him, her brown eyes twinkling with delight. She'd told him that one of her joys was getting out of the house and coming to work a few times a week. It gave her life the variety she needed to stay mentally and physically engaged.

Dave and Joy waited until she'd finished at the register, and after the customer left, Joy addressed all of the other customers in the store. "I'm sorry, ladies and gentlemen, but I'm closing for the rest of the day. Please come up to the counter now if you would like to purchase what you've chosen. And please, do come again if you haven't made up your minds yet."

Two customers came to the counter and were promptly helped by Margherita. The other three customers left the store. "Thanks for coming!" Joy said pleasantly as each of them passed her on the way out.

Once there were no more customers in the store, Margherita came from behind the counter and peered at her son and Joy with curiosity reflected in her expression.

"Mrs. Margherita Harrison," Dave said, "You're under arrest for stealing from your employer."

His mother's eyes went wide in horror. "What?" She held her hand to her forehead as if her body temperature had suddenly shot up from the shock of being accused of thievery and she couldn't bear up to the unjustness of it. Or at least that was how Dave imagined his mother's overdramatic mind was working. This was going to be interesting.

"My God," cried Margherita, as she now fanned her face. "I feel faint. I feel nauseous." She looked Joy dead in the eyes. "How could you accuse me of such a thing? I've been loyal to you since the day we met. I would never!"

"I have it right here," Joy said, thrusting her cell phone at her. "Watch it if you don't believe me."

Breathing hard, Margherita took the phone in her hand and watched the video with fascination. Her expression went from horrified to calm in a matter of seconds. "Then you had cameras installed."

"Yes, I did," said Joy. "A few weeks ago, when you weren't here. The guy told me no one would be able to detect their presence and he was right, because you never knew. How could you steal from me?"

Margherita handed Joy her phone back and then held her wrists out to her son. "Take me to jail, Chief. I'm guilty. Guilty of loving my friend and wanting her place of business to be safer. What if some hardened criminal robbed her? At least with a camera, the culprit could be identified. Who cares if she doesn't sell diamonds and other precious stones? Some people will hold you at gunpoint for fifty dollars."

She continued to hold her wrists out to Dave, who cuffed her. He allowed her to be cuffed in the front, instead of with her arms behind her.

"Sorry, Mamma, but no one is above the law," he told her apologetically.

She gave him a sad smile. "Do your duty, Chief. I did the crime. I'll gladly do the time." She then turned to Joy. "Joy, would you be a dear and get my shoulder bag out of the break room? I may need it."

Joy disappeared in the back while Dave waited for her to reappear. A couple minutes later, Joy was back and Dave gently directed his mother toward the store's exit. "Don't worry, I know a good lawyer."

She hung her head as she was led down the street with Joy on one side of her and Dave on the other. Dave was sorry he had walked here instead of driven. Now they had three blocks to walk down the streets of Port Domingo with his mother in handcuffs.

It was a Saturday morning and people were out and about, shopping, eating at Kaye's Café, buying pastries from Garrett's Bakery and getting their caffeine fix from Wide Awake coffeehouse.

Wanda Garrett stepped through the doorway of her bakery as they passed. "Lord, Chief, what are you doing with Miss Margaret in handcuffs? Is this some kind of a joke?"

"Good morning, Wanda," his mother greeted the redheaded shop owner. "Don't interfere with my son carrying out his duties. I'm the jewelry thief the *Port Domingo Herald* wrote about."

Dave had forgotten that the local newsletter—it was too small of an outfit to be referred to as a newspaper—had written about the recent petty thefts at Joy's jewelry store.

"Well, I don't believe it!" cried Wanda indignantly. She turned to go back inside. "I'm calling Gayle Winslow."

Oh no, not her, Dave thought. Gayle was Laraine's daughter. She was the editor of the *Port Domingo Herald*. Gayle was not only a journalist but a social activist. She always had a cause for which she would gladly lead a protest.

He continued on down the sidewalk, his mother smiling at everyone they passed. People ogled them but no one else interfered. He did notice a few of them taking photos with their cell phones, though. What was he supposed to do about it? In today's world everybody had a cell phone.

"This isn't for your entertainment," Joy said to a particularly nosy woman who kept taking photos. "Mind your own business."

The woman ignored Joy, took more photos, then called someone. "You're not going to believe this," Dave heard her say as she walked away.

Dave kept his mother moving. Another block and they'd be at the police station.

Dave phoned Laraine to let her know he was coming in with his mother. Laraine, ever the sensible and professional officer that she was, didn't express surprise. She was all business. "Whatever you say, Chief. I'll make sure the good cell is ready for her."

The good cell at their station was the cleanest cell. As far away from the drunk tank as possible.

They arrived a few minutes later. Once in the station, Dave turned his mother over to one of the young officers, Rosie Ortiz, who knew her. Officer Ortiz would fingerprint her and take her mug shot, give her the chance to make a call, then escort her to her cell.

Rosie couldn't help smiling at the prisoner as she took her by the arm. "Ah, Miss Margherita, I would say it's a pleasure to see you, but under the circumstances, I'll say I'm sorry to see you. You beautiful woman, you."

His mother melted with appreciation for Officer Ortiz's sense of humor and kindness, no doubt. And Dave was impressed with Rosie's multiple usages of the word *you*.

His mother smiled at her and said, "You're a sweetheart, Officer."

"Well, let's get you processed," Officer Ortiz said and led her away.

Dave ushered Joy into his office as though he was going to take her statement since she was apparently going to press charges against his mother.

What he did in his office, though, was make a few phone calls while Joy sat quietly and, he supposed, pondered her next step to take to get her friend to promise to stop trying to force her hand where her business was concerned.

Dave phoned his father and explained the situation. His father promised he'd be there as soon as possible. Then he phoned Darla, who in turn promised to inform her mother about the situation. They would also be at the police station as soon as possible.

Dave sat back in his office chair and relaxed after the last phone call. Some people had interventions for loved ones who had a drug problem. His mother's addiction was interfering too much in the lives of people she loved. Today, her family and friends were going to intervene before she overdosed. And she wouldn't be able to go anywhere, since she would be locked in a jail cell.

Joy broke the silence with "I'm beginning

to have misgivings about my plan. Is it so bad that Margherita tricked me into doing something I should have done anyway? I do feel safer with the cameras. Not that the few items that have been stolen over the years were any great loss. But the thought that the world is becoming more violent every day has me thinking that Margherita was right."

"Right or not," said Dave, "do you want her continually telling you how to run your business?"

"Of course not," said Joy.

"Then let this play out. Believe me, my mother is tougher than she looks. And rest assured, by the end she will still have the upper hand. But at least she'll think before acting the next time she tries to force her will on another unsuspecting person."

"She really got you good, didn't she?" asked Joy, curiosity etched on her face. Her spiky hair seemed to stand at attention as she awaited his reply.

Dave nodded. "And she'll crow about that, too, since Darla and I are together now."

"Congratulations," Joy said with warmth. "I like Darla. I was so sad when I heard that she had left town. I was the subject of vicious gossip after my divorce, so I felt for her. People can be so judgmental. I'm glad the two of you found one another."

"Thank you, Miss Henderson," Dave said quietly. "We're lucky to have such good people in our corner."

His cell phone sounded, indicating a text from Officer Ortiz. Check-in is done for our model detainee. And she's had her phone call, it read.

Dave rose and Joy followed his lead. "We can go see her now."

Joy hesitated. "I hope I can be convincing. All I want to do now is hug her, poor baby. It was embarrassing enough for her walking here from the store."

They left his office and as they were walking through the lobby, Darla and her mother and his dad were all waiting for them.

His dad, a tall, rawboned man in his late sixties with thick salt-and-pepper hair that he wore in a buzzcut since his army days, walked up to him. His brown eyes met his. "I was her phone call. How is she holding up?" he asked.

"Dad, I told you this isn't real. It's to get her to see reason and quit being so..."

"Herself?" was his dad's response.

Dave was beginning to feel like his mother had already won this battle. That was how she was. She was such a charming person when she wasn't interfering in your life that you wound up forgiving her for anything.

"Miss Henderson," Dave said motioning for Joy to join him and his dad for a moment. "Would you show my dad the video?"

"Video?" Miss Evie cried, getting up to look at the screen as well.

While Miss Evie and his father watched the video on Joy's phone, Dave took the opportunity to hug Darla.

"Thanks for coming," he murmured in her ear.

Darla, wearing jeans, a long-sleeved blouse and Chucks, hugged him tightly.

When she looked up at him, her eyes were alight with affection for him. He loved seeing that in her gaze and feeling the way her body relaxed when she was in his arms. He'd fought hard to come to this point in their relationship and he was one grateful man.

Everything about her these days spoke to her sense of satisfaction with her life and it never failed to make his spirits rise to be in her presence.

"I'm going to be honest with you," she told him. "I love your mom, and it's going to be hard for me to tell her she has to stop interfering in peoples' lives. She does it out of love."

"Not you, too," Dave said, smiling at her. "Joy, Dad, now you. Our side is already weak. I would have phoned Maria. She would have been gung-ho for an intervention. But she's all the way in Pensacola."

Darla took his hand and they turned to face the other three people standing in the waiting area of the lobby. His dad and Miss Evie had finished watching the video.

"Okay," he said to his dad. "Do you still feel like we shouldn't do anything about Mom's behavior?"

His dad sighed heavily. "Something definitely has to be done. She's gone too far."

"I feel like a traitor," Miss Evie said to them. "She and I are both guilty of going behind your backs in our attempt to get you two together, and she's the one who's being punished for it. Lock me in that cell, too."

"If you want to go in there, you can," Darla said.

"Darla!" Dave spoke up.

But Darla was too busy laughing at the astonished expression on her mother's face to listen to him.

Joy interjected with "All I want is for her to admit she was wrong for what she did and to promise me that she'll stop acting like a puppeteer pulling my strings!"

The others were watching her intently. *Here*, Dave thought, *is a woman who's tired of being manipulated.* Therefore, he was committed to helping her get satisfaction.

"We should do it for Miss Henderson," he told the others, who were seemingly on the fence about what they intended to do.

Darla, her mom and his dad looked at one another, trying to feel each other out, he supposed. All of them appeared undecided.

Then Miss Evie said, "Okay, we're with you, Joy. But, Dave, put me in the cell with your mother. At least I'll be there to hold her hand and commiserate with her so she'll know I want to take a share in the condemnation."

Dave laughed. "Miss Evie, this isn't the

witch trials. We're only trying to get her to see reason."

"Let's just do it and get it over with," his dad said with resignation. "As it is, we've given her too much time to think. I've been married to her for over forty years and I know how cunning she can be. We're toast already if we don't get in there and start swinging."

"He should know," said Miss Evie.

So they went into the lioness's den.

They were a solemn group as they walked down the hallway leading to the temporary holding cells.

His mother was the only detainee today. When they got there, she was sitting on a cot whose sheet had recently been changed, eating a pastry and turning the pages of a fashion magazine. Dave wondered who had provided her with contraband not normally seen in a holding cell. Her connection could be any number of his officers. They all loved her. But his money was on Officer Ortiz. She had once told him that his mother reminded her of her *abuela*, her grandmother.

He unlocked the cell door and Miss Evie went inside. He relocked the door. His mother got up and hugged her friend. "Evie," she cried. "Thanks for coming to see me."

Miss Evie gestured to the cot, and the two of them sat down.

"Mamma," Dave addressed his mother. "Miss Henderson has something she wants to say to you. I advise you to listen closely to her because your freedom depends on it. Do you understand me?"

"I'm old, not lacking in intelligence," his mother said.

"You're not old," Dave said. "You're sixty-four years old. That's not old by any means. Now stop being contentious and listen."

She made a zipping motion on her mouth and turned her attention to Joy. She and Miss Evie held hands.

Joy cleared her throat. She wiped her sweaty palms on her skirt and faced his mother. "We've known each other for over ten years now, Margherita. Ever since I opened the store and you came in, seemingly looking around but really hoping to find employment. I liked you at once when you just came out and told me you were looking for a job. And you were funny and self-deprecating. Over the years you've offered me your opinion about how I run the business. Some I took freely because they were good ideas. Like the display and how it could attract more people by being more eye-catching and how to pleasingly decorate the windows to entice people to come inside. But when you insisted that I needed security cameras, I drew the line. I didn't think I needed them because I've never suffered great losses in the store from theft. If someone pilfered something I figured it was a kid who wanted something pretty to give to his mom or girlfriend. I just hoped whomever got the gift enjoyed it. Because that's what I want to do, spread joy."

"Hence your name, Joy," his mother said, not with sarcasm but with genuine warmth. "I always liked your name, Joy."

Laying on the charm, Dave thought, but continued to listen. Maybe Joy was getting through to his mother.

Joy sighed. "I know you love me, Margherita, and that's why you did what you did. But your actions were also underhanded and not how you should treat a true friend. You do not go behind someone's back and pull that kind of trick on them, and then expect to be forgiven for it because it was done out of love! I don't need that kind of friend. I want a friend who's going to be completely honest with me, not an operative who goes on secret missions to save their friends without their knowledge. This isn't a TV show. This is real life!"

"I'm sorry, Joy," his mother said, her tone soft and full of regret. "I knew it was wrong. That's why I returned everything. But it was also exciting. I started feeling like a cat burglar. Like Cary Grant in *To Catch a Thief.* I went a little crazy, I admit. I had to rein myself in toward the end because it was beginning to be too much fun."

Tears rolled down her cheeks. Miss Evie handed her a tissue from her purse.

Joy was still holding on to his mother's shoulder bag and she stepped forward and handed it to her through the jail's bars.

If this were a real arrest, Dave wouldn't have permitted it.

Everyone was silent for a few minutes as his mother wiped her tears. She blew her nose loudly, or perhaps it was the acoustics in the cells.

His mother looked up at them from her

seat on the cot. "I'm too much. I realize that. My personality is big. Everything about me is, how do you say? Multiplied. When I came to this country, all I wanted to do was fit in, so I ingratiated myself with people I liked. I took care of them. I made myself indispensable. All because I was insecure and just wanted to be liked. Not to be looked down on because I didn't sound like them. Or because I didn't look like them. I've been doing that for years. And it became a habit I'm having a hard time breaking. I go all out for people I care about. It's who I am. But you know what? I'm too old for that anymore. I don't have the energy. So I'm going to make a concerted effort to tone down who I've been for nearly my entire life. Maybe I'll take up swimming every day instead. I hear it's good for the body and the mind and the spirit."

Dave's phone buzzed with a call from Laraine.

"Yeah, Laraine?" he answered pleasantly.

"Dave, you're not going to believe this. The lobby is full of protestors carrying Free Miss Margherita signs."

"Being led by whom?" Dave asked. As if he didn't know.

There was a pause, then Laraine let out a huge sigh. "My firstborn. Wait till I get my hands on her!" And she hung up.

Dave returned his attention to what was happening in front of him. His mother continued to weep, but the tears were slowing. Joy had gone to the cell and was now trying to shake the iron bars.

"Let her out, Chief, I can't stand to see her in there a moment longer!"

"Then you're not pressing charges?" Dave asked. He was an officer of the law, after all, and had to do things correctly.

"No, I'm not pressing charges," Joy stated firmly.

Everyone must have needed to let off some steam because cheers erupted. His mother got off her cot and she and Miss Evie did a little dance.

Dave hurriedly unlocked the cell door, and his mother came out and hugged everyone, especially Joy, who was crying now. His mother and Joy clung together and they were whispering something to each other that he couldn't hear, but it must have been words of positivity because they were both smiling and crying and hugging some more.

His father, stoic man that he was, even looked misty-eyed. His dad walked up to him and said, "You think she's going to change?"

"There's a possibility," Dave said encouragingly.

His father nodded. "I'd better get her home. She's probably worn-out from all these emotions floating around here." He looked up as if he could spot the emotions and Dave smiled to himself. Sentimentality made his dad uncomfortable.

He himself was fine with it.

He looked over at Darla, whom he found was already looking at him. They smiled.

"I have a graduation to go to this afternoon of the first class of our youth program. You want to go with me?"

She sidled up to him. "What time?"

"Two o'clock. It's going to be held right here in the big conference room. Just the parents and the graduates and some of our officers. The ones who aren't out patrolling. We'll have refreshments," he added as though that would entice her, when he could see from the expression in her eyes that he was reason enough for her to be at his side this afternoon.

She looked down at her outfit. "I'll put on something nicer."

She looked gorgeous to him in her jeans. But he did like it when she wore a dress, so he didn't protest. "Pick you up at one-thirty, then?"

"I'll be ready," she promised.

"Would you two stop flirting?" Miss Evie said as she walked between them, making sure they separated. "Take me home, please. This place is making me nervous."

"Because you're beginning to like it?" Darla teased.

"No, because it has the feel of a mausoleum. Dave, you should let Darla decorate."

Dave laughed. "This is a jail. It's supposed to be a place people are trying to get out of as soon as possible, not vacation in."

The three of them laughed. And then Darla got her mother out of there as swiftly as possible.

CHAPTER SEVENTEEN

"MOMMA, THAT'S THE fiftieth time you've played that song. I love it, but it's starting to eat into my brain," Darla complained as she walked downstairs wearing a nice dress and heels, grumbling about another round of Aretha Franklin's "A Natural Woman." She entered the great room and found her mother dancing.

Of course, her mother didn't hear her comment because she was too wrapped up in the music. And she had to admit, her mother had some good dance moves.

She walked over to the Yamaha desktop audio system, whose speakers were connected to her mom's cell phone via Bluetooth. She hit the pause button. Now she had her mother's attention.

It was a few hours after they'd gone to the police station for Miss Margherita's intervention and since then, she'd done a few chores around the house. Her mother, like a lovesick teenager who had grown up in the sixties, had been listening to Aretha Franklin's greatest hits. About an hour ago, she'd hit the loop function on this song and now the tune had become an earworm in Darla's head.

"Aw, Mom," her mother groused, as if she truly were the teenager and Darla was her fed-up mother. "You grown-ups just don't understand."

Darla laughed. Her mom was in a hot-pink tunic whose hem fell just below her knees, black leggings and was bare-footed.

"I don't know exactly what's going on between you and Mr. Jenkins…"

"He told you to call him Theo."

"He's my employer, so I'm going to call him Mr. Jenkins."

"Are you still going to call him Mr. Jenkins when we get married?" her mother asked with a mischievous grin.

Darla's mouth fell open in surprise. She abruptly shut her mouth, which made her lips issue a popping sound. "When did this happen?"

"He asked me a few days ago, but I told

him to hang on to that beautiful ring he offered me. I needed time to think. You know after your father died, I resigned myself to living out my life without a significant other. But that was before Teddy came back into my life. I think I can live with a man now. If I'm not too set in my ways."

"You're both set in your ways," Darla said, being totally honest, which was the way she and her mother communicated with each other these days. "But in my opinion, you and Mr. Jenkins make the cutest couple!"

She couldn't help her enthusiasm because she had been imagining them fulfilling a long-held dream the two of them had obviously carried from their high school days.

Her mother laughed. "Child, *cute* is the word. You ought to see Teddy trying to be romantic, which he's truly rusty at but I enjoy his attempts. He thinks every time he sees me I should be presented with fresh flowers. He writes poetry for me. That gets me right in the heart." She sighed. "*Heart* being the key word. Your old momma is in love."

Hence the Aretha Franklin marathon, Darla thought. She went and hugged her mother. "You're not old! And I'm happy for you. I'm even happier for Mr. Jenkins. He's finally rejoining the world."

"Oh, honey, he may have seemed like a recluse," said her mom when they parted. "But he is very much in touch with the world. He's a good, kind man. A man who has been alone far too long, yes. But it hasn't made him insular or incapable of being empathetic toward the rest of us. He knows his own mind, and you know what else? Although he's not a big churchgoer like I am, he's very spiritual. He believes that ultimately the kind of man he is matters. I like that."

"So when are you going to take pity on him and tell him yes?" Darla asked.

"We're having dinner at his place tonight. I'll tell him then," her mother replied as she was walking over to turn her music back on.

The doorbell rang.

"That'll be Dave," said her mom, smiling at her. "Have fun!"

So Darla left her mother to enjoy Aretha Franklin. She and Dave were going to a graduation. She loved being included in his work life. It gave her a glimpse into their future together.

"THE DAY YOU caught me speeding in my mom's car and told me I belonged to you all now," Damien Spivey, one of the four graduates of the six-month-long Port Domingo Police Department at-risk youths program, Stay on Course, said to Dave, "I thought you meant I was going to jail."

Following the ceremony, Darla and Dave were standing with Damien and his mother, Teresa, near the refreshment table. They were holding plates with little sandwiches on them and sipping from cups of soda.

Darla was sure no one else noticed the slightly embarrassed expression on Dave's face when seventeen-year-old Damien was just trying to say thank-you. Even when he deserved the accolades, Dave was uncomfortable receiving them.

She'd met Teresa a few minutes before the ceremony had begun, and Damien's mom had told her she'd been at her wit's end trying to cope with a child who constantly disobeyed her and was heading down the wrong path—one that would inevitably lead to prison if something didn't change. Enter the police department's youth program, which consisted of a boot-camp-style exercise program, provided tutors if their grades were failing and encouraged them get a part-time job to help their parents provide for them. Many of the kids came from one-parent households. In Damien's case, his mother was a widow with three children, Damien being the eldest.

Around them in the conference room, parents, teens and police personnel were gathered to congratulate the first graduating class of the program. All of the four graduates, three boys and one girl, were seniors in high school, and all of them had been awarded college scholarships to further their education and help them get a degree that would in turn allow them to make a living, advantages that hopefully would help them stay on course in life. Which was why, Dave said, the other police personnel and he had chosen the program's name, Stay on Course.

"I can't believe how stupid I was behaving," Damien continued. "Thanks for everything, Chief Harrison."

If Dave were the blushing type, Darla was sure he'd be red in the face right now. "You can thank your mother for signing you up," Dave told Damien. "She was the one who took a risk with us. This was an experimental program that we put together hoping to help some teens focus. You did, and that's why you're going to be pursuing a criminal justice degree soon. I'm proud of you, Damien."

Damien laughed. "Remember when you chased me through town after I took that lady's purse?"

Dave gave Damien a grimace that raised one of his eyebrows higher than the other. "You would have outran me if not for someone backing out of his driveway."

Teresa gently boxed Damien's ear. Obviously she hadn't heard that story before.

"Ow, Ma," Damien protested, exaggeratedly rubbing his ear.

His mother laughed, too, in spite of meting out punishment in the middle of their conversation. Darla supposed she was one proud mother, to have her son who was becoming a criminal turn his life around so much so that now he had aspirations of becoming a police officer.

Dave said, "I don't believe we need to keep an eye on you with a mother like yours. She'll make sure you stay on the straight and narrow."

"I will certainly do that, Chief Harrison," Teresa said with a stern look in her son's direction. "We're going to track down that woman, and you're going to apologize to her."

She took him by the arm. "Thanks for a lovely ceremony, Chief. Come on, Damien."

When they were out of earshot, Darla said, "She loves her son."

"She certainly does," Dave agreed.

He lowered his head and whispered in her ear, "And I love you. When are you going to marry me?"

She countered with "When are you going to ask me to marry you? You just keep saying, 'When are you going to marry me?' But I don't know whether to take you seriously or not."

"Oh," said Dave. Darla could imagine a lightbulb appearing over his head. "You're a traditional woman. I need to get a ring and propose on one knee for you to believe I'm serious."

"A ring would help. Please excuse me for a moment," Darla said, walking away from him. Laraine was across the room beckoning to her and she was going to see what she wanted.

She could feel Dave's eyes on her retreating back. Darn the man. He was adorable at all times. But he was especially adorable when he was at a loss as to how to woo her. But like her mother with Mr. Jenkins's attempts at romancing her, she was equally thrilled by Dave's.

When was she going to marry him? Why, as soon as he offered her a proper proposal instead of those attempts she considered only wishful thinking on his part. They made her think that maybe he wasn't truly ready for marriage.

They had known one another for six months. She remembered thinking that she didn't know how J.J. had considered her his one true love when they had only known one another for six months. However, her six months with Dave felt entirely different. She loved Dave with all her heart. She loved who she was when she was with him. And she believed she brought out the best in him. They were honest with one another and she felt that the simple truth of how she felt about him boiled down to one fact: he had already seen her at her worst, and he still loved her. It was all up from here. She was ready and able to step into her future with him.

He would know when to seriously propose to her. She was willing to wait because she deserved the best. And he was the best.

DAVE WATCHED DARLA walk away from him. Why was he always putting his foot in his mouth with the marriage proposal thing?

He knew why he kept doing it. He was trying to judge her readiness for marriage to him. Maybe she thought he should be secure in her affection for him by now because they'd confessed their love for one another. However, she hadn't been in his shoes when a rock star had stood in her mother's house sizing him up and absolutely finding him wanting. He could read the look in J. J. Starr's eyes that had explicitly said, *What has this yokel got that I haven't got?*

Dave had been amazed that Darla had chosen him that day. Well, some part of him had been sure that Darla had changed and would not easily give up her son and her family for life on the road with J.J. She had fought too hard to convince everyone that she was home to stay. So J.J.'s chances had not been good.

However, did Darla's reasons for rejecting J.J. have anything to do with him? Had she chosen to stay in Port Domingo because she wanted a life with him? He felt kind of selfish for putting his emotional needs on par with the love of her son. But there it was. He needed to know that she had stayed because of him, too.

Don't be a fool, he chided himself. *She said she loves you. That should be enough.*

"Hey, dude, you got a minute?" someone asked him. He looked to his left at Will Kohl, the father of the only girl who had graduated today, Casey. They'd arrested her for punching another girl at her high school for bullying her. Casey had learned how to control her anger better and she'd also expressed interest in becoming a police officer in the future.

Her dad was a mechanic. A very laid-back guy whose wife had left him and his daughter. He struck Dave as a father who wanted to be involved in his daughter's life but sometimes felt overwhelmed by it all.

"Mr. Kohl," Dave said.

Will offered him his hand, and they shook. "I just wanted to say thanks, man. Casey's happy as a lark. She thinks she's found her calling, you know? I appreciate y'all." Will's Southern accent was thicker than many folks' in Port Domingo. But people in Port Domingo came from all sorts of backgrounds. They weren't all born here.

"Casey worked really hard," Dave told him. "She was determined to do her very best. We're proud of her."

Will continued shaking his hand. But then he looked down, realized he was still shaking his hand and let go. Dave could tell Will wasn't comfortable. "Thanks again," Will said and hurried away to join his daughter, who was also shy and patiently waiting for him by the exit.

The two of them hurried out after Casey offered Dave a wave. He waved back. Then he went to find Darla.

She and Laraine were laughing at something when he walked up to them. Laraine smiled at him. "I was just telling Darla that after I broke up Gayle's protest, I made her promise to cover the graduation. That's why she was here taking photos and interviewing the graduates. The graduates are going to be on the front page of the paper tomorrow."

"That was decent of her," Dave said, "seeing as how she wasn't able to free my mother from her incarceration."

Laraine laughed. "Her heart is in the right place. She's a fighter and that's what I taught her to be. Sometimes she just goes overboard."

"Like my mother," Dave offered.

Laraine smiled. "Yes, like Margherita. They're family and it's best to love them just as they are."

Dave conceded inwardly that Laraine was right. What they'd done today might have some effect on his mother's future behavior. But even if she didn't change, he would always love her. She was his Mamma, no matter what.

He and Darla locked eyes for a moment, and he instinctively knew she was thinking of her own mother, whom she'd told him was going to accept a marriage proposal from Mr. Jenkins.

They looked away, and he caught the tail end of what Laraine had been saying while his attention had been on Darla. "...pregnant."

"Pregnant?" he asked. "Who's expecting?"

"Gayle," Darla told him. "It's her first."

"Congratulations, Grandma," he said to Laraine.

Laraine waved off the congratulations. "I have so many grandchildren, it's old hat by now." Then, "I'm lying. I'm so excited, I don't know what to do!"

And they all laughed.

CHAPTER EIGHTEEN

EARLY NOVEMBER, and Dave was finally having a housewarming party at his new house. Darla had pitched in to help him pick out furniture, and she'd put her special decorative touches on practically every corner of the two-story home.

Dave didn't tell her that he'd asked her to help him because it was his fondest wish that she would be living in the house with him someday soon. He wanted her to feel as comfortable here as possible. She'd told him that her mother was signing over her house to her since she was marrying Mr. Jenkins. But he hoped that the gift of her mother's house would just provide Darla with a form of financial security, and they'd live here together.

He hadn't worried that he wouldn't like her decorative choices because, frankly, she had great taste. Because of her efforts, his home looked like one you'd see in the pages of *Better Homes & Gardens*, or some other magazine that he'd consulted in the past, hoping to get some useful decorating ideas.

His family and Darla's, along with close friends, were invited. He told them not to bring housewarming gifts because he already had everything he needed. All they had to do was just bring themselves, and kids were welcome, too.

The party was being held on a Saturday at five o'clock in the evening, so many of his officers would be available to attend. The police station was being run by a skeleton crew. But as was his habit, he would be checking on operations throughout the day. He was always on call.

Marla, Bastian, Miss Evie and Mr. Jenkins were the first guests to arrive in Darla's car. Dave wondered where Jerry was, but he was more than likely driving from Pensacola and would need more time to get there.

Dave walked onto the porch to greet them, wearing jeans, his brown cowboy boots and a dark blue long-sleeved shirt that Darla had given him. He liked the thick, soft yet crisp cotton material and, in turn, thought of her whenever he wore it.

The beautiful November day boasted an almost cloudless sky with plenty of sunshine, and the temperatures were in the low seventies. In his opinion, this part of Florida rarely got cold enough to turn on the heater.

His property had several mature trees on it, and a big oak tree cast its shade on the front of the house. He walked down the steps when he saw Bastian climb out of his mother's car and started running toward him. He scooped Bastian up into his arms and the boy hugged him tightly. Dave set him back down almost immediately because, although Bastian was still a demonstrative child who liked giving hugs, he required them to be brief because as he'd told his mother, "I'm not a baby anymore."

"Hey, big man," Dave said with warmth as Bastian gave him his signature fist bump.

"Hey, D.," Bastian said with a grin. Dave didn't know why he'd started calling him D. He didn't ask him because children were entitled to their own idiosyncrasies, just like adults. What was odd to him might be perfectly normal to Bastian.

Bastian ran up onto the porch.

"Bastian, stay there, don't go inside yet," Dave heard Darla call. She probably didn't want him entering the house without her because she was a fastidious person and feared Bastian might break something or get sand on the runner she'd picked out for the foyer. There were hardwood floors throughout the house. Dave didn't care if that happened. A home was supposed to be lived in.

He and Darla exchanged a quick kiss when she got to him.

"Hello, sweetie," she said.

He loved it when she called him that.

"You look beautiful."

She did a quick twirl for his benefit, smiling the whole time. "Why, thank you, handsome."

She was wearing a dress that was one of his favorites on her: a deep bronze, simply-styled long-sleeved dress that was modest but still made his heart beat double-time. The color complemented her skin tone so well. And grateful man that he was, the hem fell just above her knees and displayed her shapely legs to perfection. She completed the look with three-inch heeled sandals in the same shade.

"Jerry says he's going to be running late," she told him. "But he'll be here."

"Oh, good," he said, forcing himself to take his eyes off her so that he could give his attention to his other guests who were getting closer now.

Darla went on inside with Bastian.

Mr. Jenkins, who had his cane with him but didn't seem to be leaning on it too heavily, had Miss Evie on his arm. "Beautiful home, Chief," he said.

Dave shook his hand. He admired Mr. Jenkins. Not only was he soon to be Darla's stepfather, but he was also responsible for the college scholarships the Stay on Course graduates were receiving. When Mr. Jenkins had moved back to his hometown, he'd told Dave, he had made it his business to contribute significantly to it. Along with the Nishimura Group's contributions, the program was funded for at least five more years. That meant they could steer more kids onto the right path in life.

"Thank you, sir, and welcome. You two go on in and make yourselves at home."

Miss Evie stopped to kiss his cheek. He'd noticed her eyeing the yard. It wasn't in the best shape, this being wintertime, but he'd spent a bit of labor on the landscaping. He'd even built a matching gazebo in the back-yard, which was painted the same color as the house. Besides the large deck in the back, it would be a nice place for someone to curl up with a good book, which he knew Darla enjoyed doing.

Miss Evie, though, was a gardener at heart. She gestured to the plants in the flower beds on opposite sides of the front steps. "Wild petunias, winter jasmine and begonias," she identified them, her tone slightly envious, Dave thought. "Love them. Pansies and vio-las, too. They all grow well in winter in this area. Good job, Dave."

"Coming from you, that's quite the compli-ment, Miss Evie," Dave said. He made sure the couple got up the steps safely, as they were the most aged of his guests.

Inside, the house smelled of all the deli-cious food he'd ordered from both the Symi-nettes' seafood restaurant and Kaye's Café. Tandi Syminette, who managed her family's restaurant, and Kaye Johnson, owner of

Kaye's Café, had delivered the food themselves just a short while ago. Kaye had been invited to the housewarming but told him she had to work. Dave had given each of them quick tours of the house.

His guests naturally gravitated toward the enticing smells. And they ended up in the kitchen. Dave had set out plastic forks, knives and spoons in small containers that resembled paint cans in bright colors. Next to them were napkins, paper plates and cups. All of this was arranged on the huge island next to the catered food. In a nearby corner was a fully stocked DIY drinks cart. He'd placed a chalkboard on the wall beside it on which he'd printed a few drinks recipes to help the guests mix their own. There were soft drinks and juices for the kids. Desserts were provided by Garrett's Bakery.

"Everything looks great," Darla said as she grabbed a chicken wing, placed it on a napkin and handed it to Bastian, who appeared ready to dig into the food. He immediately began eating it.

Dave was about to thank her when he heard more cars pulling up. He'd left the front door open and could see his dad's pickup and his sister's SUV from the kitchen. "Looks like my family's here," he announced. He might have been anxious if not for the fact that his family and Darla's had already spent time together. For his mother's birthday party last month and a Halloween party at Maria's house in Pensacola. Bastian and his nephew, Ben, and his niece, Sadie, had enjoyed themselves. It hadn't been the first time Bastian and Ben had met since they were both Little Leaguers who had played against each other in a tee ball game over the summer.

His mother and Maria came into the house and, judging by their expressions, were impressed with his home. The two of them were pretty much the same height, around five-eight. His mother said her people came from tall-stock Italians, like her idol, Sophia Loren, who was five-nine. Both of them had thick, dark wavy hair, like he did. His mother's was streaked with gray now. Maria's was still a vibrant dark brown.

They were dressed similarly in casual slacks, blouses and white athletic shoes. His mother was carrying Sadie in her arms. Sadie, too, was looking around.

Maria came to him and hugged him. "Sorry, Grant had to work." She glanced around again. "I'm impressed. I thought I was going to walk into a bachelor pad. But somehow, you found a good balance."

Dave hadn't told them that Darla had done the decorating.

The two families had met in the middle and were saying hello to one another, hugging, and introducing those among them who had yet to meet.

Dave noticed his mother introducing Mr. Jenkins to his dad. His mother, who was a member of the charitable group Silver Seniors, had been touched by Mr. Jenkins's generous donation to the organization. Poor man. Now that he was a target of his mother's interest, he might have more of a sensory overloaded time here than he'd bargained for. Darla had told him that sometimes Mr. Jenkins had a hard time with crowds, especially loud crowds. But Darla had also told him that Mr. Jenkins and her mother had signals they'd set up so that if Mr. Jenkins felt overwhelmed he'd communicate it to her and then she would immediately remove him from the situation.

"You have to see Darla if you want to talk decorating," Dave admitted. "She's the one behind this." And he gestured all around him.

"Darla!" his sister practically yelled in Darla's direction. Darla was standing near the bifold patio doors that led to the deck. The children obviously were trying to open them to go outside. He should have known the backyard would attract them due to the playground he'd constructed for them. There was a wooden swing set complete with a slide and a wooden cedar sandbox filled with white sand from the beach, seashells included because Sadie loved the beach. There was also an all-weather cornhole set and plenty of bags for tossing. And deeper in the yard was a backyard volleyball set. The kids were going to burn off a lot of energy.

He hurried in Darla's direction, but his sister beat him to her. "Dave says he has you to thank for decorating this gorgeous house, so I'd like the grand tour from you. Please?"

He could see from the light in Darla's eyes that she was delighted by the request, so he told her, "I'll show the kids the backyard."

They met each other's eyes and agreed by silent consensus. They had signals, too!

And he turned his attention to Bastian, Ben and Sadie, who was already pulling on his left pant leg to be picked up. She'd been in need of lots of cuddles lately. He would ask Maria about that later. He picked her up before opening the bifold patio door and leading them outside.

Once outside, the kids eagerly ran down the back steps to the playground. Sadie abandoned him so quickly it made his head spin. She made a beeline for the sandbox.

He sat down on the top step to watch them. He was sure his mother would be happy to answer the door when the other guests arrived. He thought it more important to keep an eye on the kids. He patted his jeans pocket to make sure what he'd put in there earlier was still there. Then he settled in.

DARLA WENT LOOKING for Bastian after she and Maria came back downstairs after the tour. Maria went to join the other adults. Darla noticed that the numbers had grown quite a bit in their absence. Several officers were there with their significant others or their entire families, like Rob Conrad, who was there with his wife, Kayla, and their two kids. Kayla was around nine months pregnant now, but she was one of those hardy women who took it all in stride, or at least she appeared to be. Darla remembered she had not been that cheerful when she'd been nine months along. She'd been uncomfortable, easily irritated and practically lived in the bathroom.

Marley would have been here, but she'd begged off because her ankles were swollen and she'd been told to get bed rest by her obstetrician. Darla had sympathized with her when Marley had told her the doctor said at her age, thirty-four, she'd just missed being classified as an "advanced maternal age" pregnancy, which began at age thirty-five. Darla thought, at the rate she was going, if she ever had another baby, her pregnancy would be considered a "senior moment."

Curiously, though, when she looked at Kayla, she found herself yearning for another child, maybe a girl this time. A sweet little girl like Sadie. Or an energetic child who loved everybody like Skye. Anyway, a child who would have her own unique personality and look like a cross between her and Dave.

As she was walking through the kitchen, she spotted Dave sitting on the top step that led down to the yard. She opened the door to the deck and stepped outside.

"There you are," she said to Dave. She closed the door behind her, then she looked across the yard and saw Bastian and Ben chasing one another around the playground. Sadie was contentedly filling a red plastic bucket with shovels of white sand. Several other children she hadn't been introduced to yet were also having a good time on the playground. "I think most of the people you invited are here."

Hearing her, Dave got up and stretched his legs. "Oh, great. How did the tour go? Maria didn't talk your ears off, did she?"

She smiled up at him. And naturally, he gave her a warm hug. They'd been apart for a few minutes, after all. "Nah, she was very sweet. She asked me when I was going to marry you and give her a niece or a nephew, but I'm used to that question from friends and family. Marley and Kaye are literally keeping me updated about how long you and I have been in each other's orbits. Not dating, but since we went for a coffee. It's been eight months now, in case you didn't know."

Dave chuckled. "That long, huh? It doesn't seem that long. Feels like I just met you today."

He pulled her closer to him. The kiss came naturally. It was as if they were magnetically drawn to one another. They took full advantage of these few seconds of alone time.

When they parted, they gazed into one another's eyes. Dave said, "I love you."

"I love you, too," she said, smiling and wondering if she looked as dazed or starry-eyed as she felt.

"When are you going to marry me?" he asked for the umpteenth time, and for a moment the magic between them was lost because she had come to the conclusion that when he asked her that question it was because he was still straddling the fence and wasn't sure he was ready for commitment.

This time, however, he reached into his jeans pocket and retrieved a diamond solitaire, got on his knees after taking her hand in his, gazed lovingly up at her and said, "I'm not playing with you, darlin'. Will you marry me?"

"Say yes!" Darla heard her mother shout.

Darla looked behind her. Where had they all come from? She hadn't even heard the door open. But around twenty people stood behind them, looking on expectantly, the deck door wide open.

Even the kids had come over to them. Bastian stood at the bottom of the steps with excitement written all over his face. Ben held on to his sister's hand. For her part, Sadie was pulling against him, eager to get back to her sandbox. She was too young to appreciate the moment.

"Shh," Ben urged her. "Remember cousin May's wedding and you threw flowers at everyone?"

"It's true," Maria said. "She didn't toss them on the aisle. She threw rose petals at everyone as she walked down the aisle. But excuse me. Darla, the floor is yours."

Silence reigned. Dave was still smiling at her. And Darla had begun to wonder how much longer his knees were going to be able to take the punishment of those hardwood planks the deck was made of, so she cried, "Yes, I will!"

Dave didn't immediately spring up. He took

his time and slid the ring onto her finger. It was a perfect fit.

Then he got up and kissed her soundly to the backdrop of friends and family whooping and hollering as though they had just won the Florida Lottery.

After the kiss, Dave picked her up and spun her around. He was beaming, and she knew she was grinning so hard, her jaw was beginning to ache.

In the midst of their elation, though, she distinctly heard Dave's cell phone loudly ring. He spun her around a few times more before putting her down and answering.

The expression on his face went from delirious happiness to intense anguish in the bat of an eye. "Everybody, quiet, please!" he barked.

A hush fell over the guests and the mood went from jubilation to concern.

"You hold on, buddy, I'm coming," he said and fairly leaped from the deck to the ground and began running toward his pickup truck.

"Dave!" Darla cried.

"I'll call you as soon as I can," he promised, not stopping for a moment. "Rob, call the EMTs and let them know there's been a car accident near here. On Magnolia, not two miles from here. And get whoever's on patrol to meet me there. Go!"

Rob didn't waste time. He got on his cell phone and did as he was bid. Kayla, holding her belly and appearing as if she were close to tears, stood nearby.

Darla's thoughts immediately went to Jerry and the fact that of all the guests who'd been invited to the housewarming, he had not shown up. Jerry was very dependable. If he said he was going to do something, he did it.

She went inside to grab her purse. She retrieved her cell and dialed Jerry's number. It went straight to voice mail. She tried again and got the same result.

Her mother had followed her inside. She and Mr. Jenkins stood in the kitchen near the cabinets with her. "What's wrong, baby?" asked her mother.

"Where do you suppose Jerry is?" Darla asked.

"ON MAGNOLIA, about two miles from your place. Guy just ran into me and floored it. Think I'm passing out...smell smoke..."

And those were the last words that Jerry said to him.

Dave was driving so fast, it seemed like the trees he passed were actually whizzing by him. It didn't take him long to find the spot. Traffic on this back road was sparse, thank God. At this moment, there was none. He saw Jerry's black BMW had been T-boned by a Mercedes. One that looked very familiar to him.

Dave parked on the shoulder of the road and ran across the street to Jerry's car. He peered inside on the opposite side of the car because the Mercedes's front end still had Jerry's driver's side pinned. The driver of the Mercedes was conscious and was yelling for help. Dave knew that voice.

He hated the owner of that voice. He concentrated on getting help for Jerry. Jerry had said he smelled smoke and now Dave saw that there was smoke coming from under the hood of Jerry's BMW.

He yanked on the passenger-side door and it came open. He climbed inside and checked Jerry's condition. As far as he could see, Jerry's seat belt was still fastened and his airbag had deployed. The driver's side door was bent inward toward Jerry's left side due to the impact with the Mercedes. "Jerry!" Dave cried. "Jerry, can you hear me?"

He silently thanked God when Jerry came to and asked, "Dave?"

"Yeah, buddy, it's me. I'm going to get you out of there." Dave felt because of the smoke he had no choice but to move Jerry, even though the medics might advise against it. Where there was smoke there might possibly be fire.

Dave carefully reached inside and moved the center console that was in the way of his dragging Jerry out of the car. Then he unbuckled Jerry's seat belt. "Jerry, are you stuck? Do you feel any pain in your extremities?"

"My side hurts a little," Jerry said. "Just pull, Dave. I'll help as much as I can."

So Dave eased his arm around Jerry's waist and the back of his right leg, where his knee bent, and gently pulled him toward him. He could feel Jerry trying to scoot in his direction. A few seconds later, Jerry's feet touched the ground on the right side of the car and Dave helped him stand. It was at that instant Dave heard the sirens. The EMTs were very close.

They weren't there yet, though, and there was still the matter of the smoking engine of the BMW. "I'm taking you across the street to my truck, but sounds like the medical professionals are almost here."

The two of them slowly walked across the street and Dave helped Jerry onto the passenger side, where Jerry leaned his head back and closed his eyes.

"Don't go to sleep," Dave told him.

"What about the other guy?" Jerry surprised him by asking. Everything he'd been through because of a reckless driver and he was still concerned about him.

Dave could hear the other driver calling for help. "Help me, I'm stuck. Somebody help me!"

"Are you sure you're not going to go to sleep if I leave you alone for a few minutes?" Dave asked Jerry.

"Swear, man. I'm not about to go to sleep. I ain't trying to die tonight. Go help the other guy. I'm cool."

When he got to the driver's side door, Raff was trying to light a cigarette, only the side of his face showing, but his hands kept shaking. Dave didn't understand why the Mercedes's airbag hadn't deployed. He knocked on the driver's side window, then peered in and saw that Raff's seat belt wasn't fastened. And there was an open liquor bottle on the floorboard beneath the glove compartment. Dave marveled that, after the impact, Raff was still conscious, but maybe all the alcohol he'd drunk had acted as a stimulant to keep him awake.

Dave tapped on the window again, getting Raff's attention. Raff turned to look at him. His nose looked like it was broken. He gave Dave a crooked smile. "Chief, is that you?" he asked drunkenly. "Fancy meeting you here!"

Dave started to say something cutting, but he was distracted by loud sirens as the EMTs pulled up. The techs, one woman, one man, jumped out and ran over to the Mercedes.

"Mr. Cramer, the man he hit, is in my truck," he told them. "Mr. Chandler here is fully conscious and trying to get a smoke"

The two techs looked confuse for a moment, then the woman said, "No problem,

Chief." She glanced at her partner. "Divide and conquer?"

Her partner nodded and she stayed with Raff while he jogged across the street to attend to Jerry. After a few minutes the two of them consulted with each other, and apparently decided that Jerry's condition warranted immediate attention, put him on a stretcher, switched their sirens back on and took off. Soon after they departed, another emergency vehicle showed up. A couple of his officers in a patrol car were behind the emergency vehicle.

"There's your chariot, Raff," Dave said, standing near the driver's side window of Raff's Mercedes. Raff looked at him dully.

Dave moved away from Raff's car and allowed the people best suited for medical emergencies to do their jobs. He crossed the street to his truck.

The officers got out of their cruiser and approached him. "Standard procedure, Chief?" one of them asked.

"Yes," Dave said, knowing they were more than capable. They would take photos of the cars, inside and out, and of the condition of the road, including the tire tread marks left by the cars' wheels.

After speaking with the officers, he climbed into his truck and dialed Darla's number. The phone rang only once before Darla answered. "Is it Jerry?" were the first words out of her mouth.

"How did you know?"

"He didn't show up. That's not like him. How bad is it?"

"Raff Chandler ran into him on Magnolia Road. But Jerry's alert and he's on the way to the hospital now. He was conscious when I got to him and he was conscious when the EMTs arrived. I didn't see any bleeding except for a few scratches, and his nose got banged up a little, probably from the airbag deploying. He sounded coherent when we talked. I'm heading to Pensacola now."

"We are, too," she told him.

"Then I'll meet you there," Dave said.

"Thank you for saving my brother," she said, and he could tell she was about to cry.

"Jerry didn't need saving, sweetheart. But Raff Chandler is going to need saving. He's going to prison this time." And Dave realized he meant every word.

CHAPTER NINETEEN

DARLA THOUGHT JERRY appeared a bit over-whelmed by all the attention he was receiving. They were still in the ER exam room. Tests had been administered and now they were waiting for results.

Darla and Dave were in the room with him now.

These lights, Darla thought, *make people look sicker than they are.* Jerry, whose skin was normally a healthy reddish-brown like her own, seemed washed-out. Or maybe she was imagining it because she could have lost him. That hospital gown wasn't helping. And they'd put thick baby-blue ankle socks with slip-free soles on his size twelve feet. He reminded her of an abnormally large two-year-old.

Jerry frowned at her. "Would you please stop staring at me like I'm one step from the grave? I'm fine. I'll probably be sore in the morning, but otherwise I'm fine. Wait until you hear the results of my tests. They'll probably make me spend the night, because I may have a concussion, but I'll be a free man in the morning."

Dave stayed out of the conversation for the most part. He was leaning against the wall with his legs crossed at the ankles, casually looking down at his cell phone. In those cowboy boots he made her think of a twenty-first-century version of Yul Brynner in *The Magnificent Seven*, a film she loved even though it was made decades before she was born. Except, of course, Dave wasn't bald.

She knew it had to be something important he was looking at because of all the people in her life, he was the least addicted to his device. Business all the time.

Jerry cast his eyes in Dave's direction. "Don't you think it's weird that the same man who tried to sue you ran into me?"

Dave stood up straight and raised his gaze to Jerry's. "Port Domingo is a small town, so no, I'm not surprised. This is the fourth time we've arrested him and he keeps breaking the law. This time, though, I'm going to the source."

"What, or who, pray tell, is the source?" Jerry asked.

"His father, the judge?" was Darla's guess. She and Dave had discussed Raff Chandler at length. It appeared his violations were increasing in severity. He'd been arrested three times in the past year for driving under the influence. Now, though, he was caught not only driving while under the influence, but also for being in possession of an open container and consuming an alcoholic beverage while operating a vehicle. Besides that, he was driving with a suspended license and he could have killed someone when he T-boned them. Lucky for Jerry, vehicular homicide hadn't been added to his charges.

"Do you really think a Florida Supreme Court justice is allowing his alcoholic son to run rampant?" she asked.

"Girl, you talk like Momma when you say things like 'run rampant,'" Jerry complained good-naturedly. "Why don't you just say *running wild without supervision*? Raff Chandler is way over twenty-one. He's like fifty-something, at least. So his father probably has no say in how he lives his life."

"That's not Dave's point," Darla insisted.

She met Dave's eyes. Hers asked him to explain.

Dave cleared his throat. "No, what I'm getting at is the judge may be using his influence to save his son from serious prison time. The lower judges may be currying favor. Branford Chandler is a Florida Supreme Court justice, after all. You scratch my back, I'll scratch yours. That sort of thing. And as for not putting Raff in rehab somewhere and throwing away the key, the Chandler name, which is an old Southern name, by the way, would be sullied. I'm so tired of rich people getting away with things your average citizen never would."

Darla put her arm about his waist and lay her head on his arm because his shoulder was a few inches too high. "So you're going to talk to his father?"

Dave nodded. "I'm going to give it a try."

"You were at his house when you and Raff got into it," she reminded him. "But he works in Tallahassee. How are you going to know where you can find him to have a conversation with him?"

"I may be a small-town policeman," said Dave with a smile, "but I know people."

"DAVE, HOW ARE YOU, BOY?" Robert "Bobby" Canady said as he shook Dave's hand over his desk at the Capitol building in Tallahassee, Florida. Dave had gotten there early, at eight o'clock in the morning. He knew Marshal Canady operated on military time.

"I'm fine, thank you, Marshal Canady," Dave said respectfully. "And yourself?"

"Good, good," said Robert.

Robert Canady had once been a major in the marines. He'd held several high-ranking positions with civilian police as well. He and Dave had known each other for over ten years. They had kept in touch because Robert was Cameron Canady's dad, and Cameron had been Dave's best friend.

Robert presently held the title Marshal of the Florida Supreme Court. He was in charge of security for the entire courthouse, the building and grounds that made up the Florida Captitol where the Florida Supreme Court presided. The Courthouse had been in its current location since 1949.

Robert was in his sixties. He was a tall, distinguished looking African American man with medium brown skin and a shaved head. He wore a thick black moustache that

Dave now noticed had some silver in it since the last time he'd seen him.

Robert gestured to the moss-green leather chair in front of his desk. "Sit down," he said. "What brings you here today?"

They both sat and Robert eyed him expectantly with laughter in his brown eyes.

Dave got right down to it. He knew Robert liked things laid out for him, succinctly yet thoroughly. So he told him what favor he was asking for today and why it was so important to him.

When he'd finished, Robert sat quietly for a few moments, thinking. Then he said, "And you didn't just phone and try to get an appointment with him because you figured he wouldn't give you one, am I correct? Not if you're going to accuse him of being his son's enabler."

Dave nodded. "That was my thinking, sir."

Robert thought for a while longer. Then he took a deep breath and released it. He smiled slowly. "Frankly, I don't know how you manage to do as good a job as you do. Yes, I hear things. It's not easy being a policeman nowadays. Plus, to have Raff Chandler tearing around town like some toddler whose nanny can't control him...you're a much more patient man than I am. So I'm going to help you out."

He leaned forward and turned his desktop computer screen toward him. Then his nimble fingers flew across the keys. "Mmm, Justice Chandler is scheduled to play golf this afternoon at two. I will contact him and if he's willing to see you, he will greet you kindly. If not, don't push it, son."

He quickly wrote a note on a Post-it and handed the slip of paper to Dave. "Now, when you approach him, you've got to have ID out and ready. He has a bodyguard assigned to him and he's very vigilant, shall we say. I suggest you get there before he starts playing because he hates to be denied his golf. Gets kind of irritated. I'm told he enjoys a pregame drink in the clubhouse before he hits the course. I hope it goes well for you."

Dave rose and shook Robert's hand again. "Thank you, sir. You're a lifesaver."

"Nah, I'm just a father appreciative of someone who knew and cared about my son. You're a good guy, Dave. And even though some people don't think so, good guys deserve to win."

Dave took that as it had been given—graciously.

As he was going out the door, Robert called, "And next time, don't stay away so long."

Dave turned and smiled. "I wouldn't think of it, sir. In fact, I just got engaged to a wonderful woman and I'll be sending you and Mrs. Canady an invitation."

"We'd be delighted to attend, son," said his best friend's father, which made him inordinately happy.

About five and a half hours later, he was standing in the clubhouse of an exclusive golf course perhaps ten minutes from the courthouse. He could see how it would be convenient for Justice Chandler to golf here.

The clubhouse looked like an upscale restaurant. It was elegantly appointed with white tablecloth-topped tables, a crystal chandelier in the center of the huge dining room, and the waitstaff wearing crisp white shirts and black pants.

He was approached by a slender woman in an expensive-looking black dress and heels. Her skin was like porcelain and her short black hair was slicked back from an angular face. "Good afternoon, Officer," she said.

Dave had worn his uniform today, hoping it would ease his entrance into the judge's world.

"Are you a member?" Her pale blue eyes held little warmth.

Dave was looking around the room. He'd met the judge on several occasions, and he spotted him now at the center table, where he was conversing with three other males in their senior years. A few feet away, a big man was sitting at a table alone, drinking from a bottle of water. Dave pegged him as the bodyguard.

"No, I'm not," Dave told the hostess. "I'm just here to speak with Judge Chandler." He held his ID in his right hand.

"Is His Honor expecting you?" was the next question from the hostess.

Her voice had been rather loud when she'd asked that question. Justice Chandler looked suspiciously in their direction. The man Dave believed was his bodyguard did more: he got up, whipped his jacket out of the way and pulled his gun from a shoulder holster. He didn't point it at Dave, but he did hold it at the ready by his side.

Justice Chandler rose. "It is all right, Arturo," he said quietly. "I know this gentleman. You can relax."

The bodyguard, six-four, Dave guessed, and two hundred pounds of muscle, sat back down. But his gaze never left Dave.

The justice was kind enough to wave Dave over to his table. As he was walking over, the judge got the attention of one of the waiters and requested a chair for Dave. While the chair was being brought, Branford Chandler smiled warmly at Dave, then regarded his companions. "Gentlemen, this is Dave Harrison, the chief of police of my hometown."

Dave felt he should let Judge Chandler know the nature of what he wanted to talk with him about. "Sir, I'm here because I'm concerned about your son."

The justice held up a finger for Dave to wait a moment. The extra chair was there. The justice's friends got up without complaining, and soon everyone was seated at the round table with adequate space between them.

"Dave, it just so happens that my son was whom we were discussing. These men are my sounding boards. We know about all the skeletons in each other's closets. You can speak freely. I suspect you didn't drive over a hundred miles for something unimportant to you. So I'm willing to hear you out."

Dave hadn't anticipated an audience. However, he'd come this far and he meant to have his say. But before he could begin, a waiter stepped up to the table and asked if he could bring him anything.

"Please, Chief, order whatever you wish," the judge generously offered.

"No, thank you," Dave said kindly to the waiter. He just wanted to get this over with.

The waiter went away, and Dave cleared his throat. "Sir, I believe you've been informed about Raff's recent accident."

Judge Chandler, who was in his early seventies, of average height and build, with thinning snow-white hair that he wore rather long and had a tendency of pushing behind his ears. He had a deep voice and a pronounced Southern accent.

"His lawyer is keeping me abreast of Raphael's actions. Forgive me if I take issue with your referring to him as Raff. His mother, who was an art enthusiast, God rest her soul, named him after her favorite Italian painter, and I call him by that name out of respect for her."

"I didn't know," Dave said. "He refers to himself as Raff."

"Yes, anything to irritate me. Do you have any children, Chief Harrison?"

"No, I haven't been lucky enough, yet, to marry and have children," Dave told him.

"Lucky?" the judge asked with a chuckle. "I suppose some men think of having children as lucky while others feel decidedly cursed with them. I am from another generation, Chief. When my wife and I had Raphael, it was during a time when men, especially men of means, had very little to do with the upbringing of their children. That was left to the little woman and whatever staff she chose to help her with the task."

His cohorts nodded their white heads in agreement, a couple of them laughing softly. Dave wondered where the judge was going with this. He hoped he wasn't about to tell him that he'd washed his hands of Raff a long time ago. If he had, no wonder Raff was the way he was. An unfeeling father was enough to make any child act out, whether that child was five or fifty.

"I regret that Raphael and I do not have much of a relationship. I never knew what to do with him. And after his mother died, I certainly lost interest in him. You don't get to be where I am today without neglecting some aspect of your life, Chief. I neglected Raphael. I'm not proud of it, but I don't let it keep me awake nights, either. I have a responsibility to give the people I serve the best of me."

"Yes, sir, I hear you have a fine reputation," said Dave, trying to keep the sarcasm out of his tone.

He must have succeeded because Judge Chandler smiled at him and said, "A well-earned reputation. The only thing that has ever sullied my reputation is my son. Do I resent him for it? No, I do not because the boy can't help himself. He is who he is. What kind of an influence do you suppose I can have on him now when he has spent years building his own sordid reputation? I can't tell him anything."

"You can tell him you love him," suggested Dave fiercely.

The judge started to say something and Dave interrupted him with "A few minutes ago, you said I had the floor. But you've been the one to speak. No wonder you're a judge. Now, please, listen to me. Raff needs to go to rehab and you're the only one who can send him. If that solution doesn't please you, and you want a more permanent solution, which it sounds like you do in order to get the burr out of your butt, said burr being your beloved son, then I ask you to inform your colleagues—all of the judges who keep giving him a get-out-of-jail-free card—to let him take his lumps and go to prison. Now, you can sit there and say you are not influencing the judges to go easy on him, but we both know how your good-old-boy network operates. They curry favor with you. You do them a favor down the line. I'm asking you to be a real father to your son and help him to have a quality life. He's a reckless drunk. He could have killed someone last week. And he probably doesn't even remember the incident today! If you don't want to take the time to help him, think of your wife. Do it for her memory, just as you call him Raphael out of respect for her."

Everyone at that table looked appalled by what Dave had just said, including Judge Chandler. Dave thought the man would gesture to his bodyguard to drag him out of the clubhouse, but the judge was silent.

Then his face got red. His colleagues regarded him with concern. Dave hoped he hadn't come all this way and caused a Florida Supreme Court judge to have a stroke.

Judge Chandler drank deeply from his glass of water, burped and placed the glass back on the table. He regarded Dave with an irritated expression on his face. Dave thought he was about to lambast him with a barrage of heretofore unheard-of insults.

Instead, the judge said in a soft voice, "I'll have my attorney start commitment procedures at once. He might yet be saved." He got up and motioned to his bodyguard, who immediately got to his feet and began walking in their direction.

To his friends at his table, he said, "I'm afraid golf is out of the question today, fellows. And, George, next time you're paying for drinks, you cheapskate."

His friends chuckled. Dave figured they were as relieved as he was that the judge wasn't having a medical emergency, but was taking action on behalf of his only child.

When the bodyguard reached his client, the judge told him, "We're leaving, Arturo."

Dave turned to leave as well, figuring he'd done his part and the judge had finally been goaded into action. But the judge wasn't finished with him.

"Chief Harrison," Judge Chandler called him back.

Dave turned around to face him. "Sir, if I was a bit harsh, I apologize."

"Nonsense," said Judge Chandler. "I had it coming. I needed to be told exactly what you told me. I love Raphael. But I've never told the boy I love him. I have neglected him all these years, while building myself up. I've let him down. I'm an atrocious father, and Annabelle would be ashamed of me!"

He shook Dave's hand. "Port Domingo is lucky to have you."

"Thank you, sir."

"You know," Judge Chandler said contemplatively, "a man like you can do well in Tallahassee."

Dave was quick to quell the judge's interest in his career. "Sir, I'm very happy doing what I'm doing."

Judge Chandler looked slightly disappointed,

but a smile soon returned to his face. "There is something to be said about a man who's happy with his job. Safe trip back home, then, Chief, and thank you for coming and talking some sense into me."

Dave left before the judge figured out just how nervous all of this had made him. However, he was thrilled that it appeared he'd actually gotten through to him. The sooner Raff received help for his alcoholism, the better for him, and for Port Domingo.

He was just glad that Jerry was doing well and there were no lasting physical effects from the crash. Now he could concentrate on him and Darla. She'd asked him why he'd finally asked her to marry him and "meant it," in her words. Actually, he'd meant it every time he'd asked her. What had been lacking was faith. Faith in her love for him. Faith that he was really her first choice. He'd gone to his mother for advice, and she had told him by not exercising faith in his and Darla's love, he was, in essence, blocking his blessings.

He had never heard the term before. She told him she'd gotten it from Miss Evie, who'd said if a person didn't have faith in their prayers being answered, then they were standing in the way of their own happiness. That was what Dave had been doing, according to his mother. He should propose and do it right, she told him. Then get out of the way of his doubts and believe that Darla loved him, then he would get what he asked for: her unequivocal love.

He'd proposed. Darla had said yes. Now, as he walked to his truck after leaving the clubhouse, he felt elated. Nothing could stand in their way.

EPILOGUE

DARLA WAS SLEEPING the sleep of the innocent, the sleep of someone happy with her life and who eagerly looked forward to the future, when she was awakened by a pinging sound. She stirred. Morpheus held tight, and she pulled the covers up around her shoulders, not willing to give up without a fight. It was December, and though the temperature in her mother's house was neither too hot nor too cold, she enjoyed snuggling under blankets.

More pinging. She yawned and forced her eyelids open. The room was dark aside from moonlight shining through sheer curtains. She reluctantly rolled over and switched on the lamp sitting on the nightstand beside the bed.

She heard the noise again and realized that someone was throwing something at her window. She sat up and swung her legs off the side of the bed and felt for her slippers. The wooden floor was usually cold to her bed-warmed feet.

At the window, she peered down. Luckily the moon's glow made visibility possible at that hour: 2:33 a.m., according to the alarm clock.

Dave stood on the lawn below, dressed in pajamas, a robe and, of all things, his cowboy boots. He looked so ridiculous she couldn't help laughing as she raised the window. One of the "pebbles" he'd been tossing at her window hit the screen that covered the lower part and she glimpsed it. It was an M&M's candy.

"What are you doing tossing chocolate candies at my window at this time of the night?" she asked, laughing.

"It's hard to find pebbles at this hour," he said, "so I improvised."

"What are you doing here?" she asked, trying her best to sound irritated when she was actually delighted. But it wasn't wise to encourage him. He might try to climb up here.

"I missed you," he said. He gave her that begging, puppy-dog expression that she couldn't resist, and he knew it. "Come down. Let's take a walk."

"We're getting married in about twelve hours. You can see me then. And stop looking at me. According to our mothers, who are well-versed in wedding superstitions, you're not supposed to see me before the unveiling tomorrow. Besides, if I try to sneak out, I'll have to walk past my mother's bedroom and she's a light sleeper."

"Our mothers are going too far with their rules."

"We agreed that we'd get married in the church and follow all the traditions. We're jumping the broom as a nod to my ancestors not being allowed to marry each other. And we're breaking a glass into a million pieces according to the Italian belief that the number of pieces denote how many years we'll be happy. Therefore, that glass is going to be broken into smithereens!"

"Let's thumb our noses at tradition," Dave pleaded with her. "Come down, Rapunzel!"

She melted at the passionate tone of his voice. "Fine. Five minutes, and then, you have to leave."

She closed the window and put on her robe. She was wearing pajamas, as well. She looked down at her fuzzy slippers. They were too froufrou to wear outside. She went into her closet and selected her Chucks and sat down on the bed to put them on.

She felt like a disobedient child as she tiptoed past her mother's bedroom door. She knew there was a board that creaked at the top of the stairs leading to the first floor, and she managed to avoid it.

As soon as she opened the front door, Dave pulled her into his arms and she inhaled his heady, masculine scent, allowing herself to relax.

"You smell good," he said in her ear.

They hugged tightly. "So do you," she softly said. "Now, talk to me. What's bothering you that you drove all the way over here at two in the morning?"

"I've been hit by the 'too much happiness' bug. You know, you wonder when your luck is going to run out when everything is going your way. I couldn't sleep for thinking something awful is going to happen to prevent the wedding tomorrow."

"This is not the Dave Harrison I know and love," she murmured. "When have you ever let luck dictate your life? You make your own luck! Do you remember what you told me the first day we sat down together? We were having coffee after my run-in with Joyce and you told me, 'Darla, you know who you are as a person. Don't let what someone else might think of you color your own opinion of yourself. Know who you are and stand by that. Be proud.'"

"That is pretty inspiring," Dave joked.

She kissed his chin. "So, now, go home and get your rest, because tomorrow we're going to be husband and wife. I have spoken, so let it be."

"This is why I love you so much," Dave told her. "You build me up. You don't let me get away with anything."

"No, I don't, and I never will. I will always tell you when I think you're being silly. Plus, if you don't get out of here soon, my mother is going to come down here and hit you with her shoe. She promised to do it if you didn't abide by the rule to stay away tonight."

"You're not serious," Dave said, incredulous that her sweet mother would get violent with him.

"Oh, yes, she is serious!" cried her mother, who was standing in the doorway behind them. Darla laughed when she saw her mother was actually wielding a shoe, but it was a fuzzy, pink kitten-heeled slipper. Not being very tall, her mother added inches to her height at every opportunity.

"This might not look like much of a weapon, but my aim is true and I've got it in for you, boy! Interrupting my beauty sleep and stealing kisses from my daughter... You can have plenty of kisses after the wedding. Now, go home, or you'll feel my wrath!"

Laughing, Dave hastily kissed Darla's cheek and leaped down the front steps. "I'm going, Momma Evie. I love you!"

"I love you, too," her mother told him. "Just make sure you're at the church on time, as the song says!"

DAVE WAS DEFINITELY at the church on time. In fact, he was early. Father Rodriguez, whom Dave had known since he was a boy, was the only person who arrived before he did. And Father Rodriguez was elated to be marrying him and Darla because it was his opinion that not enough people were marrying nowadays.

He and Darla wanted a simple ceremony

even though they took advantage of all the pomp and circumstance a church provided. His best man was Rob. Her maid of honor was Kaye. No groomsmen or bridesmaids. Everyone they loved was in attendance. Their parents sat down front. Mr. Jenkins was her mother's plus-one. Sebastian and Marley were there. Jerry walked Darla down the aisle in her father's place. And the children got to participate. Bastian and Ben were ring bearers, Bastian with his mother's wedding ring on a decorative pillow and Ben with Dave's. And Sadie followed them doing what she did best—throwing rose petals at the guests instead of tossing them in the aisle.

Darla was gorgeous in a white off-the-shoulder lace wedding dress, her hair in soft curls that fell down her back. He wore a royal blue herringbone linen three-piece tailored Italian suit.

When he and Darla finally stood before one another, he couldn't take his eyes off her. She was smiling, but he saw that tears already sat in her beautiful glimmering eyes. They held hands as Father Rodriguez intoned, "Dearly beloved…"

After Father Rodriguez pronounced them husband and wife, they kissed and then jumped the broom to the thunderous applause of those gathered to share their special day. Then his father brought the wineglass that was to be shattered to him wrapped in a linen napkin and Dave did the honors. He crushed the glass into many pieces with his hard-soled Italian loafers. More applause.

After that, Kaye sang, "How Sweet It Is (To Be Loved by You)" by James Taylor. She had the whole church rocking while he and Darla walked down the aisle hand in hand. Dave saw that most of his officers were in attendance. Robert Canady, Cameron's dad, and his wife, Ariana, were there. Joyce and her husband, Raymond, were there. Laraine and her husband, Fredrick, who was a retired policeman. Even the mayor was there with his wife, Bette, who was beaming at him and Darla.

Later, as they danced at the reception, he held Darla close and whispered, "You ready for a life with me?"

"I've been ready," she said with confidence. She tilted her head up and looked him in the eyes. "Just promise me that you will keep things like not telling me our honeymoon destination to a minimum. I like to know what to pack when I go on a trip."

"I told you, things for a warm climate. It'll be in the seventies. You might need a sweater at night."

She pursed her lips. "Let me guess. Is it somewhere in the Adriatic Sea?"

"Molto bene," he said.

She laughed, throwing her head back and really letting her joy loose, so that it affected him, too, and those around them on the dance floor.

"We're going to Italy!"

"Aw," he said jokingly. "You spoiled the surprise."

Tears sat in her eyes. "I've never been outside of the United States. No, wait a minute. Italy. Your mother's home country. Is she coming, too?"

Dave laughed even louder. "My mother is not going to get anywhere near our honeymoon destination. It's just you and me for two weeks, soaking up the sun and reveling in the sights, old and new. But honestly, mostly old because Italy isn't called the Old Country for nothing. They've got ancient ruins up the wa…"

He might have continued if not for his wife getting up on her toes and kissing him to shut him up. He didn't mind being shut up that way. Not in the least.

* * * * *